A DEATH IN WINTER

Also by Michael J. McCann

A DEATH IN WINTER

A March and Walker Crime Novel

Michael J. McCann

The Plaid Raccoon Press
2020

A DEATH IN WINTER
Copyright © 2020 by Michael J. McCann

ISBN: 978-1-927884-19-5 (paperback)
ISBN: 978-1-927884-20-1 (e-book)

Cover image: Winter Solstice 2019 © by Michael J. McCann
Author photo: © by Michael J. McCann

Visit the author's website at www.mjmccann.com

To the memory of my father,
whose dictionary I'm still using
after all these years, having not
returned it as I promised I would.

LATE JANUARY 2020

Chapter

1

Matthew Scanlan sat on a stool in the back of his shop, knitting.

Outside, the snow continued to fall. There was no wind to speak of, so the large, moist flakes came straight down, as they'd been doing since just after midnight last night. As they would continue to fall, according to weather forecasts, for the next several days.

Music played quietly over the shop's sound system, but Matthew's mind was elsewhere. On Melville and Hawthorne, specifically, and the book he was trying to write. Years after having abandoned his tenured position in the English Department of McGill University as a specialist in American fiction, it still bothered him that students persistently expected realistic behaviour from characters in what were clearly romances rather than novels—

A bell rang sharply, startling him. The front door closed with a bang and someone stomped snow from their feet. Matthew put aside his knitting and stood up.

"Oh, hey," the man said, coming forward, "glad you're open. It's pretty dead around here."

"Yeah, it's not spring yet, is it?" Matthew leaned his hip against the end of the counter next to his cash register and card readers. "Can I help you find something in particular?"

The man glanced around. "Oh, clothing. No. No, I'm looking for the Crosby Hotel."

"Sure." Matthew pushed away from the counter and walked to the front window. "Where's your car?"

"Down at the corner." The man looked at the racks around him. "Next to the church."

"Well, you're headed in the right direction. Straight through the intersection, down a block to Bedford, which is a T, and turn right. At the end of the block, on the north side of the street. Can't miss it."

"Thanks." The man turned to a rack of sweaters. "Boy, these look really warm."

He was a small man, standing about five feet six inches and likely weighing about 150 pounds. He wore a light car coat over a blue suit with a white shirt and a dark blue tie. Inadequate toe rubbers covered black wingtips that looked expensive. He was in his late fifties, maybe early sixties. Greying brown hair, clean-shaven, deep lines on his forehead, sad eyes.

"They're warm, all right," Matthew said. "I knit them myself. They're curling sweaters. Also known as Cowichan sweaters."

"Very nice." The man stripped off his car coat and suit

jacket, draped them over the rack, and pulled one of the sweaters off its hanger. It bore a variation of a common thunderbird motif favoured by traditional Cowichan knitters.

The man tried it on, but it was too large for him.

"Jeez, it feels good." The man reluctantly took it off again. "There's something wrong with the heater in my car. Go figure, eh? You pay a million bucks for the thing and something always has to go wrong."

Matthew went to the rack and removed another sweater with a similar design. "This is a small. It might fit better."

The man traded sweaters with him and tried it on. "Oh yeah, that's nice." He buttoned it up.

"Some people put zippers in," Matthew said, "but I prefer buttons."

"Okay." The man waved his arms around, pleased with the fit.

"I use organically coloured, hand-spun, one-ply yarn that I get from a local farm. Excellent quality wool."

"Good."

"They're designed as an outer garment, of course. Spring and fall wear."

Taking it off, the man put on a pair of wire-frame reading glasses and looked at the price tag attached to the cuff. "Two hundred bucks."

"Regular two-fifty," Matthew said, "but still on sale since Boxing Day."

"I'll take it." The man put away his glasses and handed the sweater to Matthew. His eyes wandered around the shop. "Just menswear, huh?"

"Yes."

"A haberdashery. Not something you'd expect to find in a little whistle stop like this."

"You've never been to Westport before, I take it."

"Never been east of Bowmanville. Hey, these are nice; rustic-looking." Matthew watched him select an Adirondack barn coat from another rack. It was part of an L.L. Bean line that Matthew carried because they sold particularly well in the fall. The man tried it on, and once again it was too large.

"Shoot." He took it off, looked around, and then held out his hand. "Let me put that sweater on again."

Matthew handed it over, noticing a monogram on the man's shirt: *AD*. He wore a Rolex watch on his wrist. After buttoning up the sweater, the man threw on the barn coat and held out his arms.

"Now it fits. That feels great. I'll take both of them." He removed the coat and sweater. "You don't have any boots, do you?"

"Sorry." Matthew took the man's purchases down to the back counter. "You could try the hardware store. He carries some, but I don't know if he's open now. Snow day."

"Okay. I'll stop and see."

Matthew rang them up. The total for both items, with tax, was $310.75. The man peeled six fifties from a large wad of cash. He dropped a twenty on top and said, "Keep the change."

As Matthew searched under the counter for a large bag, the man shrugged back into his suit jacket and wandered up to the front of the store to look out the window. Matthew straightened, a bag in his hand, and saw a car pass in the street outside, headlights flashing in the growing dusk.

The man turned abruptly. "You got a bathroom in here I could use?"

"In back, just past the change cubicle."

The man moved quickly. "Here?"

"No, that's the stairs to the second floor. Over there." Matthew pointed.

The man found the door and locked himself into the tiny washroom.

Matthew wandered up to the front window. He watched the snow falling in the street. The days were still very short, about nine and a half hours long, but now that it was exactly one month past the winter solstice they were gradually getting longer. In microscopic increments, of course. But heading in the right direction. At least that's what he kept telling himself, especially on days like today.

The washroom door opened and the man emerged. He held out his suit coat. "Put this in the bag, will you? I'm going to wear the new stuff. No sense buying it and then freezing."

Matthew switched the clothing around, and the man hastily removed the price tags and put on his new sweater and coat.

"Thanks a lot." The man grabbed the bag and left the store. Once outside, he stood on the front porch and looked down the street in the direction the car had passed a few minutes ago. Then he took out a cellphone and cautiously went down the steps, which Matthew had cleaned an hour ago and were once again covered with snow.

Matthew glanced at his watch and saw that it was only a few minutes short of five o'clock in the afternoon. There was almost no light left in the sky. He locked the front door and flipped the Open sign around to Closed. He watched the man jab at his phone, curse, and throw a despairing look at the snow-filled heavens. Cellphone reception in the village was good, so Matthew figured he was probably watching the classic body language of someone with a dead phone battery.

He turned off the music and the lights, gathered up his knitting, and went upstairs.

Chapter

2

Ontario Provincial Police Detective Inspector Ellie March sat in an Adirondack chair on the back deck of her four-season cottage on Sparrow Lake, smoking a cigarette.

Before sitting down she'd brushed the snow from the chair and used a small plastic shovel to clear off the deck so that her dog, Reggie, would also have a place to sit. A large German shepherd, he lay next to her, resting his chin on his paws. Only his eyes and ears moved.

The frozen lake was silent. The snow came down steadily. Since midnight last night there'd been fifteen centimetres of it, with another fifteen expected over the course of the day.

She drew on the cigarette, tipped back her head, and

exhaled slowly. She shivered, despising the cold with every fibre of her being. She was outside only because it was a hard and fast rule that she would never smoke inside the cottage. Otherwise she wouldn't come out here unless somebody paid her to do so.

There was a sudden, noisy flurry. Blue jays rounded the house and landed in a tree a few metres from the deck. Arguing among themselves, they began to take turns at a big feeder on a pole halfway down to the lake's edge.

The feeder was a Christmas gift from her next-door neighbour, Ridge Ballantyne. He'd ordered it for her from a store in Brockville between strokes. Ridge was now in an assisted-living facility in Kingston, supported by friends from the old days when he was an instructor of music at Queen's University and a celebrity on the local club scene. Not to be confused with the old-old days, when he was an international celebrity as a member of one of the most popular psychedelic folk bands of the 1970s.

His cottage—better described as a lodge—was up for sale. The asking price was just short of a million dollars. Ellie missed Ridge, but she knew he wasn't coming back. The second stroke had been worse than the first one, which she'd witnessed early last summer, and he needed the close proximity to medical care that only a city could provide. The lodge was a luxury, in terms of privacy and solitude, that he could no longer afford.

The jays flew off. There was a moment of silence. Reggie suddenly lifted his head and turned his ears. Ellie waited. Finally, she heard it as well—a car approaching on the lane that ran behind the cottages.

She and the dog listened as the vehicle slowed, paused, and turned into her driveway. Jack Riley, who lived up at the corner where the lane met the road, had plowed it out for her this morning, and she wondered if someone might be taking advantage of it to turn around and head back up the way they had come.

No. The engine stopped; a door opened and closed.

Reggie growled, a low noise in the back of his throat.

Someone walked down along the side of the cottage. Ellie put the dog inside and leaned over the railing.

"Can I help you?"

He was in his late sixties, maybe early seventies. His wavy grey hair was combed back off his forehead, and his smile was friendly. He wore a six-button navy topcoat over a navy suit, a blue shirt, and a black tie. He picked his way through the snow in zippered galoshes until he stood below her.

She could see the tail-end of his vehicle, a green-and-slush SUV that looked like it might be a Land Rover. From where she stood she couldn't see the licence plate.

The man looked up. "Hi. I'm supposed to meet somebody. April Pressley?"

Pressley was the Brockville real estate agent managing the listing next door. Ellie had spoken to her a couple of times and had accepted a business card with a number to call if something came up.

"If you have an appointment," Ellie said, "I'm sure she'll be along soon. It's been snowing all day, so she may be running a little late."

"Yeah, it's pretty relentless. I drove through it on my way here from Toronto."

"You came from Toronto?"

"Yeah. It's a good job I like to drive, huh?"

"What was the 401 like?"

"Not too crazy until just before Kingston, then it got really messy. Some kind of accident. Mind if I come up and chat while I wait?"

Ellie shrugged, holding up her cigarette. "As long as this doesn't bother you."

The man reached inside his suit jacket and pulled out a pack. "I could smell it. Thought I'd join you."

As he came up the stairs Ellie brushed the snow off her other Adirondack chair and motioned to it.

"Thanks. My name's John David Lippincott, by the way. Please call me Jay." He showed an appreciation of old-fashioned etiquette by waiting until Ellie stuck her cigarette in her mouth and held out her hand before removing his glove to shake it.

"I'm Ellie March. Interested in the place next door, are you?"

He lit a cigarette and waited until she sat down before easing onto the edge of his chair. "I'm looking for a summer place. I have a nice property in upstate New York near Lake Placid, but I'm tired of crossing the border right now, and I'd rather not go back there until they get their politics sorted out. Anyway, I thought I'd take a look at this one."

Ellie studied him for a moment. He certainly appeared as though he could afford to buy the place. She wondered whether he was another former rock star, perhaps one of Ridge's friends from a previous life, but quickly decided that he didn't have the look.

"What do you do for a living, Jay?"

He smiled. It was amiable and open, and it included his eyes. "You don't think I'm a retiree? An old geezer with nothing but time on his hands?"

"Too much of a spring in your step for that, I'd say."

"You're a police inspector, aren't you? I've heard of you."

She dropped her cigarette butt into a snow-filled coffee

mug next to her chair. "Have you, now."

"I'm a businessman. Semi-retired, I guess you'd say. Not quite all the way out the door yet."

"What kind of business?"

He drew on his cigarette and looked out across the snow-covered lake. "Helicopters. My company builds them and sells them to governments, corporations, military, police. The OPP's a customer of ours."

"Then I may have ridden in one." Ellie put on her mittens. "I'm going to guess you'll vouch for their safety so I won't worry next time I have to go up in one."

He laughed. "You bet I will."

They heard tires crunching as another vehicle slowed in the lane and stopped.

He stood up. "Hopefully that's Ms. Pressley."

Ellie held out the mug. He dropped his cigarette into it.

A voice called out, "Mr. Lippincott?"

He paused at the top of the stairs. "It was a pleasure to meet you, Ellie March. I hope we'll have another chance to talk again soon."

She stood up and watched him go down the stairs. Leaning on the railing, she saw April Pressley struggling through the snow toward the side door of Ridge's lodge. Jay Lippincott called over to her, waving. Pressley waved back.

"Sorry about all the snow," she sang out. "They were supposed to be here this morning to clear the driveway for us."

"No problem." Jay high-stepped through the drifts as she unlocked the door.

He turned, waved again to Ellie, and followed Pressley inside.

Something about the guy just didn't sit right with her.

Ellie looked at Reggie, who was watching her from the warm side of the sliding glass door.

Something about the guy was definitely off.

Chapter

3

Dante Tassone glanced at his watch and saw that it was twenty minutes past four o'clock in the afternoon. Tea time. He stood up and crossed the room to the cellarette, where he poured himself a drink, neat, and took a sip.

"Anything else?" He slid his free hand into his pocket, enjoying the taste of his late uncle's very fine single-malt scotch.

"Just one more," David Gallo replied, "and that will finish up the domestic holdings."

"I feel like I've been signing my name all afternoon. I should be a movie star or something."

Gallo smiled politely. "I appreciate your patience, Mr. Tassone."

Dante strolled over to the window. The view of Upper

Rideau Lake was spectacular. Gabriel Tassone, Dante's late uncle, had chosen a truly beautiful location in which to build his Xanadu. The mansion was, indeed, a stately pleasure dome, and if it had been within a short limo ride of Woodbridge instead of four hours away in the middle of nowhere, he might have felt somewhat jealous that he wasn't inheriting it.

As it was, Gabriel had been more than generous in rewarding his nephew for his years of loyalty and service, and Dante had no complaints whatsoever about the will.

The funeral mass, held yesterday in the local Roman Catholic church, had been well attended. Many of the family had made the trip from Toronto to pay their last respects. Gabriel would have been pleased.

He also would have been amused by the various unmarked surveillance vehicles trying unsuccessfully to remain inconspicuous in the parking lot of the school next door as they photographed and filmed the comings and goings of everyone at the church, their engines running to fend off the cold, exhaust trails drifting upward and outward.

Laughably obvious.

A few of his cousins had found it entertaining, but the whole thing had left Dante feeling rather depressed.

We all do what we have to do.

"Do you have other meetings today?" he asked Gallo, not turning around.

"No, this is the last one. Then a full slate again tomorrow."

Dante finished his drink. Leaving the empty glass on the cellarette, he strolled over to the table at which he and Gallo had been working for most of the afternoon.

"What's this one?" He picked up the next document

Gallo had set out for him.

"Mr. Tassone held a controlling interest in a numbered corporation that operates several copper mines in northern Ontario."

Dante scanned the document, which transferred ownership of the controlling interest to him. He knew that Leonardo and his team had already reviewed everything Gallo, as executor of Gabriel's will, had put in front of him today. If there had been any problems with any of them, they would not have made it into the pile he and Gallo had laboured through this afternoon.

Dante picked up his pen and signed it at the places Gallo had flagged with green Post-it Notes.

"Thank you, Mr. Tassone." Gallo added the document to the stack in front of him and bent down to retrieve his briefcase.

Dante put the pen, his personal Mont Blanc, in his pocket.

"Your son looks well," Gallo said, stuffing files into his briefcase.

"Thank you."

"He mentioned something about staying at a bed-and-breakfast in the village. I thought he was in the hotel with you."

"No other vacancies. Anyway, he has his own friends and his own life."

"Yes, of course. I regret he wasn't terribly pleased with his portion of the legacy."

Dante shrugged. All the young family members named in the will had received an equal lump sum of $50,000. Ricardo had not been happy about it, believing that he deserved far more than the others, given the importance of his position within the family business. Dante had tried to talk to him about it, but the conversation had gone nowhere. Ricardo was a very stubborn person.

Gallo stood up and held out his hand. "Thank you once again, Mr. Tassone. Will ten o'clock tomorrow morning suit your schedule?"

Dante shook the man's hand. "Yes, that will be fine."

"The international holdings are a little more complicated, I'm afraid, so Mr. Arcuri might want to sit in with you to advise. He and I have gone over everything, of course, to smooth out the wrinkles, but just the same . . ."

"Fine, fine. Have a good evening."

When he was alone in the room, Dante took out his cellphone and turned it on. When it had booted up, he looked in vain for a message from Lonnie. There was nothing at all.

Had he made it to the village yet? He was supposed to let him know as soon as he arrived.

What was this urgent matter his old friend had so desperately wanted to talk to him about, face to face?

Chapter

4

The following morning, which was a Wednesday, OPP Detective Constable Kevin Walker stood in the parking lot behind the Westport hardware store, arms folded, watching Identification Constable Jayne Witten crawl around on her hands and knees, picking through the snow around the body with tweezers and a plastic evidence bag.

"I wouldn't have that job for a million bucks," said Detective Constable Sarah-Anne Mulvahill, her breath puffing out in little clouds. "I'd be cross-eyed and buggy inside of ten minutes."

The hardware store was located at the corner of Bedford and Church Streets at the north end of the village. A settlement of about six hundred people within the broader municipality of Rideau Lakes, Westport consisted of three streets running east-west and four running north-south. The paved lot behind the hardware store formed an L-shape, with one entrance on Church and the other on Bedford.

Joseph Lappin, the man who'd discovered the body earlier this morning, earned a living cutting lawns in the summer and plowing snow from people's driveways in the winter. His Ford F-250 and its eight-foot plow were his pride and joy, and he held the contracts to clear the snow from the lots and driveways of most of the businesses in the village. A life-long bachelor who loved to talk if you got him started, he was reliable and prompt, and he would often come back more than once if a storm persisted throughout the day.

He took great pride in claiming to be a descendent of Thomas Lappin, a Carrive blacksmith in Forkhill parish, County Armagh, who was immortalized in poetry for having withstood a five-day beating at the hands of the yeomanry for supplying local rebels with pikestaffs in the 1790s and refusing to give up the names of his customers.

"Loyalty's the thing," Joe liked to say while reciting a few lines of the verse in question. "We don't get nowhere in life without it, now, do we?"

Shortly after eight o'clock this morning Joe had worked his way east on Bedford to the hardware store, where he started in on that side of the L. As he described it to the responding officer, Provincial Constable Roberta Raymond, he'd noticed right away the car in the back corner of the lot—in the heel of the L, as it were. Normally he didn't care whether he plowed them in or not. Unless the driver was there, of course, trying to get out. In which case he might give them a hand if they needed it.

Otherwise, they got plowed in.

This particular car was covered with a night's-worth of snow and there were no footprints visible around it. Without hesitation, he lowered his blade and stepped on the gas.

On his third pass, close to the back wall of the hardware store, he noticed an odd shape in front of him under the snow. He slowed, hesitating. He was tempted to drive whatever it was into the snow bank he was creating down at the far end, but he worried that it might be something heavy or frozen, a large chunk of ice or metal perhaps, and he didn't want to damage his blade.

As he told it to Bobby Raymond, it was only after he got out of his truck that he noticed the fetal shape, like someone asleep under a white quilt, knees drawn up and arms folded in. He brushed enough snow away from it to see a face, cloudy eyes open and staring, before hurrying back into his truck to call 911.

Watching Jayne Witten tweezer up something small and drop it into an evidence bag, Kevin took off his toque and shook the snow from it.

"How come you're not playing hockey this year?" Mulvahill asked.

"Oh, you know." Kevin put his toque back on, moving it around so that the OPP crest was centred on his forehead. "The kids are keeping us busy right now. There never seems to be enough time left over for other stuff."

"Admit it. You like playing with them a hell of a lot more than you like playing with us."

"Well, yeah."

"Here's the haul so far," Identification Sergeant Dave Martin said, joining them. "Looks like they searched his clothing and went through his wallet after beating the crap out of him." He passed Kevin a sealed evidence bag.

Kevin looked at an Ontario driver's licence that had been issued to Alonzo DiMaria, date of birth November 4, 1962, with an address on Woodbridge Avenue in Vaughan, Ontario. The photo matched what Kevin had seen of the victim's face, more or less.

One at a time, Martin held up other evidence bags in his collection. "Health card, credit cards, rewards points cards, the usual wallet stuff."

"And teeth," said the coroner, slipping into their informal circle. "Three of them."

"Four," Witten called out, holding up her evidence bag.

"I don't suppose you have any idea right now on time of death," Kevin asked.

Dr. Linh Phong dimpled at him. "Too frozen! The pathologist will want to take his time thawing the poor man out, so we'll just have to wait a day or two for some of that very important information you guys always like to have."

Kevin nodded, having investigated a homicide involving a frozen body once before, five winters ago.

"I'm willing to bet, though," Dr. Phong went on, "that cause of death will be cerebral haemorrhage from repeated blows to the head. He was severely beaten. Mostly kicked, from the looks of it. Terrible."

Dr. Phong, a thirty-something of Vietnamese descent, was the new coroner for Lanark-Leeds. She was a welcome replacement for Dr. Fiona Kearns, who'd run for office in the recent federal election and, to the dismay of many who knew her, became the new Conservative Party member of Parliament for Renfrew-Nipissing-Pembroke.

A family doctor in Brockville, Dr. Phong was famous for her sunny disposition and her encyclopaedic knowledge of pharmaceuticals, their various benefits, and their attendant drawbacks. She was very good with small children and the elderly. That is, as far as living customers were concerned.

"Maybe an interrogation gone wrong," Mulvahill said, banging her gloved hands together to restore the circulation in her fingers.

"It would have been late yesterday afternoon or early evening." Dr. Phong sighed. "The body's frozen solid. It was minus-twenty overnight."

Kevin looked at Mulvahill. "What time did the store close?"

"The owner said he let his staff go home at two and he locked up and left at three. Said there wasn't a single customer after lunch."

"The way the snow's been falling," Martin said, "I'm not surprised."

"Thirty centimetres so far; another five today and ten more tomorrow." Dr. Phong watched with interest as Constable Witten lifted a pair of wire-frame glasses from the snow and dropped them into another bag.

Kevin's cellphone rang. He took a step back from the group, looked at the call display, and answered. "Walker."

"Walker, this is Carty." Detective Sergeant Tom Carty was commander of the Leeds County Crime Unit, which made him Kevin's immediate supervisor. "Something's come up. I'm not going to make it there."

Something in Carty's voice, which was usually brusque and even, caught Kevin's attention. "Everything all right?"

"No, not exactly. I went off the road. I'm inside an ambulance right now, en route to hospital."

"God, Tom. What happened?"

"I hit a whiteout on a curve just north of the detachment

and went off the pavement onto the shoulder. Ended up fishtailing into the ditch. They're telling me my ankle's pretty badly broken."

"I'm very—"

"Listen up, they're letting me make two calls, and this is the second one. I talked to Callaghan, and Prez Raintree will attend your scene as incident commander."

There was a fumbling at his end. "Yeah, okay. Fine." Then: "I gotta go. Apparently we're five minutes out, and they're taking me right into surgery as soon as I get there. You and Prez will have to carry the football on this one."

"Yes, sir. I'll check in on you as soon as I can."

He was talking to a dead line.

He walked back to Mulvahill. She and Bobby Raymond were watching Dave Martin direct his team as they worked around the car that had been plowed in. A check on the licence plate had already told them it belonged to their victim.

"Carty can't make it," Kevin told Mulvahill. "Prez Raintree's en route."

Constable Raymond's face lit up. "Sergeant Raintree!"

Mulvahill gave her a look. "You a fan or something?"

"Traffic," Kevin said. "He's her commander. You know what they're like."

Mulvahill chuckled. Turning her attention to the body, the smile slipped away as she noticed the sweater beneath the torn and blood-spattered barn coat. She moved forward along the line of cones marking a safe path through the snow.

"That looks familiar," she said, crouching.

"What does?" Kevin asked.

"The sweater. I've seen them before. There's a guy sells them, here in the village."

"Oh?"

"Yeah. His store's one block down." She looked up at Kevin, breath puffing. "Our vic's from out of town? Maybe he just bought it."

Kevin nodded. "Let's go find out."

Chapter

5

The sidewalks had not yet been cleared by the municipality, so they trudged down the middle of Church Street side by side, their boots squeaking on the flattened snow. Paddy's Threads was the next block down, Mulvahill explained. On the left, just past the United church on the corner.

"I've never been in this store," she said, "but I met the guy at the Perth Fair on Labour Day. He was giving a knitting class."

"Were you working the booth there?"

Mulvahill nodded. The OPP often ran information kiosks at local events in order to conduct outreach in rural areas where they provided police services. In both the Lanark and Leeds detachments, detective constables were expected to participate.

"Two weeks before I transferred," she said.

Kevin smiled at her. "Any regrets?"

"Hell, no. I've got my own office, don't I?"

When Detective Constable John Bishop had returned from vacation at the end of last summer, Tom Carty engineered with his counterpart in the Lanark County Crime Unit what had amounted to a trade: Bishop for Mulvahill. Bishop took with him to the Lanark detachment seven years' more experience and a questionable attitude, while Carty received in exchange a younger detective with lots of energy who needed a fresh start.

Her request for a transfer granted, Mulvahill was assigned to the Leeds County detachment satellite office in Rideau Lakes to replace Bishop as the designated detective for the area. She moved into the tiny cubbyhole Kevin had recently occupied while filling in for Bishop, and while it was cramped and stuffy, it had a door that could be closed whenever you felt a little privacy was desirable.

A luxury hard to come by at their level in one of the largest police services in North America.

"This is a nice village," Kevin said. "Good people."

Mulvahill looked up. The sun was high, and the light trying to find its way down to them was turning the cloud-heavy sky a pale yellow colour. Snowflakes gathered on her eyelashes. She wiped them off with the edge of a gloved finger.

They reached the corner and stopped to wait for a car to creep through the snowy intersection in front of them. Its exhaust plumed out behind it in a lazy cloud.

"Rural's rural," she said. "Driving all over the place just to get from one call out to another."

"Yeah, true enough."

While the Lanark County detachment of the OPP policed over 3,000 square kilometres of eastern Ontario, with a scattered population of about 59,000 people, the Leeds County detachment covered about 2,100 square kilometres and 38,000 people in 20,000 households. Lanark deployed a total of 73 uniformed personnel compared to 59 working out of the Leeds detachment. Mulvahill had moved to a slightly smaller jurisdiction, but she didn't really see a difference. Rural was rural, indeed.

Paddy's Threads was open, so they walked in and identified themselves to Matthew Scanlan. Taking the lead, Mulvahill held up her cellphone to show him Alonzo DiMaria's driver's licence photo.

"Yes," Matthew said, "he was in here yesterday afternoon. My only customer of the day, as it turned out."

Kevin looked around the shop. It sold menswear exclusively, everything from underwear and socks to belts and braces, shirts and trousers, cardigans and sports jackets, and the curling sweaters that had brought them down from the crime scene.

"He bought one of these from you?" Mulvahill asked, pointing at the rack.

"Yes, and a barn coat. He came in asking for directions to the Crosby Hotel, but he was underdressed for the cold weather and decided to get something warmer."

"What did he talk about?"

Matthew shrugged. "I don't know; nothing much, really. We talked about the weather. I asked him if he'd been to Westport before, and he said he'd never been east of Bowmanville. He asked about boots, and I told him I didn't carry them but he might be able to find something at the hardware store if it was open. Why?"

Kevin leaned against the corner of a wardrobe displaying

navy sports jackets and grey flannel trousers. He'd never met Matthew Scanlan before.

"How long have you had this store, Mr. Scanlan?" he asked.

"This is my tenth year."

Kevin studied him for a moment. He was a small man. His dark hair and stubbled beard were starting to show some grey. His eyes were light blue and friendly, and his manner of speaking was slow and precise.

"Who owns this building?"

"I do. I live upstairs."

"Back to your customer," Mulvahill said. "Did he act at all unusual? Nervous or worried about something?"

"No. Maybe a little distracted. Definitely cold. He said the heater in his car wasn't working properly."

"How did he pay for his stuff? Which card did he use?"

"That was something unusual. It was cash. Six fifties and a twenty. From a big roll he took out of his pocket."

Mulvahill raised her eyebrows at Kevin. No cash had been found in the victim's clothing or in the snow around the body. It would seem that whoever killed him had taken the money with them.

"So he bought the clothes, paid for them with cash, and left? That was it?"

"He used the washroom before he left. Then he decided to wear the sweater and barn coat instead of his suit jacket and top coat. I put those in a big bag for him."

"His car was parked out front?"

"He said it was down at the corner. Beside the church." He frowned at Mulvahill, remembering. "A car went by in the street. Before he left. You asked if he acted at all unusual. When he saw the car go by, he suddenly moved away from the window and asked to use the washroom. It was kind of abrupt. As though he didn't want whoever was in the car to see him."

"Did it stop?"

"No, it kept on going. I never saw it again. Of course, as soon as he left, I locked the door and went upstairs." He paused. "When he left the store, he tried his cellphone. It looked as though the battery might be dead."

Mulvahill looked at Kevin again. So far the victim's cellphone hadn't been found.

"Can you describe the car to us?"

"Sorry. All I saw were the headlights."

"Anything else you can remember?"

"No, sorry. That's pretty much it."

Kevin handed him a business card. "If anything else comes to mind, give one of us a call."

"I will." Matthew accepted a card from Mulvahill as well. "Why are you asking all these questions? Did something happen to him?"

"A little while after he left your store," Mulvahill said, "someone caught him in the parking lot behind the hardware store and beat him to death."

"Oh my God," Matthew said. "That's horrible."

Mulvahill zipped up her coat. "Damned right it is."

Chapter

6

Ellie March shrank down inside her OPP-issue winter parka and tucked her mittened hands into her armpits as Dr. Phong briefed her on the victim's identity, the probable cause of death, and a very tentative time of death.

"We'll know more when he's thawed out, in a day or so." Dr. Phong smiled as Dave Martin joined them. "You seem to be having very little luck this morning, Sergeant."

"You know," Martin groused, "I normally don't mind working crime scenes in the winter, but this one's a definite loser. All that we can find are the tire treads from the plow. The guy scraped right down to the asphalt and destroyed everything else. Why couldn't he have come in from this side," he pointed at Church Street, "instead of this side where all the evidence was?"

Ellie looked at the snow between the location of the body and the lot entrance on Church. Other than a narrow set of footprints along the side wall of the hardware store left by personnel accessing the scene from that end of the L, the white surface was pristine. No other boot prints, no tire tracks, no nothing. Just twenty centimetres of untouched snow, with more falling as every minute passed.

She opened her mouth, but Martin cut her off.

"Don't even say it. Of course we're going to process the rest of this. But I stand a better chance of winning the lottery and retiring to Saint Lucia than finding anything under that snow. It all happened over here, on this side. End of story."

"What about his cellphone?"

"We found what was left of it in the dumpster. No battery; no SIM card; circuit board wrecked. After we get a warrant we can see if he stored data in a cloud account of some kind. Other than that, we're screwed."

Dr. Phong looked down at the parking lot entrance, where the body removal vehicle had just arrived. "Time for Mr. DiMaria to go to Kingston. Excuse me, please."

She shuffled away, her large white boots squeaking and her breath trailing over her shoulder in swirling horsetails.

"Finally we get a coroner who's not only competent but really nice," Ellie said, "and you have to be Mr. Grump-and-Fuss."

Martin scowled. "I'll make it up to her later. I'm really a very nice guy."

"I know that. But she doesn't know that. She thinks you're a foul-tempered troll."

"No, she doesn't."

Ellie patted him on the shoulder and followed Dr.

Phong down to the Bedford Street entrance. Except for the area immediately around the car, which Identification Constable Witten was still photographing and processing, Dave Martin had cleared the rest of the lot at this end of the L, so it was safe to walk on. Dr. Phong was going over the paperwork with the driver of the vehicle that would transport Alonzo DiMaria's body to Kingston General Hospital. Once it reached the KGH, it would be signed into the custody of Dr. Carey Burton, the forensic pathologist who would perform the autopsy.

Ellie watched a black Town Car approach from her right on Bedford Street. The car stopped in front of her and the rear window went down.

"Excuse me, ma'am. What's going on?"

Ellie bent down and looked in at a man in his late fifties. She took in the dark suit and tie, the neatly trimmed, iron-grey beard, and the enormous watch on his left wrist. Beside him, another man peered at her over gold-framed reading glasses, a newspaper folded across his knee. She glanced up front at the back of the driver's head and the profile of another man in the front passenger seat.

"This is a crime scene," she said. "Please clear the street immediately to allow emergency vehicles to pass. Thank you."

The man who had spoken to her looked over her shoulder and immediately became upset. He seemed to be about to ask another question, but clenched his jaw instead, glancing at the man beside him.

"Anything I can help you with?" Ellie asked.

The man shook his head. The window went up and the car began to move.

Ellie stepped back, making a mental note of the licence plate number as she watched the Town Car roll slowly away.

Where the hell was Carty's replacement? She wanted this street blocked off right now to keep the rubberneckers away. Maybe Dave Martin didn't mind winter crime scenes, but that didn't stop her from absolutely hating them.

Chapter

7

Dante Tassone leaned over the sink and washed his hands. He shook off the excess water and ran his fingers through his hair several times to smooth it back from his forehead. It was thinning and more grey than sandy brown now that he had passed his fifty-ninth birthday.

He studied his face in the bathroom mirror. His broad, high forehead was creased with horizontal lines matching the crow's feet at the corners of his eyes, lines that offset the vertical creases at the bridge of his nose and the corners of his mouth. He was looking old. More and more he could see his mother's face superimposed on his own: her small mouth, her narrow blue eyes, and the high forehead.

He dried his hands. Stress was aging him. Stress, and now, suddenly, the loss of his closest boyhood friend. If

Leonardo were correct, based on what he had seen in the parking lot behind the crime scene tape, it would be a body blow Dante was not sure he could absorb. He hoped against all hope there was some mistake, that Lonnie had merely been delayed for some reason and had not been able to call.

He dropped the hand towel into a hamper inside the bathroom door and left the washroom, heading toward the salon in which he and David Gallo had been reviewing the international holdings Gabriel had willed to him. Businesses not only in Italy but also in Germany, the Netherlands, and Australia were now passing into Dante's hands. A global network of legitimate enterprises through which to launder the funds generated by the family's other, less legal, operations.

"I take it you're getting everything you wanted," a shrill voice called out from the staircase on his right.

Dante sighed. He'd been hoping to conclude his business with Gallo here in Gabriel's mansion on the Rideau without having to talk to her, but apparently he was not to be afforded even that slight favour by the gods in heaven that controlled his destiny.

"Yes, thank you, Mollie."

"How nice." She swept down the stairs and floated before him, eyes filled with malice, mouth curving with mischief. "There's nothing that pleases me more than to see a gangster get what's coming to him."

"Yes, well, if you'll excuse me, Mr. Gallo's waiting patiently for my return."

She put a hand on his chest. "Just a minute. I have something to say to you. You've successfully avoided me so far, but your luck's run out and now you have to listen."

He tipped his head to one side, suggesting that she get

it over with.

She was small and carelessly dressed in jeans, sneakers, and a pink denim shirt over a black T-shirt. Her frizzy silver hair stuck out in all directions.

"You don't like me, Dante, and I don't like you either. But it's important that I underline to you, right here and now, that I'm quite satisfied with what Gabbie left me, and I sincerely hope that no one else will take it into their nubby little Italian brain to challenge the will in court."

"You should discuss it with Mr. Gallo," Dante said, "but I can assure you I'm not aware of any potential problem."

"What about your son? I'm hearing that he's, shall we say, a trifle agitated."

"Ricardo is fine."

She curled her hand into a tiny fist and rapped it on his collarbone. "He better be."

Dante gave her a tight smile.

"I'll probably keep this place," she said, pirouetting, taking it all in, without a care in the world. "After all, I was the one who talked him into building it."

"I'm aware."

"Good for you. Awareness is a wonderful thing. I have to say, I'm really very productive here. The house, the surroundings; all very conducive to good writing."

"You won some kind of award last year, didn't you?"

She curled her lip. "First of all, it was two years ago; second of all, it wasn't some kind of award, it was the Man Booker Prize, for chrissakes; and third of all, I didn't win the damned thing."

"I'm sorry," Dante said.

"No, you're not. Not that I give a shit what you think. Anyway, this place is good for me, so I'm staying. I'm actually working on a new novel. A sequel to an earlier one, so I expect it to be another bestseller." She spun on her heels. "Anyway, I won't wish you good luck because I don't care if a satellite drops out of the sky tomorrow morning and lands on your head, but I will say Sayonara, which is Japanese for 'Don't let the door hit you on the ass on your way out.'"

Dante watched her sweep down the hall and around the corner, out of sight.

Please, gods, let those be the last words I ever hear from the mouth of that woman.

His cellphone chimed. He took it out and looked at a text message from Leonardo:

I'm in the sun room. I have an update.

It took a bit of searching to find the sun room, but eventually he made it there. He sat down opposite his friend. Glancing at Giorgio Marino, his personal security man, who was sitting in an armchair in the corner reading something on his smart phone, Dante clasped his hands together between his knees.

"Tell me."

"It was him. They're taking his body to Kingston for an autopsy. They notified Stella. I spoke to her briefly and said that you'd call."

Dante covered his face with his hands.

Stella was Lonnie's wife.

Leonardo crossed his legs. "Did he tell you what he wanted to talk to you about? What it was that was so important he'd drive all the way here in the middle of a snowstorm?"

Dante shook his head.

After a few moments, during which Leonardo maintained a respectful silence, Dante lowered his hands and exhaled loudly.

"How did it happen?"

"He was beaten to death. That's all I know right now."

"Damn it. This is stepping over the line, Leo. Lonnie has always been out of bounds. Everybody knows this." He glanced at Giorgio, who was maintaining a respectful silence. "Call Dom, Leo. See what he can tell us."

"I will, but he probably won't talk to me. He doesn't trust me. He prefers to talk to you only."

Dante nodded. "Yeah, but call anyway. If he won't answer your questions, tell him to call me."

"Yes, Dante."

"Out of bounds," Dante repeated, standing up. "I won't tolerate it."

Chapter

8

Kevin looked on with amusement as Sergeant Preston Raintree watched the removal crew load the body of Alonzo DiMaria into the back of their vehicle and close the doors. Raintree pulled off his glove and shook hands with the driver and his assistant, then shook hands with Dr. Phong before stepping out of the way so that the vehicle could leave the scene.

Raintree walked up the parking lot and shook hands with Dave Martin. He waved at Identification Constable Witten, who was still processing Lonnie's car, and finally made his way over to Kevin and Ellie.

"I'm Prez Raintree," he said, holding out his hand to Ellie. "I don't think we've met."

"Ellie March." She shook his hand, leaving her mitten

on because it was too damned cold to take it off.

"You, I know." Raintree pumped Kevin's hand, his grip firm but not aggressively so.

He was a big man, almost as tall as Kevin, with a barrel chest and narrow hips. Snow dusted his Russian-style fur cap and the sergeant's chevrons on the epaulettes of his duty jacket. He carried his sidearm on his left hip and his portable radio on his left breast, indicating that he was left-handed.

"So what's the story here, anyway?"

Kevin briefed him on what they knew so far about Alonzo DiMaria, which was limited at this point to his basic personal information and the manner of his death. "We're still not sure why he's here."

"Or who beat the crap out of him."

"That's right, sir. I sent Sarah-Anne down to the Crosby Hotel to see if he ever made it there."

Raintree pursed his lips at the victim's car, a three-year-old Lexus that was still half-buried in snow plowed onto it by Joe Lappin. "Looks like the answer to that one might be in the negatory."

"Could be, sir. We'll see." Kevin turned to Ellie. "I ran the other plates you gave me. I think we may have a connection."

Raintree frowned. "What plates?"

"A Town Car stopped down at the end of the lot," Ellie said. "Before the street was closed off." She gave him a look. "They wanted to know what was going on. I told them to beat it." She looked at Kevin. "What'd you get?"

"The vehicle's registered to a business called Wooden Bridge Investments. The address is on Woodbridge Avenue in Vaughan. Looks like it might be only a few blocks from the condo building where our victim lived."

"Wait, wait, I know this." Raintree grinned. "'Rule 39: there's no such thing as a coincidence.'"

Ellie looked puzzled.

"You know. Leroy Jethro Gibbs."

Ellie stared.

"*NCIS*," Kevin supplied. "The TV show."

She shook her head. "Whatever. Kevin, you're following up on this Wooden Bridge company?"

"Yeah. I'll let you know as soon as we get something."

"Fine. What about the other plate?"

"Registered to a John David Lippincott with an address in York Mills. Apparently that's the second-richest neighbourhood in the city." He shrugged, embarrassed by her stare. "I Googled it."

"So who's this guy?" Raintree wanted to know. "Is he connected to this too?"

"That's what I want to find out." When Ellie left the cottage this morning, Jay Lippincott's Land Rover was still parked in her driveway. She'd been able to make out the licence number by deciphering the shapes of the letters and numerals beneath the caked brown slush.

"Do you want me to keep digging on him?" Kevin asked. "Verify a link between this and the helicopter company?"

"Not at the moment."

"All right," Raintree said, his eyes following Dave Martin as the identification sergeant walked over to see how Witten was making out. "Anything you need, just let me know."

"I'll do that," Ellie said.

Raintree strode off, making sure to step in Martin's boot prints as he went over to see what they were up to.

"In case you're wondering," Kevin said, "he speaks four languages—English, French, Spanish, and Ojibwe—he's a provincial chess champion, and he's a member of MENSA. He just has a lively sense of humour, that's all."

Ellie frowned, her thoughts elsewhere.

Chapter

9

Mulvahill stamped the snow from her boots and crossed the front lobby of the Crosby Hotel to the front desk. The smell of food assailed her nostrils from the dining room off to the left. She unzipped her duty jacket and took off her fur hat.

"Hey Garnett," she said to the kid behind the desk, "I thought you just worked in Perth."

He blushed, pushing blond hair off his forehead. "My uncle owns both hotels, so sometimes I'm here and sometimes I'm there."

"Okay, then." Mulvahill dropped her hat on the long mahogany counter. Garnett Carr lived in Stanleyville, a small hamlet just north of Westport on the Lanark side of the county line. He was nineteen, good-looking, and very shy.

Over the past few years that Mulvahill had been working in the Lanark crime unit, Garnett had been a willing informant whenever she wanted to know about the comings and goings of various individuals at the hotel in Perth. It was her lucky day, she decided, that he was down here in Westport today.

"I need to know if an individual named Alonzo DiMaria checked in yesterday."

Garnett slid onto a stool, pulled out a keyboard tray, and began to type. "What's the last name again?"

Mulvahill spelled it for him.

"Nope. Sorry."

"Nothing under that surname at all?"

"Zip."

"What about Maria?"

Garnett typed. "Nope."

"Hmm."

"We had a lot of checkouts yesterday and this morning," he said, wanting to be helpful.

"Is that right?"

"Yeah. There was a big funeral on Monday at St. Edward's. A lot of out-of-towners."

"Really. Who died?"

"The guy in that big place on North Shore Road."

"You mean the one on the Upper Rideau? The big mansion with all the glass and steel?"

"Yeah. Gabriel Tassone." He pronounced the surname with three syllables: Tass-OWN-ee.

Mulvahill grunted. Now that she thought about it, the name rang a bell. Tom Carty had sent her a heads-up that intelligence types were going to be coming into her bailiwick on Monday for something or other. She hadn't paid it much attention because she considered intelligence work a little beyond her pay grade. If the pointdexters came up with something she needed to know, she'd find out about it soon enough. Or so her reasoning had gone at the time.

"Couvillon House was all booked up too," Garnett said. "And the motel out on Salem Road."

Mulvahill was vaguely aware that Couvillon House was a bed-and-breakfast place on Church Street. She and Kevin had walked past it on their way to Matthew Scanlan's shop earlier, although she hadn't paid it any attention.

Top Star Motel, on Salem Road, was a dive. She couldn't picture people attending a billionaire's funeral who would stay there willingly. Stranger things had happened, though.

She remembered that she'd also been asked to check on the black Town Car. "What about four guys, middle-aged business types, in a black limo?"

"Sure, they're still here. Three of them, anyway. The fourth guy with them is staying out on the highway. He drives the limo."

"And you know this how?"

Garnett shrugged. "He helped carry in the bags. They were talking about it."

"Okay. Tell me about the ones here."

"One guy took our suite on the second floor and another's in the room next to it. Third guy's across the hall."

"Names?"

Garnett worked the keyboard and mouse before turning the monitor around so that she could see the screen. She took out her notebook and wrote down *Dante Tassone, Leonardo Arcuri,* and *Giorgio Marino,* along with their particulars.

"Thanks. I wonder if this Dante Tassone is related to the Upper Rideau Lake Tassone."

"Gabriel. It's what I understand. I took the call for the reservation on Sunday. The secretary said they were coming up here to attend Mr. Dante Tassone's uncle's funeral." Garnett turned the monitor back and cleared the screen. "Why? Do you think the old guy was murdered or something?"

"Nah. Just a routine check." Mulvahill zipped up her jacket and grabbed her hat. "Stay out of trouble, Garnett."

"I will."

The smell of the food assailed her again as she headed to the front door and reluctantly walked out into the cold.

Chapter

10

Sergeant Raintree accompanied Dr. Phong down to her car, a black Mercedes sport utility vehicle parked a block away and around the corner on Main Street. She knocked the snow off the back, opened the hatch, stowed her kit, and grabbed a snow brush. While she cleared the windshield, Raintree used his arm to wipe off the side windows.

They met back at the hatch. She tossed in the brush and slammed it shut.

"Hopefully it'll start," Raintree said.

"It's a very good car. I've never had any problems with it." She pulled off a glove and held out her hand. "Very nice to see you again, Sergeant."

"Same here." He shook her hand. "Could I ask you a question? I know you want to get going."

"Sure." She got in the car and started the engine. She left the door open, since there was too much crusted snow on top of the rubber gasket for her to lower the window. After a moment, the annoying chime stopped.

"What have you been hearing about this new coronavirus coming from Asia?"

"Not much so far," she replied. "Are you worried?"

"You never know with these things." He put his arm on the top of the door and leaned down so she could hear him over the noise of the revving engine. "I've been following the releases from the World Health Organization. There are more than three hundred cases in China already, and it's spreading to Thailand, Japan, and South Korea."

"A week ago the United States had their first case," Dr. Phong said. "Someone coming back from Wuhan. But you mustn't worry too much right now. It's winter, and these viruses turn up. Hopefully it'll run its course."

"Apparently on Monday the CDC deployed their own testing kit separate from what the Chinese are using, but it's turning out to be defective. They're trying to use three genetic sequences instead of two like the Germans are doing, for example, but the third sequence is giving out inconclusive results. It's not working. I don't like the way this is looking."

"I know. It *is* concerning, I agree." She cranked the heater fan up to full blast. "You're the only police officer I ever heard of who even knows about WHO outbreak news releases, let alone reads them."

"Time on my hands, I guess."

"I doubt that."

"Drive safely, Dr. Phong."

"Thank you."

He stepped back to let her close the door, then moved

behind the car as she shifted into gear and eased away from the snowbank. Surprisingly, she had enough traction to make it out into the middle of the street.

Since she was required to attend the scenes of any number of deaths, winter and summer, Raintree figured that a reliable vehicle was essential equipment for a coroner as well as for law enforcement personnel. Evidently the Mercedes was worth the money she'd spent on it. He watched her drive away before heading back to his crime scene.

Trudging past the Crosby Hotel, he told himself not to be worried about things he couldn't control. The weather, viruses, the whims of GHQ and regional command. Stuff like that.

He slipped in a rut left by a car tire and waved his arms around to maintain his balance. He resisted the urge to curse. Cursing was not only a waste of breath but a waste of emotional energy, as far as he was concerned. Mental discipline; that was the key.

And always being quick to laugh.

Approaching the barricade at the corner, he realized he was enjoying himself. He liked the challenge presented by a major case. While his heart was touched by the pathos of the poor frozen victim, so badly beaten and left overnight to be covered by a blanket of snow, the feeling didn't cloud his judgment. He'd seen plenty of dead people in his time, back home and down here, and he was hardened to the reality of death.

He almost slipped again and thought of Tom Carty. *Not a good idea to go breaking your ankle like that, Prez, my boy.*

He signed back into the crime scene, taking the time to exchange a little small talk with the uniformed constable in charge of the clipboard. His mind still on Carty, he ducked under the tape and lifted a hand to Ellie March, who was taking shelter in the front entrance of the hardware store. She didn't see him, and she didn't look toward the sound of his boots kicking through the snow.

He didn't particularly like Carty. There wasn't anything specific, just the natural dislike felt by two dogs that instinctively know they'll end up in a fight. He'd heard talk that Carty wasn't popular as commander of the crime unit, that he tended to persecute detectives he didn't like and was incapable of showing loyalty to the team as a whole.

He'd probably be laid up for a while with the ankle. When the detachment commander ordered Raintree here to fill in for Carty, he told him to expect a transfer into the position for the foreseeable future. The assumption being that when Carty returned to active duty, they'd find another seat at the table for him somewhere else in the region.

He smiled. *Detective Sergeant Preston Raintree, if you please.* Better than traffic sergeant, as far as he was concerned.

The next step up the ladder.

Chapter

11

Ellie munched on an egg salad sandwich as she listened to the voice of Inspector Norm Callaghan, commander of the Leeds County OPP detachment, drone on and on through the speaker on her cellphone. He ran through the various reasons why he couldn't possibly provide any more resources than were currently assigned to the DiMaria case: the winter flu bug had swept through the detachment, affecting not only two members of the crime unit but also numerous constables in the Emergency Response Team and other sources of backup; people were on vacation; and there was also Tom Carty's unfortunate accident, which would likely keep him on the sidelines for the next several weeks.

"It's that time of year," Callaghan said in his

Newfoundland drawl, "and there's nothin' we can do about it."

"Understood." Ellie popped the last bite of sandwich into her mouth.

"Maybe the chief can help you." Callaghan then launched into a monologue about his new boss, Chief Superintendent Jordan Malcolmsen, commander of the East Region. Malcolmsen had recently replaced Leanne Blair in that role when Leanne had moved from the region to General Headquarters. She had been promoted to deputy commissioner and appointed provincial commander of Investigations and Organized Crime. This was the command area within GHQ that included the Criminal Investigation Branch, in which Ellie worked, the Organized Crime Enforcement Bureau, the Provincial Operations Intelligence Bureau, and other areas of responsibility.

Leanne had replaced Cecil Dart, Ellie's rumoured rabbi in the force. Dart had been appointed commissioner, replacing Ted Moodie. Like Dr. Fiona Kearns, the former coroner for Lanark and Leeds, Moodie had entered politics in the last federal election and was now the Liberal member of Parliament for a large and powerful Toronto riding.

It was an elaborate and rather serious game of musical chairs that Ellie very much preferred to avoid.

Jordan Malcolmsen was an appointee who'd moved up from the Indigenous Policing Bureau at GHQ, where he'd overseen a number of innovative measures including outreach initiatives, programs to support aboriginal youth, and enhanced Native awareness training. The brainiacs at headquarters considered him a rising star, but within the region the jury was still out. For some, particularly the old guard, he was too young, too good-looking, and too damned smart to trust.

Ellie sighed as Callaghan finally came up for air. "I'll check in with him."

While Ellie held functional authority as a headquarters major case manager in charge of the overall direction of the investigation, the region held the actual line authority. Flowing down the chain of command stovepipe on their side, the region was responsible for providing investigators, equipment, administrative support, and everything else necessary in an operational sense to conduct the investigation.

As detachment commander, Callaghan was Malcolmsen's managerial boots on the ground, so to speak. The crime unit belonged to him, and passing the buck upstairs to his boss was not particularly surprising, given the human resource problems he had just described to Ellie. What was a little surprising was that Callaghan was willing to allow her to go over his head, rather than make the telephone call himself. It seemed he was having a few communication problems with his new regional commander.

Not that Ellie particularly cared. Regional personality conflicts were none of her business. Just as long as they didn't interfere with the management of her cases.

She ended the call and put the cellphone in her pocket. Slipping her mittens back onto her cold hands, she retreated into the doorway of the hardware store in a vain search for shelter from the wind, which was starting to pick up a bit. She watched Mulvahill round the corner, joining Kevin Walker across the street in front of the sandwich shop from which they'd all bought lunch a short while ago.

Kevin handed her a brown paper bag and a cup of coffee. Ellie watched the breath stream out in a cloud from Mulvahill's mouth as she laughed at something he said and began briefing him on what she'd learned at the hotel.

After a few moments, they walked single file through a gap in the snowbank and crossed the street.

"Sarah-Anne has something for us," Kevin said as they joined her in the doorway.

"Our vic didn't make it to the hotel." Mulvahill hunched her shoulders against the cold. "At least, he didn't register. Matthew Scanlan, the guy who sold him the sweater and coat just before he was killed, told us DiMaria had asked him about buying boots, and he told him to try the hardware store. He must have stopped here first, and that's when they caught him and beat him to death."

Ellie nodded.

"I asked about the guys in the limo," Mulvahill continued. "One is Dante Tassone," she said, giving the surname the three-syllable pronunciation used by Garnett Carr. "He took the suite upstairs. Next to him is Leonardo Arcuri, and across the hall is a Giorgio Marino. All three gave addresses in Woodbridge, Ontario. Check-in last Sunday afternoon; check-out was originally for this morning but it's been extended two days."

"I see." Ellie frowned at the threads of snow lifting off the snowbank and blowing along the surface of the street in front of them. "What about the fourth guy?"

"Not there. Looks like he got a room in the flea trap out on the highway. There was a big funeral Monday. A lot of people came from Toronto for it, including these guys. Tassone's apparently the dead guy's nephew. Most people checked out and left, but Tassone and his crew are still here."

"Hmm." Ellie closed her eyes for a moment, thinking.

"The desk clerk said that Couvillon House, the B and B just down the street here," she pointed, "was also full as well."

"Is it your understanding," Ellie asked, "that there are vacancies at the Crosby now?"

Mulvahill shrugged. "Probably. Sounds like it."

"Good." Ellie looked at Kevin. "I'm going to see if I can get a room. It's ridiculous for me to keep driving back and forth in this weather."

"What about Reggie?" Kevin asked.

"Riley has a key. I'll ask him to let him out to do his business."

Mulvahill frowned.

Ellie caught the look, and felt compelled to say, "My office door stays locked when I'm not there, and I'm the only one with that key."

Mulvahill reddened.

Kevin said, "I think we'll go down and check out the B and B."

"Sounds like a good idea." Ellie shot her cuff to look at her watch.

"You know," Mulvahill said, trying to rally from her embarrassment, "whoever killed our vic did a pretty thorough job of searching the poor bastard for something or other. If they didn't find it, I think they're probably still around here, looking for it."

"You might be right," Kevin said.

Turning up the collar of her duty jacket, Ellie reluctantly stepped out of the doorway into the wind and snow.

"Let me know what you find out," she said.

Chapter

12

Couvillon House was down on the right side of Church Street, one door before the corner of Spring. A three-storey Victorian red brick house, it was formerly the residence of a nineteenth-century jeweller whose descendants ended up in Wisconsin. It was now a bed-and-breakfast establishment with six guest rooms, a dining room, and an Irish-style pub bar.

Kevin showed his warrant card and badge to the woman behind the front desk. "Are you the owner?"

"I'm Angélique Couvillon," the woman replied. "What's this about?"

"Just a few questions." Kevin looked around. "We understand you were very busy last weekend."

"No vacancies, right up to yesterday morning. People

were here for the big funeral."

"Yeah, we heard about that. Anyone check out last evening or this morning?"

"Check-out time is noon," she said. "No one left last evening. No one this morning, either."

Kevin glanced at Mulvahill. If the killer had been staying here, they might not have left yet.

"So you still have some guests?"

"Is this about the guy who was found dead up the street?"

"News travels fast."

She shrugged. "Matthew called. He's upset about it."

"Scanlan?" Mulvahill raised an eyebrow. "You two are friends?"

"You could say that." She tapped at the keyboard, her eyes on the screen. She was in her late forties, maybe early fifties. Her wavy, shoulder-length hair was a touched-up auburn colour. Her features were sharp and devoid of emotion. "We still have two guests."

"Did Alonzo DiMaria stop in here yesterday? Maybe looking for a room?"

Angélique shook her head.

"Can you tell me the names of your two remaining guests?"

"No." Angélique turned the monitor around.

Mulvahill wrote down the names *Rick Tassone* and *Dom Calutti* in her notebook, along with their particulars.

"They're in the bar right now," Angélique said, "if you want to talk to them."

On the right was a staircase that led to the upper floors. On the left was a doorway into the kitchen, from which the pleasant odours of lunch were still evident. On the far left was another doorway through which the faint sound of a television could be heard.

As Mulvahill wandered off in that direction, Kevin asked, "What kind of guys are they?"

"Those two?" She looked at him with steady hazel eyes. "They're not tourists and they're not businessmen; not in the usual sense."

"What do you mean?'

"They're not on an expense account, that's for sure. The young one, he spends without thinking about it. Like money is just air that he breathes in and out. The older one's obviously an employee. He does what he's told."

"Thanks." Kevin followed Mulvahill through the far doorway. At the front of the house, on their left, was a dining room that looked out onto the street. They walked straight ahead into the pub. It featured dark panelling, a short bar, and a few tables. Two men sat on high stools at the bar, watching a hockey game on a widescreen TV on the wall. It was a replay of a game from the night before. Behind the bar, a young woman polished beer glasses, her eyes down.

"Excuse me," Mulvahill said, "which one of you is Rick Tassone?"

The older man turned slightly on his stool. "Who's asking?"

Mulvahill badged him. "OPP, Detective Constable Mulvahill. This is Detective Constable Walker. Are you Tassone?"

"I am," the younger man said, his eyes still following the action on the TV screen.

"Show me some identification, please. Both of you."

The older man lifted a haunch and took out his wallet. He handed his driver's licence to Mulvahill.

"This says you're Domenico Calutti and your address is

in Woodbridge. Is that correct?"

"Dom. Yeah." He took it back, returned it to his wallet, and returned his wallet to his back pocket.

"And you, sir?"

The other man sighed, unable to suppress the impatience of youth. He tore his eyes from the hockey game and pivoted on the stool, removing a billfold from the inside pocket of his suit jacket. It was a slim, black leather job that didn't seem to contain any currency. The card slots, however, were filled. He took out his driver's licence, held it up, and handed it over.

"Ricardo Tassone," Mulvahill said.

"Rick."

"You ever talk to the police before, Mr. Tassone?"

Rick returned the licence to his billfold and slipped it back inside his jacket. It was a calculated performance, an attempt to emphasize his superior social status. There was a small square shape visible in the right front pocket of his trousers that Kevin guessed was a money clip holding folded currency.

"Actually, no. Never have. To what do I owe the pleasure?"

"Are you related to a Dante Tassone who's currently registered at the Crosby Hotel?"

Rick rested his elbow against the bar. He was a small man, small-boned and fine-featured. His dark, wavy hair was stylishly mussed, and his beard was trimmed close to his face in order to achieve the three-day stubble look that had remained popular with men for far too long.

"My father," he said. "What's he done now?"

Mulvahill leaned her hip against the bar. "So you were here for the funeral on Monday, is that right?"

"Yep."

"You related to Gabriel Tassone?"

"My father's uncle. Ergo, my great uncle."

"Where were you last evening?" Kevin asked.

Rick lost the affability he'd been affecting. "Why the hell should I tell you that?"

"Because we're investigating the murder of a man named Alonzo DiMaria. He was beaten to death last night behind the hardware store up the street from here. He was from Woodbridge; you're both from Woodbridge; I'm betting you knew him. Where were you, Mr. Tassone?"

Rick looked at Dom, as though to share his frustration at the stupidity of cops, but Dom had his eyes down, studying his fingernails.

Rick shrugged. "I was attending a reception at Gabriel's mansion on the lake. You know, a thing for everyone who stuck around to meet with the estate executor. A chance to drown your sorrows because the old geezer ripped you off in his joke of a will."

"From what time to what time?"

Rick looked at Dom. "When did we go up there, about two thirty or so?"

Dom nodded. "Nearly three."

"In the afternoon?" Mulvahill frowned.

"Yeah," Dom said. "And I brought Mr. Tassone back here around midnight."

"So, three to midnight. Did either of you leave during that time?"

"No," Rick said.

Mulvahill looked at Dom. "What about you?"

"I was there the whole time, hanging out in the kitchen with Mr. Dante Tassone's driver. I don't drink when I'm working, but we sampled pretty much everything to eat that went out to the others."

"Food tasters," Rick joked, "in case of poison."

"Yeah." Dom smiled, but it didn't reach his eyes.

Mulvahill looked at Rick. "Did you know Alonzo DiMaria?"

"Sure. Lonnie. He worked for my dad. His accountant. Too bad he's dead. I hope you're going to catch the guy who did it."

"You don't seem too broken up about it."

"I'm good at hiding my feelings."

"What else are you hiding, Mr. Tassone?"

Rick snorted.

"When were you planning to head back home?" Kevin asked.

"Originally it was going to be this afternoon, but it's not safe to drive in this weather." Rick looked at Dom. "We're paid up here until tomorrow, so we'll see what it's like in the morning."

Dom said nothing.

"Unless," Rick added, "you're going to tell us we can't leave town until further notice. Isn't that what the cops usually say when someone gets offed?"

"You read my mind," Kevin said.

Chapter

13

Matthew frowned at his needles, busily working on a sleeve for his current sweater project. He was knitting down from the armhole, working in the round, deep in concentration, when the telephone on the counter next to the cash register began to ring.

"Damn." He piled his work into the bag at his feet and stood up to grab the portable. "Paddy's Threads."

"Matty, it's Angélique."

"Hey, there." He drew the stool over with his foot and sat down again. "How are you doing?"

"The police were here, asking questions about that guy who was in your store last night. The one they found dead this morning."

"The same detectives? Walker and Mulvahill?"

"Yes."

"I told them he was asking about the Crosby, not your place."

"Yeah, I know. They were more interested in the two guys who are still here. They asked them a lot of questions. In the pub."

Her tone was as even and businesslike as always, but he could sense the tension beneath the surface.

"I'm sure it's just routine. Getting everyone's story on the record."

"I guess so. I really can't believe someone would get murdered here. In a city, yes. But not here. It's unbelievable."

"Do you want me to come over?"

"No." It was quick, firm, and decisive. "There's no need."

"What about later. Maybe for dinner? What's on the menu?"

She snorted. "Pub fare. It's all these guys want. Cheeseburgers, French fries, and beer." She hesitated. "No, maybe another time, Matty. I don't have a good feeling about this, but I can handle it. I just wanted to hear your voice."

He smiled. "Likewise."

"How's your new sweater coming?"

"Not bad. I like the way it's turning out." The design Matthew had chosen featured stylized herons and zig-zag patterns above and below suggesting a river or stream. He was working with three colours—natural cream, sand, and a very nice blue his supplier had hand-dyed using indigo plants.

He waited, but she didn't say anything else.

"Three and a half weeks to go," he offered.

"Yes. I can't wait."

After much discussion, soul-searching, and internal deliberation, they'd decided to go on a Valentine's Day weekend trip together. The 14th fell on a Friday this year, and the following Monday would be the annual Family Day holiday in Ontario, so they'd decided to close up shop and travel to the Canary Islands. Four days in a luxury hotel with a beautiful beach, spectacular food, tours to interesting museums, and, well, more beach. It would be their first time away from the village together, completely alone, with no distractions and all the time in the world to find out where their relationship might take them.

He heard her mutter something under her breath.

"Problem?" he asked.

"Ah, I have to go. The young guy, Moneybags, wants a different bottle of single malt. *Cochon.*"

Matthew chuckled. "Call back again as soon as you can."

The call disconnected in his ear. He stood up and dropped the portable back into its base. His foot moved the knitting bag as he sat back down on the stool, but he didn't reach for his work. He leaned against the edge of the counter and looked out the window at the snow.

This was his tenth year in Westport, and he'd grown comfortable with the slower pace and the familiarity of the village. A native of Montreal, he'd grown up in a small apartment above his parents' sandwich shop on Atwater Avenue, a block from the old Montreal Forum. "The best onion burgers and grilled cheese sandwiches in the city," his sister Cécilia loved to brag to the customers lined up out the front door every lunch hour.

He was a city boy, a street rat who spent his free time in the winter hanging around the back doors of the arena hunting for autographs and his summers riding his bicycle along the waterfront, taking pictures of the ships with a cheap camera he'd received as a birthday gift.

He was also a dreamer, and by the time he'd finished high school, reading had become an overriding passion. His grades were high enough to earn him an academic scholarship to McGill University, where he completed an honours degree in English literature. Another scholarship took him away from home for the first time, across the border to Cambridge, Massachusetts, where he earned a Master's degree at Harvard with a specialization in American fiction. Then it was on to Chicago and a doctorate, then back to McGill, completing the circle, to accept a position with the English department.

He put in the time, working his way up the ladder, until tenure was achieved and his career path was set. He published articles, wrote a book on the serialized novels of William Dean Howells and other Gilded Age writers, and generally burrowed into the warm insulation of academic life to make a home for himself.

He met Joyce Williamson at a party in 2006. She and her business partner, Terri Farrell, were doing a tour publicizing their book about the threat posed to ancient historical sites in the Middle East by Al-Qaeda and other terrorist organizations. Farrell was the investigative reporter and Joyce the photojournalist, and Matthew was quite intimidated at first, but Joyce apparently thought he was cute and they struck up an acquaintance. When the book tour was done, she came back to Montreal and they took it from there.

They had been married for two years when Joyce returned to Iraq with Farrell on another assignment, and this time she didn't come back. Travelling to Diyala

Province, known to be dangerous for outsiders, they were assessing the threat of destruction faced by Tell Ishchali, an ancient archaeological site southeast of Baghdad, when they disappeared. Six months later their bodies were found in a shallow grave along with a dozen others, all executed by Al-Qaeda. Once famous for its antiquities and its orange groves and date orchards, Diyala was now forever engrained in Matthew's mind as a place of hatred and murder.

He tried, but after a while he could no longer stay in Montreal. He sold their condominium, quit his job, said goodbye to his sister and her family, and moved to Ottawa. He rented an apartment and lived on his savings for a winter. Looking back, he couldn't remember clearly what he'd done to pass the time.

One Saturday evening in the following spring he was listening to Cécilia on the phone as she scolded him about his lack of direction and inability to snap out of his chronic funk when she suddenly said, "Why don't you go back to that family history research you used to work on with Papa?"

He dismissed the idea at the time, not really interested in it, but a month later he found himself in front of a microfilm reader in the Library and Archives building on Wellington Street, poring over census records and taking copious notes. That summer a field trip was in order to Westport, where his father's ancestors had settled in the late nineteenth century, and after several follow-up visits he spotted the big brick house on Church Street that was up for sale.

By this time he'd been holding down a part-time job in a menswear store in the ByWard Market, within walking distance of his apartment. He'd always enjoyed clothing and liked dressing well, and one brilliant idea seemed to lead to another. He bought the brick house and moved down to Westport that fall. He spent the winter on renovations and business planning, and he launched Paddy's Threads the following spring.

From the beginning, Angélique Couvillon had been a friendly face around the village, showing an interest in how the new store was doing and encouraging him to attend the informal business council meetings she held once a month in her dining room. Through her he met the other merchants in the village and grew more comfortable within the community.

At the same time, his interest in tracking down his family history continued to grow, and his blue Toyota hatchback became a familiar sight on back roads in the township as he photographed the places where his ancestors had built shanties and struggled to clear the land in order to grow enough crops to feed their families.

Unfortunately, his sense of direction was not very good and he got lost a few times, ending up in places like Maberly or Sharbot Lake without a clear understanding of how he'd gotten there. He told these stories of wrong turns and bad guesses to Angélique, who was by now inviting him to regular lunch dates at Couvillon House, and one day she surprised him with a gift.

"It's a GPS device," she said, watching him strip off the wrapping paper and pull open the box. "It plugs into the cigarette lighter in your car. Just enter your destination and it'll give you turn-by-turn directions."

He wasn't much of a technology guy, but he deeply appreciated the thought. However, she wasn't done with him yet.

"Give me your phone."

Miraculously, he'd thought to stick it into his jacket pocket before coming up from his store. He watched her power it up, rolling her eyes at him because he seldom had it on. Once it was ready she tapped and swiped, eyes narrowed in concentration.

"I'm downloading a GPS app," she said. "It's one that works even when you don't have any bars. I know you like to get out of the car and wander around, taking pictures." She wagged the cellphone at him. "Make sure you have this with you, and you won't get lost on foot, either."

"Thanks," he said, dubiously.

"It updates automatically. Use it, all right?"

"I will."

He smiled now at the memory and decided that Angélique Couvillon was helping him find his way on more than one level.

Over time, her own story had come to him in bits and pieces, as stories often do when the subject of them is unwilling to talk about the past. She grew up in a farmhouse on the Perth Road, a few kilometres north of Westport on the hardscrabble granite ridge known locally as Foley Mountain. Her father, Frank Couvillon, was a handyman who installed roofing and siding. French was his preferred language when at home, and Angélique grew up fluently bilingual.

Her mother left them when she was eleven. Her older brothers and sisters likewise departed for greener pastures, but Angélique remained behind to look after Frank, who'd fallen off a ladder while she was in high school and shattered his pelvis. It didn't heal properly, and he remained confined to a wheelchair for the rest of his life.

When she was twenty she became involved with a man whose name Matthew never learned. It lasted a year. The man assaulted her father and robbed him of six hundred dollars he kept in a shoebox under his bed. Someone told Matthew they thought he was now living in Kingston.

Shortly after Frank passed away, Angélique took up with a man who lived down the road. Separated from his wife, Marcel Campeau drove a delivery truck for a local lumber yard. By all accounts, he was a friendly, patient man who was good to her. She gave birth to a son, Alexandre.

The third time Matthew and Angélique spent the night together, late last summer, she reluctantly told him what happened to her family.

"Alexandre had just turned six. He was in Grade One and liked it. He was a smart little boy and easy to manage. Marc was a good father."

Matthew waited, staring up into the darkness.

"I was riding my bicycle one morning, along the Parish Road, and I got hit by a car."

"Good lord."

"She came up behind me and swerved when a squirrel ran in front of her. Knocked me into the ditch. I woke up in the hospital with a broken leg and a concussion."

"That's terrible."

"It's life. Anyway, while I was still in hospital Marc's ex came around to the house. It was a Saturday. She had a shotgun with her."

Matthew waited for her to gather herself.

"She shot Alex and Marc. Killed them both, then killed herself."

"My God. I'm so sorry."

"They told me later she was looking for me as well. She didn't know I'd had the accident and wasn't at home. Otherwise I'd be dead too."

Unable to return to her house, which was still a crime

scene, and unwilling to move back to her late father's place, which had fallen into disrepair after she'd moved in with Marc, Angélique took a room at the Crosby Hotel and started looking for work.

Sharon Franklin, who owned the hotel with her husband, felt very bad about what had happened and hired her as a housekeeper. She also kept the media away from Angélique until interest in the story had died down.

To her surprise, Angélique discovered she liked being in a hotel. She liked staying busy. She liked meeting new people passing through from somewhere else, people who didn't know her, people to whom she could be friendly without any commitment beyond the moment.

Marc Campeau had been renting the place where they'd lived and had left nothing of value behind, but Angélique had retained ownership of her late father's property. She sold it and put the money into the big Victorian brick house on Church Street, which had been up for sale for several months.

She converted it from an oversized, drafty residence to a bed-and-breakfast guest house that gave her purpose and direction, brought her out of her shell, and re-engaged her with the rest of the world. Through it she quickly developed sharp business skills, an interest in the community around her, and an ability to make friends once again.

Matthew was thankful that he was one of those friends.

He pulled out his knitting and went back to work.

Chapter

14

"I can give you Twenty-Eight," Garnett Carr said, turning the monitor around so Ellie could see photos of the room. "It's on the second floor; private bathroom, queen-size bed, and a view of the lake. They'll probably shovel it off soon so people can go skating. See? Nice pine floor."

"Sure, that's fine." Ellie handed over her OPP corporate credit card. "Book me in for the next two nights."

It made sense for her not to drive back and forth between Sparrow Lake and Westport in this kind of weather. It was fifty-five kilometres one way, and while that was nothing in fine weather with clear highways, a three-day snowstorm with at least one more day of it in the forecast was turning the roads into potential deathtraps.

She could probably make the drive home safely if she

crept all the way there, and she could manage the case from her cottage via telephone, but there was something about this one that was compelling her to stay on site.

Something about a bunch of rich old men from Toronto all showing up at the same time in the same place in small-town eastern Ontario in the middle of the worst snowstorm of the winter.

Garnett returned her credit card. She put it into her wallet and bent down to pick up her go bag, which she'd retrieved from the trunk of her Crown Vic. It contained several changes of clothing, toiletries, and other various necessities that she always kept on hand for contingencies such as this one. As she straightened and took her room card from Garnett, she saw two men enter the foyer, knocking snow from their boots and removing hats and gloves.

It was the two from the back seat of the black Town Car. The bearded one, who'd spoken to her through the window, saw her and nodded in recognition. The other man removed his galoshes and overcoat at the rack inside the door and went into the dining room.

After removing his boots, the bearded man walked over to her, unbuttoning his navy overcoat.

"Are you Tassone or Arcuri?" Ellie asked, without preamble.

He smiled politely, a handsome, poised individual with perfect teeth and confident eyes. "My name is Leonardo Arcuri. And you are?"

Ellie showed him her warrant card and badge. "I take it your friend is Dante Tassone?"

"Are you a police detective?"

"Detective inspector," she said. "OPP. I understand that you and Mr. Tassone are here in the village as a result of the passing of Mr. Tassone's uncle. Is that correct?"

"Yes. I'm Mr. Dante Tassone's attorney. May I ask you a question?"

Ellie looked at him.

"Has something happened to a man named Lonnie DiMaria?"

"If you mean Alonzo DiMaria, then, yes. He's been murdered. What can you tell me about it?"

Leonardo grimaced, rubbing his forehead. "I was afraid of that. When I saw his car . . . Lonnie worked for us. Specifically, for Mr. Tassone."

"In what capacity?"

"He headed up the accounting department for Mr. Tassone's holding company, Wooden Bridge Investments."

"What was DiMaria doing here? He missed the funeral, didn't he?"

"Would you mind?" Leonardo glanced at Garnett, who was staring at his monitor, pretending not to listen. "Maybe you should talk to Mr. Tassone about this."

"Sounds like a good idea." Ellie hefted her bag. "You two will be in the dining room?"

Leonardo nodded.

"Order me a cup of coffee, black with honey. I'm going to take this up to my room, and I'll be back down in ten minutes. Sound like a plan?"

"It does."

Ellie nodded. "See you then."

Chapter

15

Ellie used the little wooden honey drizzler to sweeten her coffee as Dante watched, his expression sombre.

"What about the other two guys I saw with you in the car?" she asked, returning the drizzler to the honey pot and using a teaspoon to stir. "Names? Current whereabouts?"

"Joseph Gagliato is my driver," Dante replied. "His home address is the same as mine; he lives in a coach house on the property. Right now he's staying at the motel out on the highway."

"They don't have parking here," Leonardo explained. "He got a room out there so he'd have somewhere to put the car."

"And the other guy?"

"Also an employee," Leonardo said. "Giorgio Marino.

He looks after Mr. Tassone's personal security. I think he's next door, in the bar."

"A security guy pounding the booze?"

"Drinking coffee. He's an abstainer."

"I see." Ellie studied the two driver's licences on the table in front of her, which they'd handed over when she demanded to see some identification. "You're both from the Woodbridge neighbourhood in Vaughan."

"Do you know the area?" Dante asked, his voice politely neutral.

"I grew up in Toronto. Your local police service is the York Regional Police, and your district is number four. I know the commander, Superintendent Creighton. Have you met him?"

"We've attended a few fundraisers together. I try to be very supportive of first responders in my community, Detective Inspector March."

"I understand you came here to attend the funeral of your uncle, Gabriel Tassone."

Dante nodded.

"My condolences. How did he die?"

"Gallbladder cancer. It was in the late stages before it was diagnosed."

Ellie sipped her coffee. It was excellent. "Mr. Arcuri tells me you know a man named Alonzo DiMaria, that he was another employee of yours."

Dante nodded again. "He's the head CPA for my company. Can you confirm that something has happened to him?"

"He was found dead this morning in the parking lot behind the hardware store. Someone beat him to death last night. Any idea how that might have happened?"

Dante covered his eyes with a hand. Despite already

knowing about it, he found it very difficult to take from the mouth of a police officer.

Ellie waited.

"Mr. Tassone and Mr. DiMaria have been friends since childhood," Leonardo said.

"I see." Ellie gave her coffee a moment's attention before asking, "Was Mr. DiMaria on his way from Woodbridge to see you, Mr. Tassone?"

Dante lowered his hand. "Yes."

"Why was he driving all the way here in a snowstorm to meet with you personally? Couldn't he just have called?"

Dante said nothing, looking out the window of the dining room at the frozen lake.

"Wooden Bridge Investments; I don't know anything about that company. What kind of business is it?"

"We have a number of interests," Leonardo said. "Construction, paving, aggregate, import/export, whole-sale distribution, and we also buy and sell real estate. Wooden Bridge is the holding company for these various businesses."

"You said he was beaten to death," Dante said in a low voice.

"Yes. Mostly kicked when he was on the ground. It was brutal."

Dante's lips compressed and his eyes closed.

"Do you have a business card?" Leonardo asked. "We have nothing helpful to offer you right now in terms of information, but if something important comes up, we'll call right away."

"Sure." Ellie slid their driver's licences across the table to them, followed by her card.

She finished her cup of coffee and stood up. "By the way, do you know a man named John David Lippincott?

Goes by the name of Jay?"

Leonardo gave her a blank look. "No, sorry. Who is he?"

Ellie looked at Dante. He shrugged, uninterested.

"I thought it might be someone you do business with," she said.

"Never heard of him," Leonardo said. "Sorry."

Ellie left them to their grieving.

On the far side of the front desk there was a sun room with comfortable chairs and a wood stove. Seeing that there was no one in there, she made herself comfortable in a leather rocking chair and took out her cellphone to make a call.

After navigating several layers, she found herself talking to Colin Hailey, an old colleague who'd recently been appointed deputy director of the OPP's Provincial Operations Intelligence Bureau. After briefly sketching in the case to date, Ellie admitted she was calling for a favour.

"I seem to remember a young woman, an analyst, who specializes in the 'Ndrangheta."

"You're probably referring to Charlotte McKinley," Hailey said.

"Yeah, that's the name. It was on the tip of my tongue."

"Don't tell me you're starting to slip, Ellie. You're five years younger than I am."

"Stuff on my mind, I guess. Any chance McKinley could come down here and take a look at a few things for me? I know the weather's bad, but I could use her expertise."

"I'll see. Can I call you back?"

"Please do."

Ellie put her phone away and leaned her head back

against soft leather, rocking gently. The warmth of the wood stove was very pleasant.

She'd made a good decision to dig in here for the time being rather than risk her neck on the roads. It was a nice hotel, and there was room in her budget to accommodate the expense. Case managers were often required to find a place to stay locally when working a major crime, and she didn't anticipate any problems when the file was audited after she handed it in.

She closed her eyes and thought she might even be able to doze for a few minutes. So nice and warm.

Hopefully Reggie wouldn't miss her too much.

Chapter

16

Kevin drove slowly down Church Street on his way home. Dusk was about twenty minutes away, and Janie was expecting him. Joshua and Brendan both had colds, and she needed his help around the house at suppertime.

The plow had passed through the village again about half an hour ago, and although the snow continued to fall, the street was manageable. His motor pool Ford Fusion had a new set of winter tires on it, so he felt reasonably safe heading out onto the highway.

He understood why Ellie had decided to stay, though. She wasn't much of a winter person. The cold seemed to go right through her, and he knew she disliked driving in bad weather. Something about having gone off the road in a cruiser during a snowstorm when she was a provincial constable working traffic, years ago.

On his right, just before Church ended at Rideau Street, he saw two men high-stepping along the sidewalk, heading north toward Spring. They were both bundled up in down-filled parkas. One wore a brightly-coloured toque over heavy dreadlocks and the other, incongruously, a cowboy hat. Toque was Black and Cowboy Hat was Caucasian.

They threw him only a brief glance as he passed, concentrating on the narrow path they were following on the snow-filled sidewalk.

Kevin watched their backs for a moment in his side mirror as they soldiered along.

Who the hell wore a cowboy hat in winter?

They were definitely not locals. He'd never seen Cowboy Hat before in his life. And according to the latest census, the population of Rideau Lakes included only ten visible minority residents who identified as Black. He'd looked it up once, in a completely different context. Leeds County overall was a predominately white community.

At various times over the past year or so he'd met all ten of them, at the Canada Day celebration in the village, minor hockey games, and a local heritage event. Mr. Dreadlocks had not been one of them.

Filing the memory of their faces away for future reference, he turned his attention back to the task of getting himself home to Janie and the kids in one piece.

Chapter

17

After supper Kevin did the dishes while Janie and Caitlyn went into the living room to watch TV. Brendan went downstairs to play a video game in the rec room. They'd had spaghetti and meatballs, and there were pots and a frying pan to scrub as well as the usual dishes, cups, and silverware, and Kevin was pretty tired by the time everything was done.

Janie was sitting on the couch with her smart phone. It was time to reorder stock for her beauty salon, and she was browsing online catalogues looking for bargains. Caitlyn was in her rocking chair, watching television.

Kevin flopped down in his recliner and put up his feet. "What's on?"

"A program about Machu Picchu," Caitlyn replied.

"Borrrring," Janie said without looking up from her phone.

Caitlyn sighed. "I've seen it before. Is there something you want to watch, Kevin?"

"Not really. Put on whatever you want." He closed his eyes, ready to doze.

"Do you want the news?"

"Doesn't matter."

"I'll see what's on."

"Turn it down, will you?" Janie said. "It's too loud."

"Sorry." Caitlyn muted the sound and flipped to the program guide.

Kevin felt himself drifting. Caitlyn was twelve, halfway through Grade Eight, and was very smart. Her schoolwork no longer challenged her, and tests had shown her to be at a Grade Twelve level in all subject areas. Even math, which had always been Kevin's *bête noire*. He'd seen her at the kitchen table not very long ago with a calculus textbook borrowed from the library, amusing herself with page after page of problems. What he remembered of the subject could be written on his thumbnail, and he'd been petrified that she'd ask him something about it. Thankfully, she hadn't needed any help.

She'd decided she wanted to become a psychologist. Kevin had no doubt in his mind that she could succeed in whatever profession she chose. They'd debated the psychology thing for a while, Kevin tentatively suggesting that something more concrete, like medicine or architecture or novel writing, might be more suited to her considerable potential, but she'd made up her mind. Mental health would be her chosen field. Helping people feel better about themselves, helping them learn how to help themselves, was what she wanted to do with her life.

Kevin had looked up how many years it would take her to complete the necessary degrees before checking out what kind of scholarships would be available to her. Lord knew they wouldn't be able to afford it otherwise.

She was saying something, but he didn't catch it.

"What?"

"I said, it's you, Kevin. You're on TV."

His eyes flew open. She'd put on the CBC all-news channel, and he was looking at a shot of himself picking his way along the middle of the snow-filled street with Mulvahill, head down, eyes on where he was walking. The banner at the bottom said, "Homicide In Village Of Westport, ON."

"Turn it up."

"—and the identity of the victim has not yet been released, the statement said, pending notification of next of kin. In other news—"

Caitlyn muted it again. "Is that where you were today? Westport?"

"Yeah. I didn't even see the media there today. Well, I saw a truck, but . . ."

"Who's that with you?"

"Detective Constable Mulvahill." He looked at footage of a traffic accident on the 401, with multiple cars off the road and flashing emergency response lights everywhere.

"I've never met her before. Is she smart?"

Kevin hesitated. Caitlyn had met several of his colleagues in the crime unit at various gatherings to which family members were invited, and had pronounced them to be a fairly motley crew. She'd said she was still looking for another detective as intelligent as her step-father but wasn't going to hold her breath. To which he'd not known exactly what to say, since he thought Dennis Leung was smarter than any of them, including himself, so he hadn't said anything.

Janie, on the other hand, filled in the gap with her usual vinegary wit, saying something to the effect that for detectives the bar was pretty low and always open.

Ha, ha.

"Smart? I suppose so," he replied cautiously, hoping that Janie wasn't paying attention. "She has a couple of kids. They live with their father." He knew it was too much information as soon as the words were out of his mouth, but Caitlyn merely nodded wisely and pressed the remote against the point of her chin.

"When will they announce the name of the person who was killed?"

"Probably tomorrow."

"Was he shot?"

"That's enough Caitlyn," Janie interjected, apparently listening after all. "You know he can't talk about work."

"Sorry. It's just that Mrs. Balmer will ask me about it tomorrow."

"She should know better." Janie looked up from her phone. "She's a damned pain in the ass."

"She's all right," Kevin ventured.

"'Oh, hellllo, Detective Walker. It's soooo nice to see you again,'" Janie mimicked Caitlyn's teacher in a sarcastic falsetto. "God. Hand me a barf bag."

Caitlyn snorted.

"A little respect, please," Kevin put in. "She works in a very difficult profession."

"Oh, come on. A difficult profession." Janie made a rude noise. "Give me a break. She just has to stand up there and read stuff from a handout. A trained chimp could do it."

"If chimps could talk," Caitlyn giggled.

"Not nice," Kevin said.

Caitlyn resumed rocking. "You know what I mean. Your job is ten times harder than hers. A hundred times harder."

"It has its days," Kevin said. "Today I froze my rear end off, for example."

"Poor baby." Janie's eyes were back on her phone.

Caitlyn frowned. "That's not what I mean. You have to deal with death. And dangerous people who kill someone and try to get away with it."

"Maybe we should talk about something else."

"Put on the weather channel," Janie said. "Let's see when this snow's going to stop."

Kevin watched Caitlyn point the remote at the satellite receiver to bring up the channel guide again. He doubted the weather would be any more cheerful a subject than what they'd just been talking about.

Chapter

18

Ellie ordered the hot turkey sandwich with a side of fries for dinner, topped off with a piece of lemon coconut cake and more of the hotel's delicious coffee.

Joining her in the dining room, albeit on the far side near the fireplace, were Dante Tassone and Leonardo Arcuri. They ate their meals in silence, essentially ignoring each other. The only other guests enjoying dinner at the Crosby this evening were a middle-aged couple seated in front of the French doors leading out onto the snowed-in patio. They spoke quietly between bites and ignored the rest of the room.

Ellie accepted a refill of coffee and watched Dante take a phone call. Leonardo discreetly moved to the next table to give him a little privacy. She saw the wrinkles at the corners of Dante's eyes deepen and wondered if he was speaking to his wife.

She had a theory about the way people smiled. If their smile didn't reach their eyes, they were potentially very dangerous. On the other hand, if their mouth remained neutral and they smiled with their eyes, they were deep thinkers but probably cautious by nature.

Her phone chimed. She took it out and saw that it was a text message from Charlotte McKinley:

I've arrived. At front desk. Where shall we meet?

Ellie had never met this woman before and wasn't quite sure what to expect. She had a very basic awareness of her background. McKinley held a graduate degree in Legal Studies with a thesis on organized crime in southern Ontario. After finishing school, she spent two years as an analyst with the Ontario Public Safety Division before leaving the provincial government to work on a multi-jurisdictional project with the Hamilton Police Service and the OPP. When that assignment wrapped up, Colin Hailey grabbed her to work in his bureau at GHQ. She was said to be highly intelligent, socially inept, and remarkably fearless.

There was a story about her ringing the front door bell of a major crime boss in Hamilton one Sunday afternoon to ask him why he'd sent an important *sgarrista*, or soldier, back to Italy on a one-way airline ticket. It seems she'd been studying the man and was a little put out at having him whisked out from under her nose.

Wait five, Ellie texted back.

She paid her bill, made a side trip to the washroom, and went to the front lobby.

Charlotte McKinley had left her overcoat on the rack inside the front door and exchanged her boots for what looked very much like a pair of ballet slippers. She slung a canvas messenger bag over her shoulder and crossed the room. She was tall and slender, and her long, straight brown hair lay across her shoulders like a mane. She was far, far too young.

"Detective Inspector March, I'm Charlotte. It's an honour to meet you."

Ellie shook the bony, long-fingered hand held out to her. "I hope the drive wasn't too bad."

"Oh, it was awful, all right, but as it happens I was visiting my grandmother in Stittsville, which is only ninety kilometres away, and so it could have been worse. I could have been in Orillia."

"I suppose." Ellie looked at Garnett Carr. "Is there anyone in the sun room right now?"

Garnett shook his head. "No, ma'am."

"Don't call me that." Ellie looked at Charlotte. "Do you want coffee?"

"That would be lovely."

"Would you have a pot brought in to us?" Ellie asked. "And maybe a plate of pastries?"

"Yes, ma'am." Garnett winced. "Sorry."

"Let's see if there's still a fire burning in the wood stove," Ellie said, leading the way.

The sun room was warm, comfortable, and empty. Bamboo blinds had been lowered over the windows. Ellie sniffed at a faint, pleasant odour of wood smoke as she sat in the same leather-covered rocking chair she'd enjoyed earlier in the day.

Charlotte settled on the couch opposite and opened her messenger bag. She removed a thick spiral notebook and a pen. She brushed aside the edges of her tan cardigan sweater, fussed at the collar tips of her white blouse, and crossed her legs. Her foot began to bounce up and down.

"I've followed your career to the *nth* degree," she said, not quite making eye contact. "Not that I'm a stalker or anything, not by any means, but women in law enforcement with your strength, perseverance, and intelligence are heroines to me." She made a face. "I'm sorry; that was too much. All the way down from Gran's I rehearsed what I was going to say now that I finally have a chance to meet you, and that wasn't it at all."

"Don't worry about it. I understand you're an expert in Italian organized crime in southern Ontario."

"Well, 'expert' makes me sound like I've published books on the subject and been the guest of honour at think tanks and that sort of thing. Actually, I am. Writing a book. On the 'Ndrangheta in particular. It should be done in April. The first draft, I mean."

Ellie recognized a severe case of nerves when she saw it. The poor young woman was petrified. "Did you have a chance to eat dinner?"

"I ate a couple of Big Macs in the car on the way down."

"So tell me about your grandmother."

"Gran? She just turned seventy-four. I was helping her celebrate. I'm the only relative she has now. She lives in an assisted-living facility. Very bad hips."

"I'm sorry to hear that."

"Yes, well, actually she's an extremely happy person. Sometimes I wish I didn't live so far away from her because I sure could use a regular dose of her optimism. Life's pretty dark." She turned a page in her notebook, which was moving up and down on her knee in time with her foot. "She's actually pretty famous, although you've probably never heard of her."

"Your grandmother?"

Charlotte nodded. "Her name's Ruth McKinley. She retired from the NRC nine years ago. When she was forty-six she won the Nobel Prize in Chemistry."

"Really?" Ellie knew very little about the National Research Council, the federal organization responsible for government research and technology, and she'd never heard of Ruth McKinley. It hadn't occurred to her that there would be Nobel Prize winners working for the Canadian federal government.

"She actually has a theory named after her," Charlotte said. "The 'McKinley Theory of Electron Transfer.' It has to do with the rate at which electrons jump from one molecule to another. It has applications in things like photosynthesis, corrosion of metals, and even some kinds of solar cells that people are building these days."

"Impressive," Ellie said.

"Extremely. Although I don't understand a word of it. I'm not scientific minded at all."

"Neither am I." Ellie saw that the foot bobbing had slowed down to a slight twitch. "Tell me about the 'Ndrangheta."

"All right. What would you like to know?"

"Let's start with the Tassone family."

Charlotte's face brightened. "Oh, yes. Of course." Her fingers found an orange-coloured Post-it Note, and she flipped to a page near the front of her notebook.

"They emigrated from the province of Reggio Calabria in southern Italy, on the toe of the boot. Their family has hundreds of acres of olive groves over there."

She turned a few pages. "These are all notes about the 'Ndrangheta in Calabria and how they've migrated throughout Europe and North America. I know a notebook like this is very old school, but I like writing stuff down. I'll skip a bit. Here we are. A Giuseppe Tassone immigrated to Canada in 1963 with his wife and two married sons, Vincenzo and Gabriel. Giuseppe was brought in to take over criminal enterprises in northern Toronto that had fallen out of 'Ndrangheta control through bad management and unfortunate deaths."

She glanced up at Ellie. "Natural deaths, believe it or not. At any rate, Giuseppe died in 1978 and control of the family business passed to his elder son, Gabriel. I won't bother with all these ranks and org structures and what not."

"Thanks."

"Gabriel preferred the loan sharking and protection rackets to the drugs, so he licensed out control of the cocaine, marijuana, and meth markets in his territory to a local outlaw motorcycle gang and kept only the heroin and other opioids like oxy and fentanyl. He used extortion and bribery to get a really significant foothold in the construction business in the Greater Toronto Area, and over the course of a few decades took over most of the road paving and aggregate distribution not only in the GTA but throughout the province. It's quite a success story."

"Inspirational," Ellie said.

Charlotte laughed. "I know; I make it sound like he was some kind of business hero. He was pretty vicious, according to everything I've learned."

Ellie held up her hand. A server walked into the sun room and set down a tray on the table between them. It held a large pot of coffee, a pitcher of cream, cubes of sugar, a pot of honey with a wooden drizzler, and a plate of assorted pastries.

"Thanks," Ellie said, leaning forward to turn the coffee

pot handle toward her.

The server nodded and, after getting her signature on the bill, left the room.

"I'm sorry, Charlotte. I forgot to ask you if you prefer decaffeinated."

"I basically live on caffeine." Charlotte held up her cup and saucer.

Ellie poured, they fixed their coffee the way they liked it, and Ellie picked up a strawberry-filled danish. "Don't make me eat all of these by myself."

"You're aware," Charlotte said, considering her options on the plate, "that Gabriel Tassone was actually living in this area? And that he just died last week?"

"Yes." Ellie polished off the last bite of danish and wiped her fingers with a linen napkin.

"His funeral was on Monday. We had someone there. I've looked through the pictures and they're interesting but not terribly earth-shaking. The usual suspects."

"Tell me what you know about Dante Tassone."

"Mmm." Charlotte struggled to swallow a large mouthful of blueberry puff pastry.

"Take your time."

"Sorry." Charlotte drank some coffee to clear things out. "I used to live on this stuff when I was in school. Blueberry's my favourite. Okay. Dante Tassone. Eldest son of Vincente Tassone, Gabriel's younger brother, which makes Dante Gabriel's nephew. He's fifty-nine; has a son and three daughters; a degree in business administration from York; took over the loan sharking stuff after graduation and ran it for his uncle for about eight years or so. A rough, dirty business, and informants have told us he was utterly ruthless. Either you paid what you owed or you paid the price in broken bones and concussions."

"There aren't very many kind-hearted loan sharks."

"No, that's for sure. He ran a chain of pizzerias as a cover for his other activities, and when he turned thirty, Gabriel promoted him to be his local *capo crimine*, the person in charge of all the illegal enterprises under his control. Dante looked after the extortion and bribery operations, plus the human trafficking and the drug trafficking, and he was responsible for keeping things trouble free across the clans. If there was a dispute of some kind, Dante often got it solved without violence. He apparently has a talent for negotiation and conciliation, despite all the early violence on his résumé."

Ellie watched Charlotte grab a chocolate-covered éclair and devour it in two bites. The woman likely weighed about a hundred pounds, soaking wet. Ellie decided that she must have the same kind of metabolism that she herself had, which let her eat pretty much anything she wanted to cram down her throat without gaining an ounce.

A second éclair followed the first, and Charlotte was ready to continue. "Dante ran that side of things for a while and then switched to the legitimate businesses that they employ to launder their ill-gotten gains. A lot of times, as I know you know, these things are just storefronts that don't really make any money on their own, but Dante really loves business and he's built them up into true powerhouses. You see their road paving crews all over the province, and their gravel trucks, and a lot of other things that belong to their company, Wooden Bridge Investments. It's really quite remarkable."

"What's he worth?"

"Good question. One that the Canada Revenue Agency would love to be able to definitively answer, I'm sure." Charlotte turned a page in her notebook. "Last year he filed a tax return on an income of nine hundred and twenty grand as chairman and chief executive officer of Wooden Bridge. The corporation itself has a current balance sheet showing thirty million in assets, two million in debt, and twenty-eight million in net worth. I won't bother going over the various individual companies unless you want me to."

"No, that's okay." Ellie set down her coffee cup. "Tell me about Dante's chief accountant."

"Um." Charlotte frowned, flipping over pages. She flipped back. "Here it is. Alonzo DiMaria. I don't have very much on him. He's a known associate of Dante Tassone. Dante's *contabile*, his *valigetta*, which translates as 'briefcase'. I have some tombstone information."

"Fire away."

"Okay. Also known as Lonnie DiMaria; fifty-eight; married with two adult daughters and one son; lives with his wife in a million-dollar condo in Vaughan; graduate of the University of Toronto; chartered professional accountant. Big-time numbers guy; investment guru; believed to have socked away a fortune offshore for Dante, his childhood friend."

She hesitated. "I'm not sure if this is the kind of thing you want to know. His father was a *camorrista* who collected extortion money for the Tassone family. As a boy, Lonnie was apparently very shy and withdrawn. He disliked sports and other physical activity but displayed a superior talent for math. Because the DiMarias lived one block over from the Tassones, Lonnie became best friends with Dante, who was a year older."

Ellie nodded. "This helps."

"What I've learned," she went on, "is that when they were boys they shared a common interest in chemistry and electronics. They built crystal radio sets and things like that. And devices with small explosive charges they'd remotely detonate in Lonnie's backyard. The police came around a few times, but it didn't amount to anything."

"Interesting."

"As adults, they share a common interest in clothing. They've been seen many times going out on shopping trips together, if you can believe it. They have the same tailor, a guy with his own shop downtown—Toronto, I mean—and they go together for fittings and what not. One of my informants watched them for two hours one time in the Eaton Centre browsing the menswear stores. She said it was like watching two old girlfriends on a shopping spree."

"Implying a sexual connection?"

Charlotte shook her head. "Not at all. Both men are as straight as can be, and as far as I can tell, they're both faithful to their wives. Never earthed up any infidelity leads on Dante at all, for sure. Leverage like that would be solid gold, but not happening, unfortunately."

Ellie waited, but there didn't seem to be anything else Charlotte wanted to add.

"Are you aware that Lonnie DiMaria was murdered last night?"

Charlotte looked thunderstruck.

"Here in Westport. His body was found this morning. That's why we're here."

Charlotte drew in a long, audible breath, then turned back a page and began scribbling in her notebook.

When the pen finally stopped moving, Ellie cleared her throat. "One more question right now, if you don't mind."

"Yes. Of course. Absolutely."

"What do you know about an individual named John

David Lippincott, a.k.a. Jay Lippincott, resident of York Mills, approximately seventy years of age, CEO of a helicopter manufacturing company in the GTA?"

"Lippincott?" Charlotte frowned. "Lippincott?" She closed her eyes, running it through her extensive memory banks. "Sorry; never heard of him. Is he important?"

"I don't know," Ellie said, discouraged. "Time will tell."

Chapter

19

"It's very sad," Dante said quietly in his native Calabrian dialect. "My heart is very heavy."

Passing through the dining room, the owner of the Crosby Hotel took a step toward him, saw that he was on the phone, and changed direction.

"No, darling, I'm sure Stella's very glad to have you there. It's impossibly hard for her right now. Stay with her and do whatever you can."

The hotel owner, whose name was John Franklin, stopped at Leonardo's table. "How was your dinner this evening, sir?"

"Ricardo's fine," Dante murmured. "Yes, I'm keeping an eye on him." He chuckled. "He's a grown man, Renita. He does what he wants to do."

"It was very good," Leonardo said, lowering the magazine he was reading. "Mr. Tassone appreciated the effort."

"Our chef enjoyed talking to him," Franklin said. "He's never done Calabrian cuisine before, but fortunately we had all the ingredients on hand to prepare the pork roast the way he described it. Was the pasta all right?"

"Surprisingly good," Leonardo said. The chef had prepared a dish called *fileja* for them, made with fresh spiral tubes of pasta and a spicy tomato and pork sauce.

"I love you with all my heart," Dante said. "Later, darling. Good night."

"He wrapped the pasta around a chopstick to make the spirals," Franklin said, smiling. "We're going to add it to the menu, I think. And the pork roast, too. Good winter fare."

Leonardo's cellphone, which was sitting on the table near his hand, began to ring.

"Excuse me, please." He reached for the phone.

"Of course." Franklin nodded and left the dining room.

Leonardo answered the call. "Yes?"

He listened. "Very well, I'll see if he can speak with you." He thumbed the Mute button and lowered the phone.

"It's Dom. He wants to speak to you."

Dante held out his hand for the phone and gestured to Leonardo to sit down at the table with him.

"Yes, Dom."

"Mr. Tassone, I'm very sorry to disturb you so soon after dinner, but it's the first chance I've had to be alone. Rick went upstairs to his room."

"No problem. What's going on?"

"First, I have to say how sorry I am about what happened

to Mr. DiMaria."

Dante said nothing.

He and Domenico Calutti had a long history together. Dom was the son of a cousin on Dante's mother's side, a man with a high school diploma, broad shoulders, and big fists who had worked his way up through the ranks to become one of Dante's most trusted problem solvers.

When Gabriel had tapped Dante to replace him at the helm of Wooden Bridge Investments, turning over control of the criminal enterprises to Dante's cousin Pietro, Dom was there to cover Dante's back, preventing any leakage of trouble from the illegal side to the legitimate business side while Lonnie, for his part, made sure the money flowed without disruption.

After Rick graduated from university and came back from having spent a year touring Italy, supposedly getting in touch with his European heritage, Dante quietly inserted Dom into his son's inner circle as a general handyman and bodyguard. Once again, Dom's problem-solving talents made him indispensable.

Rick trusted him, and his desire to keep him close suggested that he had no idea Dom had been, and continued to be, Dante's man.

"The two guys who killed Mr. DiMaria are Wolfpack," Dom said.

"Wolfpack?" Dante looked at Leonardo, who frowned.

"There are certain meetings he doesn't take me to. Late night stuff downtown. He takes Esposito instead. I've tried tailing them but . . ."

Noise began to enter the dining room from the lounge next door. People were walking through from the main entrance, glancing in at them as they passed the doorway.

"Continue."

"Two guys came up here last night," Dom said. "A Black guy and a white guy. I've seen them before coming out of clubs when Rick's there, meeting with friends. They showed up here at the B and B, all worked up about something. They told Rick they followed the guy all the way from Toronto and when they finally caught up with him they couldn't find it. When Rick asked 'What did Lonnie say about it?' the white guy said, 'Thanks to our friend here, the guy's not saying anything to anybody any more.' Or words to that effect."

Dante hissed air between his teeth.

"Rick got very upset." Dom cleared his throat. "He kind of forgot I was sitting there. He turned on the Black guy and said, 'What the fuck's the matter with you? What did you do?' Excuse the language, Mr. Tassone."

Next door, in the lounge, someone began testing a microphone and speaker system.

Check, check, check. One two. Check. One two.

"Go on," Dante gritted.

"The guy, his name's Henry Samuel by the way, went off on this rant about Mr. DiMaria being too stupid to know when it's worth his life to talk as opposed to getting killed for nothing. All kinds of crazy stuff like that. The guy's extremely violent and dangerous."

Dante said nothing.

"Before I called you, I reached out to a couple people I know." Dom paused, taking a deep breath. "Samuel's from Haiti originally. Ran a street gang in Montreal called Cheval Noir, then moved down our way along with this white guy, name of Patrick McQuillan. This guy was with an Irish gang in Montreal called West End Gang or something like that. They're part of the Wolfpack Alliance that's been moving into Toronto over the last few years. A bunch of pissed-off millennials."

"So what you're saying," Dante said, "is that this Samuel and McQuillan are responsible for Lonnie's death. Am I understanding this correctly?"

"Yes, sir. Samuel's the one who did the beating, from what I understand, while McQuillan stood around and watched."

Dante digested this information for a moment.

Next door, someone played a few bars of music on a bass guitar and said something into a microphone. It was too muffled to understand.

"Why?" Dante asked. "Why would they do this?"

"I'm not sure, Mr. Tassone. The item they wanted to get off Mr. DiMaria was one of those computer USB jump drives with some kind of information on it. Rick was really, really upset they didn't find it. He told them to find it or else."

"I see."

There was more racket coming from the lounge. Leonardo rose, but Dante shook his head.

"Is there anything else?"

"No sir, not at the moment."

"All right. Call me when you have more, or leave a message with Mr. Arcuri and I'll call you back."

"Yes, sir, Mr. Tassone. And please accept my condolences. Mr. DiMaria was a nice man. Everyone liked him."

"Not everyone," Dante corrected, raising his voice as loud music began to play next door. "Not everyone."

Chapter

20

The next morning, which was Thursday, Matthew Scanlan went outside and cleaned the snow from his sidewalk and verandah. He spread ice-melting crystals around to make it safe to walk, and he cleared the snow from the railings so that people could hold on to them as they climbed the steps up to his front door.

Thankfully, the municipality's little sidewalk plow had been around, making it easier for theoretical customers to find their way to his store.

He tipped his head back and looked at the sky, which was showing a patch of blue directly overhead. The snow had stopped falling, but according to this morning's weather forecast, it was only a temporary respite. Thirty-five centimetres had come down so far, with another ten centimetres expected to begin falling this afternoon and on throughout the evening.

He went inside and removed his boots and overcoat. *We've definitely reached deep winter*, he thought. Surely this was as bad as it would get.

Behind him, the bell rang as someone opened the front door. A rush of cold air came and went.

"Good morning," Matthew said, turning around.

There were two of them. The one in front wore a long navy overcoat buttoned up under his neck, galoshes, and black leather gloves. There were chunks of ice in his iron-grey beard. His smile was friendly but his eyes were dark and unsettling. The one behind was shorter and squatter. He wore a tweed car coat and a driver's cap.

"Are you the owner?" the bearded man asked.

"Yes, I am. How may I help you?"

"You may have heard of the unfortunate incident the night before last that cost the life of a man named Alonzo DiMaria."

"Yeah." Matthew watched the man with the cap mosey down toward the cash register at the back of the shop. "Are you with the police? I've already talked to them."

The bearded man shook his head. "My name's Leonardo Arcuri. Mr. DiMaria was a colleague of mine. I've been going from store to store this morning to ask if he might have stopped in that evening, before he died."

The man with the cap stuck his head inside the open door of the change cubicle.

"He did," Matthew said, "around four o'clock in the afternoon. I was just about to close for the day."

The man with the cap shot a triumphant look at Leonardo.

"Did he mention why he was here?" Leonardo asked.

"In town?"

"No. He just asked for directions to the Crosby Hotel."

"Nothing about meeting anyone?"

"No."

"Did he happen to leave anything here with you? Perhaps for safekeeping?"

"Leave anything? I'm not sure what you mean. He bought some clothing and paid with cash, which I've already deposited in the bank."

"Nothing else? An envelope perhaps, with something small inside?"

"No. You're the second ones who've asked me that same question. What's this all about?"

Leonardo looked surprised. "The police asked you if he left something here?"

"No. Yesterday afternoon, two other guys came in asking questions like you are. They wanted to know if the man had given me anything. To hold onto for him, or whatever. I told them the same thing I'm telling you. Just the cash. Which is now in the bank."

"Two other men." Leonardo frowned. "Not cops?"

Matthew laughed without humour. "Definitely not. A Black guy with dreadlocks and a white guy wearing a cowboy hat." He paused. "The guy with dreadlocks had a bad look in his eyes. Unbalanced. Like he wanted to take me apart just for the fun of it. I was glad when they left."

"I see. Did they say who they were or where they were from?"

"No. They weren't locals, though. That much I can tell you for sure."

"And Mr. DiMaria didn't leave anything here with you? You're certain of that?"

Matthew shrugged. "Yeah, I'm certain."

The man took out a small leather folder. He removed a business card and gave it to Matthew. "If you remember anything important, call me at the cell number listed there."

"Okay." Matthew looked at the card. "You're an attorney?"

"Yes. Thank you for your time."

Matthew watched the man with the driver's cap open the door for Leonardo, standing aside with unmistakeable deference. He watched them walk down the steps to the sidewalk and turn right, disappearing out of sight.

Feeling uneasy, Matthew turned away and began fussing with a display of silk ties.

As Dafoe said, "Fear of danger is ten thousand times more terrifying than danger itself."

Somehow, the thought failed to make him feel any better.

Chapter

21

The Crosby Hotel was at one time the house and stables of a very rich lumber king who controlled the village for several decades in the late nineteenth century. Its conversion into a hotel forty years ago had taken quite a bit of time and money, but the result was not only a selection of comfortable guest rooms and a suite upstairs but a dining room, lounge, sun room, and conference room on the main floor.

It was this last feature that had caught Ellie's interest this Thursday morning after breakfast as she looked for a quiet place to get a little work done. Her room was too tiny for anything other than falling asleep while watching TV. The sun room and dining room were occupied, and the lounge still smelled of last night's beer and greasy fast food. Garnett Carr was back behind the front desk, and when she inquired about the conference room he told her it wasn't booked for anything over the next little while.

Ellie promptly took out her corporate credit card and claimed it. She wanted a meeting place for her investigation team as the case progressed, and while the Crosby's conference room was not all that large, it was about the size of the board room in a typical OPP detachment office and would more than suffice for her needs.

Additionally, Constable Rachel Townsend had struggled over from Smiths Falls to brief the press as regional media liaison officer, and she'd be grateful to know there was somewhere indoors she could work. The briefing would happen early this afternoon, so Ellie made a mental note to give the room a wide berth until it was done. They'd already worked out the statement between them, and there wasn't much else they were prepared to hand out at the moment in terms of answers to questions, so Ellie was confident she wouldn't be needed.

As conference rooms went, it wasn't fancy. The long table dominating the room was actually four stacking tables pushed together and covered with a tablecloth, with six upholstered chairs to provide the seating. It wasn't the most elegant set-up she'd ever seen, but it would do.

She settled in at one end and took out her tablet. When she fired it up, she was relieved to find that she could remotely connect to the encrypted network she always accessed while working at home in her winterized cottage on Sparrow Lake.

Dave Martin had filed several reports on his findings related to the crime scene, and she went through these one at a time. It didn't come as a shock to her that he'd uncovered very little physical evidence to help with the investigation of Alonzo DiMaria's brutal murder.

Her cellphone began to vibrate. She picked it up, looked at the call display, and answered.

"March. Is anything wrong?"

"Hi, Ellie." It was Jack Riley, her neighbour. "Are you staying inside like I told you to?"

"Trying to. What's up?"

"This and that. The dog misses you. He doesn't like me much, but at least he's stopped showing his teeth." Pause. "I thought I'd let you know some guy stopped in to ask questions about you."

Jack Riley lived in a tumble-down farmhouse at the corner of Tamarack Lane and Lake Road in Yonge Township, just above Ellie's cottage. Riley was an old bachelor who'd taken a liking to her despite the fact that she was a cop, and she relied on him to keep an eye on things and look after Reggie while she was away.

"Oh? When was this?"

"This morning. Driving a green Land Rover. I wrote down the licence number." He recited it to her. "Said he was back to take a second look at the Ballantyne place. I saw him go by the first time he was here, couple days ago."

Ellie recognized the plate number. It belonged to the vehicle registered to Jay Lippincott. "You've got an eye for detail, Jack. You'd make a good cop."

"Don't get personal. Not sure what I've done to deserve that."

"What did he want to know?"

"Oh, a bunch of stuff. What you're like, whether you'd be a good neighbour, if you're there year-round. Trying to come off like he just wants to fit right in, like one of us. I wasn't buying it, though."

"Oh?"

"Guy's from a different species. I never met a one-percenter before, but I have now. He'd fit in here like a thousand-dollar bottle of cognac sitting on the shelf next to my Mason jars."

Riley was an expert moonshiner whose wares Ellie had sampled once and lived to tell the tale. Their relationship was solid because Ellie had promised not to turn him in to Excise. While she'd never tasted thousand-dollar cognac before, she was sure it was somewhat smoother than Riley's product.

"That bad, huh?"

"Look, I don't like to be judgmental about people, particularly those I just met. He seems like a nice enough guy. Just asks a few too many questions, that's all."

"Well, I appreciate the heads-up, Jack."

"No problem. Stay out of the snow, Ellie. You'll catch your death of cold."

"Aye-firmative. Thanks for calling."

She put down the cellphone and leaned back, rubbing her eyes.

What was going on with Lippincott? Why was he showing up, completely out of the blue, at a time when she was knee-deep in Toronto-based millionaires who'd brought their murderous tendencies all the way out here to eastern Ontario? How was he connected? What was his angle? Why was he staking out her home rather than milling around here in the village with the other high-priced hoods?

Was it a personal threat of some kind? Were they trying to outflank her? Looking for some kind of leverage in case she got too close to something they didn't want her to mess up? If so, why on earth hadn't they just sent the hired help instead of one of their own from the top echelon?

She suddenly realized she'd forgotten to ask the dining room server for a mid-morning pot of coffee. She jumped to her feet, stuck her tablet under her jacket so that no one could see the screen, and went off to take care of that particular oversight.

Chapter

22

Rick Tassone was bored to tears.

He sat alone at a table in the dining room of Couvillon House, staring at the snow outside in the street as he sipped his fourth cup of coffee of the morning.

The place was quiet. The owner was in the kitchen with her staff, and Dom had gone for a walk to pick up a few things at the drug store one block over. The nut jobs, McQuillan and Samuel, were likewise absent. In search of housebreaking opportunities, apparently.

He glanced at his phone, which sat on the table next to his cup and saucer, but he didn't pick it up. He'd already browsed the news feeds and read everything that was worth reading. He'd scanned Twitter and Instagram, checked his e-mail (who used e-mail now, anyway?), and watched a few minutes of an episode of *Game of Thrones* he'd seen before.

He felt like he'd been dropped off at an outpost inside the Arctic Circle with minimal supplies and nothing to do, and the next dogsled not scheduled to reach the place for another six months.

His mind wandered over this whole business with DiMaria, and for the hundredth time he asked himself whether his father suspected what had happened. It was inevitable that once Lonnie had discovered the first irregularity he would launch his own personal search for trouble, like a well-trained hunting dog that catches a faint scent on the breeze and suddenly focuses on that specific thing to the exclusion of everything else.

Just as it was inevitable that Rick would have to do something about it.

The call had come Monday afternoon, while Rick was upstairs in his room changing his clothes after the funeral. Tom Tedesco, the CPA for the aggregate business and Rick's key money man, called in a panic that he'd just come from a meeting with Mr. DiMaria.

"He knows, Mr. Tassone. I tried my best, but he spotted the anomalies and called me out on them. I pretended I didn't know what he was talking about, but it's no good. He's on to us."

Rick calmed him down, assuring him the whole situation would be taken care of, and hung up. After he finished dressing, he sat on the edge of the bed and called the other heads of accounting with the other firms he oversaw on behalf of his father. Two of them had already spoken to Tedesco and one other, Jordan Walters, was scheduled to meet with Lonnie after dinner that night. They were upset and worried. Rick did his best to sound confident and to smooth things over, but he knew he was in trouble.

After returning from the evening reception at the mansion, Rick took another call from Tedesco. He'd spoken to Walters after the meeting with Lonnie, and it wasn't good. Lonnie had a USB drive with spreadsheets on it that he'd gone through with Walters, pointing out all the irregularities in the books for the company Walters handled.

Why was this amount so far out of whack? What happened to the hundred K that was supposed to be here? Who was this guy, and this company, and why have I never heard of them before?

Rick got little sleep that night, worrying about what his father would do if he found out that he was skimming money and investing it in other ventures, things the old man would never approve of, and with outside partners that would definitely make him unhappy.

The next morning, which was Tuesday, Rick nibbled on toast in the dining room while he waited for Dom to come downstairs to drive him back to the mansion for his big meeting with David Gallo. Fifteen minutes, squeezed in among all his doofus cousins, who were all brainlessly happy with their token prizes of fifty K.

As he sat there, he was surprised to receive a call from Lonnie.

Rick had tried to engage him in pleasantries, but Lonnie was having none of it. He got right to the point, asking Rick if he was aware that money was disappearing from the books of the various companies he was managing on behalf of Wooden Bridge Investments.

Rick played dumb, expressing doubt that such a thing would happen.

"I'm going to have to show this to your father, Ricardo.

He needs to be aware."

Rick paused, trying to choose his words carefully. "That might not be such a good idea, Lonnie."

There was silence at the other end.

Sensing his tone had given him away, Rick tried to move sideways to neutral ground. "We could meet. When I get back. You could walk me through it. I'm sure it's nothing."

More silence, after which Lonnie said, "This was a courtesy call, Ricardo. That's all. Expect to meet with your father about this, not me. I work for him, not for you."

The line went dead.

In the car on the way to the mansion, Rick stared out the window in the back seat and tried to figure out what he was going to do. If Lonnie had some kind of a flash drive with incriminating spreadsheets on it, Rick needed to get possession of it right away. At the same time, he needed clean sets of books substituted for the ones Lonnie had been auditing.

After arriving at the mansion, he went straight into a washroom and made two calls. The first was to Tedesco, telling him to get busy putting a scrubbed set of books in place right away. Why had this not been done already, before Lonnie could notice what was going on? Tedesco didn't have a good answer for this rather pertinent question.

The second call was to one of his partners in the Wolfpack Alliance, Pat McQuillan.

"I need you to take care of something for me."

Rick had done a favour for McQuillan not long ago, smoothing over a disagreement between the big Irishman and Thomas Chen, another Toronto partner. Chen was a Triad enforcer known for his unforgiving nature, and Rick had scored major points within the group for brokering an arrangement whereby McQuillan made up for his perceived transgressions in a way that saved face all around. The Irishman owed him, big time.

Rick described Lonnie, gave McQuillan the address, and told him the objective was to secure a flash drive in Lonnie's possession.

"He's probably got a hundred of them," McQuillan said. "How will I know which one it is?"

"He's probably got it on him. In his pocket or his briefcase or something. Just grab whatever you see and I'll figure it out later."

"Will do."

An hour later, McQuillan called him back.

"Rick, it's under control but it went a little sideways."

"Just a minute." Rick was in a sitting room on the second floor of the mansion, having just finished a phone conversation with his lawyer back in Toronto. The lawyer had assured him there was nothing he could do about the will, so he might as well accept the situation gracefully and let sleeping dogs lie. He was just about to go into his meeting with Gallo, and his mood was not the best at that particular moment.

He got up and closed the door. "Tell me about it."

"We caught him down in the parking garage in his building. On the way to his office, looked like."

"We. What do you mean, we?"

"Me and Henry Samuel. He was with me when you called, so I took him along as an extra body. Unfortunately, he took a shot at your guy, and DiMaria bolted."

"Jesus fucking Christ."

"Yeah, I'm sorry about that. Look, we're eastbound on the 401 right now, just past Ajax. I have no fucking idea where's he's going but I'm keeping him in sight."

"Did you dump the moron?"

McQuillan laughed nervously. "Nah, he's sitting next to me. Asleep right now."

"Just get the drive, okay? No more shooting at him. Christ all fucking mighty."

"Yeah sure, Rick. Don't worry. I'll take care of it."

But he hadn't. They'd followed Lonnie all the way to Westport and killed him late that afternoon behind the hardware store while trying to take the USB drive away from him.

A total, complete, unequivocal clusterfuck.

Dragging his thoughts back to the present, he heard a noise in the front vestibule and thought it was probably Dom, coming back from the drug store.

For the hundredth time he wondered how far he could trust the man. He was aware that Dom was his father's man, but he'd accepted him as his personal security assistant because he was one of the best, and Rick loved to surround himself with the best of everything. He figured Dante had gifted Dom to him, like a brand-new SIG Sauer wrapped up in a box under the Christmas tree, or a Lexus from the lot of the dealership in Vaughan that his father owned.

The main problem he had with Dom was that he could never tell what the man was thinking. He was like Russia, a riddle wrapped in a mystery inside an enigma. Or like static electricity, an invisible high-voltage charge waiting to explode. Like one of those things, anyway. It was why Rick preferred to leave him behind when he went downtown to meet with Chen and McQuillan and the others, taking Esposito with him instead. Esposito was younger and not very bright, but Rick had cultivated him as a follower and he was openly loyal.

What he saw and heard wouldn't go any further, Rick felt certain.

Dom stuck his head through the doorway, waved at Rick, and disappeared upstairs with his bag of purchases.

Rick's phone began to ring. He looked at the call display: Thomas Chen.

"Fuck."

Word of Rick's predicament had spread, obviously.

Time for some serious sweet-talking.

Chapter

23

The suite was small and cramped, not on a par with accommodations to which Dante was accustomed when travelling, but he prided himself on being a man who was able to make each situation work, no matter the circumstances. As a result, he had trained himself to adapt to whatever conditions he had in front of him, as far as was necessary.

While he was downstairs at breakfast, housekeeping did their thing and moved on. When he returned to his suite, he was able to spread out his files in the tiny living room and go to work. He was stranded here for at least another day, so he'd decided to use the time to study the documents on a few of the international companies that now belonged to him. He wanted to gain a better understanding of how they were set up and how he could use them to his advantage from here in Canada.

He had finished one accordion file and was starting on a second one when someone knocked at the door: one light; one heavy; two light. It was Morse Code for L—Leonardo. His private joke.

"Come in."

His friend was dressed for the weather in a navy turtleneck shirt, grey flannel trousers, and a dark grey cardigan sweater with a shawl neck and wooden toggle buttons. Dante glanced at him over his reading glasses and took a moment to arrange the papers back into the accordion file before waving at a somewhat hideous bamboo armchair.

"Dante," Leonardo said, sitting down and crossing his legs, "Joseph and I finished canvassing the town, and I only found one place where Lonnie stopped. A menswear shop a few blocks from here."

"All right." Dante leaned forward and set his reading glasses down on the coffee table. Joseph Gagliato was the driver. When not behind the wheel of the limo, his job involved carrying out small tasks whenever he was told to take care of them. Dante had ordered him to go with Leonardo on his little tour around the village asking after Lonnie, on the premise that two were always more secure than just one.

"He knew nothing about a USB," Leonardo said. "I could see he was confused when I asked if Lonnie had left anything with him for safekeeping. He told me he'd spoken to the police earlier, and it hadn't come up."

Dante ran a hand over his hair, using his thumb and little finger to catch loose strands at each temple and rake them back over his head, out of the way.

Leonardo shifted. The chair was as uncomfortable as it was ugly. "Something more disturbing, however."

"Oh?"

"Two other men also went around yesterday afternoon, asking the same questions. One Black, one white. Samuel and McQuillan, obviously. Looking for the USB."

Dante pursed his lips thoughtfully. He'd described to Leonardo his conversation last night with Dom, including the descriptions of the two men, Henry Samuel and Patrick McQuillan. The two pieces of excrement who were—according to Dom—responsible for Lonnie's death.

Dante knew that Leonardo understood the significance of their presence here. Leonardo knew as well as he did that these men were members of the Wolfpack Alliance and that Rick associated with them. His friend understood his fear that Rick was complicit in Lonnie's murder, that it was part of some greater scheme Rick had undertaken with these lowlife bastards to further his own personal advancement.

The telephone rang. When Dante nodded, Leonardo picked it up.

"Mr. Tassone's suite."

He listened for a moment and then covered the receiver with his hand. "The policewoman, March, is asking for a meeting with us downstairs in the conference room."

"I didn't know there was one. When?"

"When?" Leonardo asked. He listened. "Ten minutes."

Dante nodded again. He was reluctant to get too far into things with the police, but he knew it wasn't going to be possible to avoid it altogether. The trick would be to steer them to the Wolfpack morons without implicating Rick. While gaining possession of Lonnie's USB drive in the process.

Chapter

24

Charlotte went into her room's washroom and closed the door. She lifted the toilet lid and sat down without lowering her pants. The washroom was so small her knees were only a few inches from the door and her left calf pressed against the edge of the bath tub. It was good, though. It provided the perfect levels of control and containment that she preferred to have when making important phone calls.

If someone asked her why she always lifted the lid instead of just sitting down on top of it, as though the toilet were a porcelain chair with a plastic top—and she fervently hoped the subject never came up with anyone, ever—she would be obliged to explain that the lid had a slightly convex surface to it which wasn't really all that comfortable to sit on. Plus, if you weighed a few pounds, it might flex downward slightly as you sat, which could be very disconcerting. On the other hand, the toilet seat itself provided a slightly concave surface that accommodated one's buttocks and upper thighs, even when encased in denim, which was much more comfortable and reassuring than the alternative.

The only caveat was that it was always important to remember the actual, specific reason you were sitting there and not just let muscle memory take over, as it were. It was very, very important not to become too preoccupied, too absorbed in the business of the call. That had happened to her once when she was at university, while calling a professor to ask for an extension on an essay that was swallowing her whole. The memory of the resultant disaster had remained with her ever since.

"Gail, it's me."

"Mack, hi. You in your room?" Gail Tolbert was an analyst with the RCMP's Criminal Intelligence Service and a close friend. When they weren't speaking on the phone they were texting each other or messaging or waiting for the other to wake up or come out of a meeting or drive to wherever they were going before resuming their constantly running dialogue.

"Yeah." Charlotte had sent her pictures of the room this morning, and Gail had thought it looked nice.

"I like the wood floors. So what's up?"

"I'm about to go into an interview with Ellie and Dante Tassone. I'm a little nervous."

"Don't be. You said she was nice, didn't you?"

"She's amazing. It's true she never smiles, at least I haven't seen it so far, but she's been very kind to me. That's a big deal. And she's very, very focused. Which is why I'm calling to pick your brain."

"I've got my notebook open right in front of me. Pick away."

"Okay. So, it kind of blew me away when she told me last night that Alonzo DiMaria was dead. I know his name's not in the news yet, but I thought someone would have heard about it and let me know."

"Yeah, me too. Thanks again for clueing me in right away."

"No problem. What I don't know is whether or not he was connected to the transfer of legacies from the estate of Gabriel Tassone to our guy Dante. Would that be the reason why he was killed?"

"Dunno. What I hear is that Dante had a small team reviewing everything, and that DiMaria and a couple of his CPAs went through a ton of financial reports and audits and stuff beforehand. If he spotted something, maybe he would have been going to tell Dante about it, but that's not what I'm hearing. All these companies are apparently squeaky clean and a really nice inheritance for this guy."

"It was a really violent murder," Charlotte said. "He was beaten to death. Kicked, mostly."

"Not their usual drive-by execution or restaurant shoot-out."

"No. Almost like it was personal. A high level of emotion. Or the unsub is deranged or something and has a low level of self-control."

"Yeah," Gail agreed. "More like a street gang thing or something."

"Yeah. Good. Okay, what about—" Charlotte's phone emitted the sound effect that told her another call was coming in. She pressed a button and saw that it was Ellie.

"Oh, crap, Gail. It's her. I'm late. I gotta go."

"Sure, no problem, Mack. Break a leg!"

"Thanks. You're the best. I'll catch you up later."

Charlotte ended the call and jumped to her feet, unconsciously flushing the toilet and washing her hands before hurrying out.

Chapter

25

"I'm not going to waste my time," Ellie said, watching Dante and Leonardo take seats at the conference room table across from Charlotte, "and I'm not going to waste your time, either. I want to know who had a reason to beat Alonzo DiMaria to death. I want you to give me a name."

"I understand," Dante said. "Who's this?"

"I'm Charlotte McKinley," Charlotte said. "I'm a civilian employee with the OPP. I'm here to assist Detective Inspector March."

Dante glanced at Leonardo, the corners of his mouth twitching. "An intelligence analyst."

Leonardo nodded.

"Were you one of the ones taking my picture outside the cathedral on Monday?"

Charlotte rolled her eyes. "No."

"A brief word on your rights, Mr. Tassone," Ellie said. "This is an interview, and in no way should you consider yourself under arrest or detention. You're here of your own free will, and you can leave at any time. You don't have to tell us anything you don't wish to say. You have your lawyer with you, and that's fine, under the circumstances. Consult with him at any point during this interview. Do you understand?'

"Sure, sure. As you say, let's not waste time."

"How about we start at the beginning, then. We understand Mr. DiMaria worked for you, and we understand he was also a friend, but what we don't understand is why it was so important for him to jump in his car and drive four hours—probably more like six, given the weather—to come all the way up here to meet with you in person. What was it that he couldn't handle with a phone call?"

"I actually don't know the answer to that question," Dante admitted. "I wish I did."

"You knew he was coming? You knew he was on his way?"

"He called. He said he had something very important to show me and it couldn't wait. When I said I was going to be here at least until Wednesday, he said he'd come up."

"When was this that he called?"

"Monday evening. Late; about ten."

"Did he give you any idea what it was about?"

"No. I asked him, because I didn't want him making the trip for something that could wait until I got back home, but he wouldn't talk about it over the phone."

"Did you have any suspicions?"

"Not that I would care to discuss at this time." Dante glanced at Charlotte, who was taking notes.

Ellie's eyes followed his. "Charlotte?"

"Since Mr. DiMaria was your *contabile*, your head accountant, we're thinking it had something to do with your finances. Yours, personally, or those of Wooden Bridge Investments, maybe. Have you been having problems in that regard over the past while?"

"Not at all. Certainly not that I'm aware of."

"We understand you'll be inheriting controlling interest in a number of limited liability corporations from the estate of the late Gabriel Tassone. Any problems there?"

Leonardo cleared his throat. "None. Mr. DiMaria set up a small team for Mr. Tassone when he was told about the legacy, and everything was given a clean bill of health. My own team reviewed everything as well, and we were also very pleased."

"There was something he apparently brought with him," Dante said to Ellie. "Something that has gone missing. I'm worried it may be the reason he was killed. Someone wanted to find it."

Ellie saw Leonardo look sharply at Dante before dropping his chin and hooding his eyes. "What kind of a thing are we talking about?"

"I'm told it was one of those, what do you call them, jump drives."

"A USB flash drive?" Charlotte asked.

"Just so. If I had to guess, I'd say it had certain financial information on it that Lonnie felt I needed to see immediately. Just a guess, however."

"How did you learn about this drive?" Ellie asked. "Who told you about it?"

Dante said nothing.

Ellie looked at Leonardo. "Your man, here, was going around the village this morning asking people if DiMaria had left something with them. Is it safe to assume it's this USB drive we're talking about?"

Dante tipped his head to one side.

"We've also learned that two other men went around yesterday afternoon on the same Easter egg hunt. More employees of yours?"

"No," Dante said flatly.

"But you know who they are?"

Dante's lips thinned.

"We know," Leonardo put in, "that they're outsiders. Undesirables. Punks. Trash."

Ellie considered this one for a moment. "Names," she prompted.

Neither man spoke.

"I won't stand for vigilantism around here. I won't stand for people getting gunned down in drive-bys like some kind of big-city Mob bullshit."

Dante raised a disparaging eyebrow. "Really, Detective Inspector. You have such a vivid imagination."

"Four people getting shot to death in a Woodbridge coffee shop is not someone's imagination," Charlotte said. "Pat Musitano's murder in Mississauga isn't someone's imagination. These things are happening for real all around you, Mr. Tassone."

Dante narrowed his eyes at her.

"If you know the name of the person responsible for kicking your friend DiMaria to death," Ellie said, "I expect you to tell me. And if you know the whereabouts of this USB, you'll inform us immediately so that we can take custody of it as evidence. Is that clearly understood?"

Dante shrugged.

"We will continue to communicate with you," Leonardo said. "It's in our best interests that the person or persons responsible for this despicable act be brought to justice."

"Lovely. One more question. How does Jay Lippincott fit into all this?"

"You've already asked me about this person," Dante snapped, "and I've told you I don't know who he is. Please do not ask me a third time."

Ellie watched him stand up abruptly and stalk from the room, Leonardo close behind.

"Interesting," she said to Charlotte. "Very interesting."

Chapter

26

"I understand it's your birthday tomorrow," Ellie said, hooking a leg over the corner of the table and slumping back in her chair, cellphone pressed to her ear. "Happy birthday, old geezer."

Superintendent Gavin Elliott laughed. "Thanks, El. Fifty-six. At least now I have an excuse for being bald."

"Bald is sexy, Gavin. Hasn't Christine explained that to you?"

"Many times. Some day I'll probably believe her. How's it going down there?"

"Still snowing. Our victim's autopsy is about to get under way as we speak."

As the director of the Criminal Investigation Branch at GHQ, Gavin was Ellie's immediate supervisor. They'd worked as colleagues for a number of years, major case managers out of Orillia, Gavin assigned to Central Region and Ellie to East Region. They'd shared the highs and lows that come with the job of leading homicide investigations in a province that saw more than its fair share of them, given the size of its population, and they'd occasionally brainstormed difficult cases together, they'd commiserated when the answers wouldn't come, and they'd celebrated each other's victories. When she'd sat in the director's chair in an acting capacity two years ago he'd worked for her with no reservations, and when he was permanently appointed to the job instead of her she was sincerely happy for him.

He was a good friend; one of the best.

"How's McKinley making out?" he asked.

"Charlotte? Fine. She's very smart. But she's too young, Gav. Shouldn't we be waiting until they reach the age of majority before we hire them?"

"They're all too young at this point," he laughed. "Seriously, though. Will she be able to help you at all?"

"Definitely."

"We're all very surprised to have an Italian OC case spring up in your neck of the woods."

"Join the club."

"Make use of your famous tact and discretion, El. This is very sensitive territory right now. There's a lot of turmoil among them at the moment and no one really knows which way Queen's Park would jump if push came to shove and they started to yell and scream about police harassment and all the rest of that song and dance."

"Understood. There's enough turmoil here as it is. We did our street canvass yesterday afternoon and all we heard was that another pair of characters had been there before us, asking the same basic questions."

"Oh?"

"And two other guys this morning, this time Dante Tassone's lawyer and driver. People here are getting pretty sick of being asked questions."

"Any useful witnesses? I mean to the homicide itself?"

"No. Mostly businesses in the immediate vicinity, and they were all closed. Residences down the street, but no one in their right mind would be outside at dusk in this kind of weather unless it was absolutely necessary. So nobody saw or heard anything."

"Too bad. Oh, by the way, I hope the room you got is nice."

"It is. I tacked on the conference room as well to use for team meetings. All within budget, boss."

"Don't forget McKinley's travel and accommodations, and her meals and incidentals. You're racking it up on me, Ellie."

"Relax. It's all covered six ways to Sunday." She paused. "I've got a question for you. What can you tell me about Preston Raintree?"

"Prez? Now, there's a character. Why?"

"Tom Carty was in a car accident yesterday morning, and Raintree's been assigned to command the crime unit down here until further notice."

"Poor Tom. I hadn't heard. Is it serious?"

"Broken ankle. He'll be laid up for quite a while."

"That's too bad. So Raintree's filling in? Is that the idea?"

"Yeah. Callaghan's pulling him from Traffic and moving him into the crime unit as commander. I haven't run into him before."

Gavin laughed. "I made the mistake of playing chess

with him once, when he was up here for something or other. Kicked my ass pretty bad. I don't like chess very much but I thought I was a decent player until he came along. Anyway, he was very gracious about it."

"Yeah, I heard about the chess. What I want to know is what kind of cop he is."

"As far as I know, he's a good one. Kind of a golden boy, is the impression I got. I'll ask around for you."

"Sure." She paused. "One thing. Have you ever heard of a guy named Jay Lippincott?"

Gavin thought for a moment. "Uh, no. Who's he?"

"That's what I'm trying to find out."

"What about McKinley, does she know him?"

"She's checking into it for me. I thought I'd ask you, just in case."

"Sorry. He probably fits in somewhere. Anyway, keep me posted. Let me know what comes out of the autopsy."

"I will. Everything seems to centre on a USB jump drive thing the vic apparently brought with him from Woodbridge. Everybody and his dog are trying to get their hands on it."

"Motive?"

"Looks like it's at the middle of it, so probably yeah. Nobody seems to know where it is right now."

"Maybe he swallowed it," Gavin joked. "They'll probably empty his stomach contents and it'll plop right out into the pan along with his lunch."

"Gavin." Ellie dropped her leg and sat upright. "You may have something there. I'll talk to you later."

She ended the call and hit Kevin Walker on speed dial.

Chapter

27

Kevin disliked autopsies. The first one he'd ever attended was also an unexplained death in winter, five years ago, and it turned out to be the first time he met Ellie March and the first homicide investigation he'd ever worked.

He'd started out all right in that one, getting through the external examination and the taking of tissue and fluid samples, the initial incisions, and the removal of the heart. He endured everything with stoicism and what he hoped was noticeable professionalism until the stomach contents of the victim, a man he'd known as a neighbour in Sparrow Lake, were dumped into a pan. The sight of a masticated bacon cheeseburger and home-cooked fries proved too much for him, and he'd ended up outside the building, vomiting into a snowbank.

Since then he'd worked very hard to overcome his revulsion toward the insides of the human body. He'd studied textbooks on post-mortem examination, familiarizing himself with the concepts and various procedures, and he'd found himself able to get through the next one without further embarrassment. After that they'd been a little easier.

Just the same, as the diener assisting in the autopsy of Alonzo DiMaria tied off the esophagus and duodenum and Dr. Carey Burton began to remove the stomach, Kevin was greatly relieved to feel his cellphone begin to vibrate against his hip.

Shedding his protective gear, he hurried through the automatic doors and sat down on a bench against the wall. "Walker."

"Kevin, it's Ellie. Have they started yet?"

He leaned his head back against the wall and closed his eyes. He could hear an edge to her voice that he knew would lead to something he wasn't particularly going to enjoy.

"Yes, they have."

"They searched his clothing, right?"

"Yes. Nothing we didn't already know about. No watch; no cash."

"Nothing taped to his body?"

"No."

"Okay. I need you to ask Dr. Burton something."

"Fire away."

"I need to know if the victim swallowed something before he was killed."

Kevin opened his eyes and stood up. There was a small team inside, observing the procedure as part of the chain-of-custody arrangements necessary to ensure that evidence connected to the body would be admissible in court. Most of them had been here before and were paying only token attention, but Prez Raintree was in attendance and had gawked at everything like a tourist leaning over the railing of a Thousand Islands tour boat, fascinated by the view.

Kevin was fairly certain that if something had turned up in the x-rays, Raintree would have pounced on it with a dozen questions.

"What kind of something are we talking about?"

"A jump drive. A USB drive about the size of your thumb."

"A USB drive?"

"Yes, Kevin. Find out."

He bit his lip. "I'll call you back."

Garbed up once again in the appropriate gear, Kevin went back inside. He waited until Dr. Burton finished with DiMaria's stomach and was eyeing his next target before clearing his throat.

"Uh, do you know if there was anything in his stomach or digestive tract? Did he swallow something?"

Dr. Burton frowned, his scalpel suspended in mid-air. "I'm not sure what you're asking me. Are you talking about food?"

Kevin avoided the eyes of Dave Martin and Prez Raintree. "No, I'm talking about a, uh, foreign object of some kind."

"Foreign object? No. No." Dr. Burton lowered his weapon and looked at his diener. "Linda, where are the x-rays? Let's look at the digestive tract from top to bottom."

The diener, Linda Chabot, crossed the room and grabbed a handful of x-rays. She took them over to a long light box on the far wall and began sticking them into place.

Dr. Burton joined her, followed by Kevin and the others.

"I've already looked at them, Kevin, but let's go over them again. Nothing in the mouth." He pointed. "Nothing lodged in the esophagus." He pointed again. "Here's the stomach; no foreign object. Didn't find one in the physical exam just now, either. Not much of anything, actually. He must have been hungry." He moved to the next x-ray. "Nothing in the small intestine. What the hell am I looking for?"

"A USB jump drive," Kevin admitted.

"You're kidding me." Dr. Burton shook his head. "Large intestines," he pointed. "No jump drive. Bowels. Colon. Likewise clear of technology."

"Thanks," Kevin said. "Sorry to interrupt your work. Just something we had to be sure of."

Dr. Burton winked at him. "No problem. But if I take out his brain and find that it's wired to some kind of circuit board, you'll be the first to know."

Kevin failed to ignore the laughter that rippled from the others behind him.

Chapter

28

Dante chose to have lunch with his son upstairs in his suite rather than downstairs in the dining room. He'd discovered that the hotel was a popular mid-day spot for locals as the lunch crowd looked for something a little better than tuna sandwiches and poutine. And while the dining room wasn't exactly packed, thanks to the weather, it was still too busy for the kind of quiet meeting Dante had in mind.

They sat on either side of the table against the wall, across from the tiny kitchenette, watching the waiter as he laid out their china and utensils. Giorgio Marino, his security man, had retreated to his room across the hall for the duration.

They picked away at Dante's choice of antipasti, an

assortment of cheeses, salami, pieces of honeycomb, olive tapenade and walnut crostini. The waiter made himself scarce, leaving behind his trolley with the other two courses.

"You met with Gallo again this morning," Dante remarked, sampling the tapenade. They would speak in English, as Rick understood almost no Italian.

"Yeah." Rick helped himself to another crostini. "Complete waste of time. Oh well. It is what it is."

"What about the others? How do they feel?"

"They're morons, so what do you think?" Rick's low opinion of his many cousins and nephews had not improved after forced interaction with them this morning. For the most part they were either too interested in the salacious side of the family business for their own good, or they were too callow and timid to admit it existed.

"Fifty grand lights them up like a Christmas tree."

"It's important that the will be processed without a challenge," Dante said.

"I know that." Rick wiped his fingertips on his napkin, his tone sardonic. "I'm trying to make a point here. Not that anyone would notice."

"I understand."

"I don't think you do. I'm an asphalt, gravel, and truck guy. How exciting. My life's ambition, already realized at thirty-two."

Dante got up and cleared away the remnants of their appetisers. Rick had ordered a pizza that would serve as the remainder of his lunch, while Dante would have a pasta plate before his main course. He served his son and then sat down with a rather basic fettuccine alfredo that was passable but not great.

"Is it the money?" he asked.

"Of course it's the money. You and I both know I could be salting away ten times what I'm making right now. Easily."

Dante said nothing. Rick's current income, after taxes, was around a quarter of a million dollars a year. The Wooden Bridge companies were exceptionally profitable, thanks to provincial government contracts and the numerous sub-contracts that kept their workforce busy and the income flowing. At his age, still single and living in a luxury condominium that was already paid for in full, Rick should have enough money to do whatever he wanted to do right now.

"I don't need you there," Dante said, understanding that Rick wanted direct involvement in the family drug-trafficking business. "I need you with me, running the companies that pay our bills and keep our skirts clean."

"It's boring, it's dull, and it's a waste of my talents."

"Pietro has things well in hand."

"He's old, Papà." Again the sardonic tone. "He's out of date. There are new ways, new ideas, approaches that can make us billions instead of millions."

"Stability is extremely important. It keeps our family prosperous enough, and more importantly it keeps our family safe. Pietro understands this."

Rick shook his head, pushing aside his plate. "He's passing up a good third of the drug trade, sticking with the biker franchise deal for pennies on the dollar. It's ridiculous."

"This is on my orders, Ricardo. It's the way Gabriel wanted it handled, and it's something I continue to believe is in the best interests of our family. I would hope you'd understand we can still make money from this very distasteful enterprise while minimizing our exposure and our risk."

"Ell-are, ell-are."

"I beg your pardon?"

"Low risk, low reward. The kind of risk management that's a sure recipe for underperformance in business." Rick pushed his chair back and stood up. He helped himself to a fresh bottle of tonic water from the mini-fridge and sat down again.

"Family first," Dante said.

"What's family's done for me lately? A lousy fifty grand. Family's overrated, Papà. It's what you do for yourself that matters. The economy helps those who help themselves."

"No, Ricardo. Family is everything." Dante rose and cleared away their dishes. He still had another lunch course left. "Would you like some of this?" He uncovered a generous serving of grilled salmon and vegetables marinated in marsala wine.

"God no, I'm full. I don't understand how you can eat so much and still stay thin like you do."

Dante smiled, as though it were a sign of affection from his son.

"I spoke to your mother last night." He sat down again and unwrapped clean utensils. "Your grandmother's feeling much better. Hopefully our prayers to God that we avoid another winter death in the family have been answered."

Rick said nothing, chugging down the tonic water.

Dante ate for a moment, preparing himself to broach the subject that was the point of this meeting. Finally, he put down his utensils, wiped his mouth, and leaned back. "Those two men," he said, "I don't like them being here."

"Which two men?"

"Don't play stupid, Ricardo. Black and white. The Wolfpack jackals."

"Papà, that's not very nice. They're friends."

"They're trash. Look, Ricardo, I'm aware that you've invested money in their activities."

Rick froze, the bottle of tonic water an inch from the table top.

"I don't approve," Dante said, "not in the least, but it's your money. You're an adult, and you're capable of making your own decisions. I just—"

Rick slammed the bottle down. "This is bullshit!"

"Don't take that tone with me. I won't tolerate it."

"Who the hell told you that? Who the hell's spying on me? Was it that damned DiMaria?"

"Tread softly," Dante warned.

"I won't stand for it. I won't put up with it."

"Listen to me very carefully, Ricardo. I've shielded you before when you ventured outside our protective circle. I've kept the attention of the police directed elsewhere. I've a certain level of tolerance for the impetuosity of youth, but a line has been crossed. Lonnie has always—always!—been out of bounds. If these two Wolfpack punks killed him, and if you're involved, I can't promise that I can continue to protect you."

Rick stood up and headed for the door. "Can't or won't?" He didn't wait for an answer, slamming the door behind him as he left.

Dante stared at the door, his heart heavy. "Probably both, son. Probably both."

Chapter

29

Ellie slipped her phone into her pocket and left the stall. She went over to the sink to wash her hands, thinking about the embarrassment in Kevin's voice as he reported the findings of the autopsy on Alonzo DiMaria. And the non-findings, in the case of the missing flash drive.

Kevin was a good detective, one of the best in the various crime units within the region for which she managed major crimes. He was physically imposing and courageous, and he was able to put himself in harm's way to carry out his duties without hesitation. He was bright and curious; he had leadership capabilities that were off the charts; and he had a good sense of humour. Perhaps most importantly, he had a high level of empathy for the less fortunate among the people they policed in Leeds County. He was a good cop and a good man.

However, despite being able to pass all the tests, whether physical, psychological, or intellectual, Kevin lacked self-confidence in a way that constantly surprised her. He often betrayed a bad case of rabbit ears, for example, unable to ignore the things people said about him, and at times he worked a little too hard to impress.

She held her hands under the blower and rubbed them dry, appreciating the warmth.

If she had to guess, she thought it might be the result of the unorthodox route Kevin had taken to enter the OPP. Instead of being hired as a rookie recruit and following the usual training and probation processes most other sworn members of the force went through, Kevin had applied for a transfer from the now-defunct Sparrow Lake Police Service when the municipality of Yonge Township had dissolved their little department and contracted out to the OPP.

Despite having nine years of service under his belt when he was accepted into the force, the last five of which he'd spent as the only detective on staff in the SLPS, Kevin had initially encountered a healthy skepticism from his fellow OPP officers, particularly because he'd been able to lateral directly into a detective position in the Leeds County Crime Unit. It was only after his colleagues and superiors saw him in action that they understood why the rank determination process had worked out in his favour.

Eight years later, Kevin still seemed to labour under the burden of impostor syndrome. He still showed signs of believing he didn't quite belong, that he didn't quite fit in.

Ridiculous, as far as she was concerned. For Kevin, the sky was the limit.

She pushed through the washroom door and bumped

into Charlotte McKinley, who was coming out of the lounge.

"There you are. I was just looking for you." Charlotte pulled out a mouthful of hair. "We should talk."

Ellie rubbed the spot on her right forearm where Charlotte's messenger bag had banged it. "What's up?"

"I've got a report for you. Um, the name you gave me to run." She looked away self-consciously as someone edged past them and went into the men's washroom.

"I'm really starting to get claustrophobic in this place." Ellie moved her chin in the direction of the lounge. "Is anybody in there?"

"Just that guy," Charlotte said, looking at the washroom door, which was still closing. "And the guy behind the bar."

Ellie shuffled around her and led the way. The guy behind the bar, whose name was Wayne something, nodded as she slid onto a stool at the far end.

"Ice water. And put whatever she wants on my room tab."

"Hot chocolate," Charlotte said promptly, sitting down on the next stool.

"Toddy?" Wayne grinned at her. He was short and muscular, clearly a workout warrior, and his teeth were large and perfect.

"No. It's too early."

He nodded and went away.

"I typed up a full report for you on John David Lippincott," she said, taking out her notebook. "I haven't logged it into the system yet, because I thought we should go over it first."

"All right."

Wayne came back with their drinks. He put a tall glass

of ice water on a coaster in front of Ellie and a mug of hot chocolate next to Charlotte's folded hands.

"On the house," he said, winking at Charlotte. "My treat."

Ellie watched him slap his cloth across the bar on his way down to the other end. "He likes you."

"Ew."

"Lippincott."

"Yes. Well." Charlotte pinched a lime-coloured Post-it Note and flipped open her notebook. "I ran a full background on him. I can give you as much or as little detail as you want."

"Give me the Reader's Digest version. Where does he fit into OC in the GTA?"

"That's just it. I can't see where he does. There's absolutely no indication, not even anecdotally, that he has any connection whatsoever to any organized crime group or member or associate, not now or ever. He's completely clean. Not even an outstanding parking ticket."

Ellie frowned, thinking.

"I'm not sure where he fits into your case." Charlotte sampled her hot chocolate and burned her lips. "Ouch."

"I don't know. Maybe he doesn't." Ellie sighed. "Give me the highlights."

"Okay. The origin story. Let's see." She frowned at her notes. "Born and raised in Toronto, attended Upper Canada College with other assorted elites and what have you. His father, John Douglas Lippincott Senior, a.k.a. Jack, owned a company called Powers Engineering, which made components for Pratt and Whitney aircraft engines. Young Jay went to U of T for his mechanical engineering degree and on to the Wharton School of Business at U-Penn for his MBA so he could follow in Daddy's footsteps."

She tried her hot chocolate again and this time found it drinkable. After a long swig, she smacked her lips. "Onward. When Daddy died, Lippincott the younger inherited millions along with control of the company. Surprisingly, he sold it and used the money to buy another company that manufactured light aircraft. It was in pretty serious difficulty, so he picked it up for pennies on the dollar. He renamed it Lippincott Helicopters, retooled the whole thing away from planes to helos, headhunted some of the best aeronautical engineers in the business away from other companies, and built the thing up into the juggernaut it is today. Guy's a multi-billionaire who pays his taxes and keeps his nose incredibly clean.

"On the personal side, in 1975 he married the former Jeanette Kennedy, the daughter of a Pratt and Whitney Canada vice-president by the name of Gerald Kennedy. They have three children. The oldest is James, born in 1977 and currently chief financial officer of Lippincott Helicopters. Next is John the third, nicknamed Trey, born in 1978. This guy runs a charter fishing boat business in Tofino, B.C. He's been married twice and has four kids. Son number three is William, a.k.a. Bill, born in 1981, currently teaching English as a second language in Tokyo. Lippincott and Jeanette divorced in 2000. She got the house and he bought another one in the same neighbourhood, only a few rooms smaller, where he lives by himself."

She gulped more hot chocolate and looked in Ellie's general direction. "How am I doing so far?"

"It's very boring. No offence."

"None taken. Like I said, there's nothing interesting here at all."

Ellie sighed. "No intelligence whatsoever suggesting criminal ties?"

"Zipperoonie."

"So why does this guy give me the willies?"

Charlotte closed her notebook. "I don't know. My thing is information, and working it with other information until it's intelligence, and using that intelligence to predict future behaviour, et cetera, et cetera. It's what I do. But I know for a fact that people out in the field who are good at field work, I mean, really *really* good at it, like you are and like other people I know, they all have a highly developed gut instinct for things I couldn't ever hope to have. I've asked around, Ellie, and they've got nothing for me. But if you feel creeped out by this guy, there's obviously something we're not seeing yet."

"Thanks, Charlotte. I appreciate the time you put into this."

"You're welcome." She smiled apologetically. "Sorry I couldn't be more helpful."

"No problem."

"I'll keep my antennae up." She put her index fingers alongside her temples. "Something's bound to pop out of the ether if we keep scanning the wavebands."

"Thanks." Ellie rapped the top of the bar and walked out.

Couldn't help but like the kid.

Chapter

30

Thursday afternoon was Matthew Scanlan's day to close the store early and take care of the weekly housekeeping chores. He also cleaned on Monday mornings before opening and tidied as necessary in between, of course, but Thursday afternoon was when he gritted his teeth and tackled the bathrooms, downstairs and up. One of his least favourite things to do.

Vacuuming was a good form of procrastination, so his first job was to run his heavy-duty Dyson around the carpet between the racks and into the change room and the washroom. Then he decided he should probably wipe down the windows on the inside and dust the shelves and refold a few sweaters and shirts.

Finally, he couldn't put it off any longer. He shoved the

vacuum back into the closet, put on a pair of latex gloves, and headed into the bathroom.

The cleaning supplies were kept in the little vanity below the sink. He squatted and opened the doors, reaching for the can of Comet toilet cleanser. He pulled it out and paused.

Frowned.

Someone had rolled up a small manila envelope and tucked it into the crook of the gooseneck pipe under the sink.

He stared at it for a moment. It was too small to hold documents, too thin to hold cash in any significant amount, and too empty-looking to hold drugs, as far as he could tell.

He ditched the can of cleanser and reached for the envelope.

He stopped and pulled his hand back.

Muttering to himself, he reached again, taking hold of a corner with his thumb and index finger. He gently pulled the envelope out of the crook.

Something small moved inside as he unfolded it.

Holding his breath, he tore open the envelope and poured the contents out into his hand.

It was a small USB flash drive. Red plastic, with a pivoting aluminum cap to protect the business end.

The light begins to dawn, Matthew thought, staring at it. *Is this the object of their desire? The thing they seek with all their hearts and all their minds?*

It occurred to him then, in a sober flash of understanding, that if Alonzo DiMaria had hid it here when he used the washroom late Tuesday afternoon, it was probably the very thing that had gotten him killed.

He decided to clean the bathroom another time.

Chapter

31

"What do you think it is?" he asked, watching Angélique turn the flash drive over and over in her hand.

"It's obvious, Matty." She rolled her eyes at him. "It's a computer jump drive. A memory stick, for data."

"Yes, yes, I know. But what do you think is on it? Why would someone have killed that guy to try to find it?"

They were sitting in the front entry of Couvillon House. Matthew had immediately thrown on his coat and boots and hurried up the street to show his discovery to her.

"I have no idea." She handed it back. "I don't know who these people are, so it could be anything. Did you look at it?"

"Not yet. I brought it up to see what you think."

"I think you need to turn it over to the police."

"What if it's something he wanted me to have? Maybe I should look at it first before I decide what to do with it."

"Are you nuts? Get rid of it, Matty. Right now."

"You're probably right."

"Of course I'm right. We shouldn't have even handled it. Now our fingerprints are all over it."

He nodded. Her natural caution was infectious.

He opened the manila envelope and dropped the flash drive into it.

A noise from across the room drew their attention.

Pat McQuillan stood in the doorway, his cowboy hat tipped back on his head.

"Your waitress dicked off somewhere. We're looking for another round of beer. How about we just help ourselves?"

"Please don't." Angélique stood up. "I'll be right there."

McQuillan touched the brim of his hat and went back into the lounge.

"Take it to the police," she said.

"I will." Matthew watched her follow McQuillan into the next room. Envelope clutched in his hand, he zipped up his parka and let himself out.

In the pub, Angélique stepped aside as McQuillan hustled past her, throwing on his overcoat. The other three men were sitting at a table. She took their orders and, on her way around the end of the bar, looked out the window.

McQuillan was hurrying through the snow in pursuit of Matthew, who didn't seem to be aware that he was being followed.

She bit her lip, not sure what to do.

Chapter

32

Matthew heard the boots behind him as he hurried across the intersection and along the side of the church down to his store. He didn't dare look over his shoulder until he was standing on his front verandah. He turned and saw the man in the cowboy hat grimly approaching, eyes fastened on him.

Matthew let himself in and locked the door. He hurried upstairs to his living quarters, heedless of the snow his boots were leaving on the carpet and hardwood floor. He grabbed his cellphone and turned it on.

It started to boot up, flashed a 2 per cent power level message, and went dead.

He thought of Alonzo DiMaria with a lifeless cellphone in his hand mere minutes before his death. Perhaps at the hands of the man who was now chasing him.

Downstairs, McQuillan rattled the door and banged on the glass.

Matthew grabbed a knapsack and stuffed his laptop into it. Gripping his keys, he slung the knapsack over his shoulder, went down the back stairs, and pushed out the door into the carport.

He heard the sound of breaking glass at the front of the house.

He got into his Toyota and started it up. He shifted into drive and eased out of the carport, praying the cold engine wouldn't stall.

He rolled down the narrow driveway between his building and the next one. When he was even with his front verandah, he saw McQuillan duck back out of his shattered front door, eyes flashing.

Matthew drove through the gap in the snowbank and was going to turn right, thinking he should try to reach the Crosby Hotel in the hopes of finding someone from the OPP, but he quickly changed his mind. The Black guy was running up the middle of the street from that direction, slipping and sliding, dreadlocks flying, a gun in his hand.

Matthew turned left instead. He accelerated and immediately began to fishtail. He turned into the skid and straightened it out. He heard a cracking sound behind him and instinctively ducked.

At the end of Church Street he swung right onto Rideau, then right again onto Concession. He drove down to the county road, where he turned left and floored it.

The village quickly disappeared behind him.

Chapter

33

Rick Tassone closed his eyes and slowly shook his head.

"We've been at this for almost an hour," Henry Samuel was saying. "I say we do it my way. I'll get her to tell us."

"Be quiet," Rick said. "Let me think."

"I don't work for you, man. We're partners. I get an equal say, and I say we do it my way."

"Hank," McQuillan said, "give it a rest."

Rick wanted to say that he hadn't brought Samuel into this thing to begin with, that it had been McQuillan's mistake and not his, but he swallowed the words. Samuel had put together a small but nasty organization since moving to Toronto, and some of the other partners valued his participation in the alliance, to an extent at least that

Rick understood the need to tolerate him. On a short-term basis.

He opened his eyes and rubbed the stubble on his chin. Angélique sat on a high stool behind the bar, watching him. Dom sat at the bar across from her, head down, hands around a glass of beer.

Couvillon House was now under their control. They'd forced Angélique to send her chef and server home, and they'd locked the doors. They'd questioned her about the flash drive, whether Matthew Scanlan had looked at its contents, if he'd told her what was on it, and where he might have gone with it. She'd been completely unhelpful.

One of the courses Rick had actually enjoyed as a business admin undergrad had been the one that taught him how to think and problem-solve using outside-the-box methods. Instead of sticking to a linear, station-to-station approach, Rick had learned how to think laterally. Step out of line, move sideways, find a different entry point, and try again.

If Samuel would only close his mouth for a blessed moment, something might occur to him.

"Shut up, will you?"

Samuel shoved back in his seat and huffed out his breath.

A neon beer sign buzzed quietly on the wall above the shelves of booze.

On Rick's right, McQuillan crossed his legs and dropped his cowboy hat onto his knee. He cleared his throat softly and spun the hat around, waiting for something to happen.

Rick suddenly pushed back his chair and stood up. He walked over to the bar and sat down next to Dom.

"We need to know where Scanlan went," he said to

Angélique, tipping his head sideways as though they were friends and he was asking her for an easy favour. "He's got my property and I really need it back. Did he say where he was taking it?"

"I already told you. He didn't say."

"Is he taking it to the police?"

"I told him he should. But what I say and what he does are two different things, so I have no idea."

He held out his hand. "I need to borrow your phone for a minute."

Angélique reached under the bar and brought out a portable that connected to her landline. "Fill your boots."

"Funny you. Your cellphone. Please."

"I'm not giving you my cellphone."

"I won't steal it, and I won't wreck it, I promise. I know how damned expensive they are to replace. I just want to look at something on it."

"No."

Samuel began to stand up.

"Dom," Rick said.

Dom left his stool and moved to block Samuel's way, putting out a hand like a traffic cop.

"Get out of my fucking way, man."

"Sit down," Dom said.

"Hank," McQuillan said, "let him run with it for a minute."

Samuel sat down.

Dom walked around the end of the bar. He stopped a pace from Angélique and looked her up and down. She wore a blue T-shirt under a red apron tied around her waist, jeans, and white Skechers. Dom's eyes lingered on one of the apron's pockets. He held out his hand.

Sighing, she pulled out her cellphone and handed it

over.

Dom gave it to Rick, who brought it out of sleep mode and went to work. It was a Samsung that operated with Android, like his. He opened her Contacts directory and found two listings for Matthew Scanlan. He pressed the first one and listened to it ring.

"You've reached Paddy's Threads. Our regular hours are ten AM to four PM Monday to Friday, eleven to three on Saturday, and we're closed on Sunday. Please leave a message and your number and I'll be happy to call you back."

The landline in Scanlan's store, no doubt. Rick was tempted to leave a sarcastic remark about returning stuff that didn't belong to him, but he refrained. He cut the connection and tried the other number.

"This is Matthew Scanlan. Please leave a message and I'll get back to you."

"No answer at the store, of course, and his cell goes right to voicemail."

"Sometimes he doesn't keep the battery charged," Angélique said.

"Mmm." Rick poked around, looking at the various apps installed on her phone.

Dom sat down again beside him and drained his glass. "Another one, please."

She took away his empty, worked a tap handle, and came back with a fresh one.

"Thanks."

"Bite me."

Dom chuckled, lifting the glass.

"Hey, shit." Rick tapped the Samsung's screen. "Look at this. You've got a tracker on his phone. What the hell."

Angélique said nothing.

Rick opened the app. It was something he'd heard of before, a spontaneous GPS tracking app that shared the other phone's location on a continuous basis. There were similar apps that were essentially spyware for monitoring the use of social apps like Skype, Facebook, Instagram, and what have you, as well as tracking call logs, messages, e-mail, and all the rest. This particular one, however, was relatively benign, limiting itself to GPS location.

"Does he know you have this?"

"Yes."

"Is he autistic or something? Does he need constant supervision, or are you just super nosy?"

"Not funny."

"No, you're right, actually. I have a cousin who's autistic. I apologize." Rick fiddled with the app. "There you are, Mr. Scanlan."

Angélique sighed again.

Rick looked at McQuillan. "It says he's on Cottonwood Drive. Outside the village. Know where that is?"

McQuillan shrugged.

"What's he doing there?" Rick asked Angélique.

She looked at her hands.

"Come on, come on. I've been very patient with you. What's Scanlan doing there?"

"He has a cottage," Angélique said, very quietly. "It's on Wolfe Lake. I don't know why he would go there. It's not winterized. Maybe he left his phone there and went somewhere else."

"I don't think so. Nice try, though."

"You won't be able to get in there anyway," she said. "It'll be snowed in. No one's there in the winter, and the plow doesn't go that way until after all the other roads are done."

"He got in."

"Four-wheel drive."

"Yeah, you may have a point."

"I saw a place," McQuillan said, "on the edge of town. We could rent a snowmobile. Get in that way."

"Fucking A," Samuel said. "Now you're talking. Let's do it."

"A snowmobile?" Rick looked at McQuillan dubiously. "A city boy like you?"

"Hey, man. I drive a hog in the summer. How much different could it be?"

"Whatever." Rick looked out the window. "It's getting late. Call and see if you can get something. Just a sec." He Googled the nearest snowmobile rental place and frowned at the results. "Green Rentals? Is that the name?"

"Yeah, I think so."

Rick tapped the prompt to call the number.

"Hi, you've reached Green Rentals, the best and most environment-friendly vehicle rental service in Rideau Lakes. We're closed now, but we'll be open again tomorrow morning bright and early at eight o'clock. Leave a message at the beep."

Rick disconnected, shaking his head. "I feel like I just stepped out of the Tardus into the middle of Baffin Island or something. What the hell's the matter with people around here?"

"It's a storm," Angélique said. "Don't they get them on the planet you came down here from?"

Dom laughed.

"Sure." Rick slipped Angélique's phone into the inside pocket of his jacket and went back to the table. "Look," he said to McQuillan, sitting down, "it's getting late. It'll be dark soon. Get a machine first thing in the morning, right at eight o'clock, and find him then."

"Sounds good."

"Find someplace else to stay tonight. I don't want us all bunched up together."

McQuillan made a face. "I'm not staying at that fucking dump out on the highway. I hate bedbugs."

"I got an idea," Samuel said.

McQuillan looked at him.

"That funky stone house up the road, remember? The red roof. I said they were obviously in Florida or something?"

McQuillan stood up, clapping his cowboy hat onto his head. "Snow in the driveway; blinds all down. Good thinking."

Samuel laughed. "I bet the beds are real big and soft. And we can loot the place before we go."

"You're evil, Hank. Fucking evil."

"Yeah, I know."

Rick watched them bundle out of the room, fastening their overcoats. The front door banged, and they were gone.

"I could use a glass of single malt," he said to Angélique. "What's on the menu for dinner tonight?"

"You sent my chef home, so I haven't a clue."

"Then you and Dom better take a look in the kitchen and see what you can put together for us, don't you think? Otherwise it's going to be a long, uncomfortable evening."

Chapter

34

After dinner Ellie locked up the conference room with the key they'd given her and took refuge in the sun room, which was currently unoccupied. It was her second day at the hotel, and the walls were starting to close in on her. The darkness on the other side of the windows felt oppressive. The snow, which continued to fall outside, increased her sense of claustrophobia.

Would it never end?

Dinner with Charlotte McKinley had been a bit of a chore. After their meeting this afternoon to talk about Jay Lippincott, conveniently timed to avoid Rachel Townsend's press conference in the boardroom, Charlotte had disappeared upstairs. After a few hours she came back down, withdrawn and quiet, and reluctantly accompanied

Ellie into the dining room.

Aware that an explanation of her behaviour seemed to be needed, Charlotte talked briefly about life on the Asperger's end of the spectrum, and she tried to explain how much she sometimes disliked being around people. Other than Ellie, of course. It was an intermittent thing for her, she said, but when it hit, it really hit. Then she'd gone quiet again and that was it for conversation. She finished her meal, excused herself, and hurried back upstairs.

Ellie didn't mind. She didn't need Charlotte to be a brilliant conversationalist. She understood, in a general sense, that adults with an Asperger's profile tended toward depression and anxiety in social situations. She didn't need Charlotte to keep her company. When it was time to work, Ellie needed her to focus on her job, at which she was proving to be very good. But when a timeout was necessary, Charlotte should be able to take one. Ellie was fine with that.

She sipped a post-prandial cup of coffee and thought about the case. While Kevin had attended the autopsy of Alonzo DiMaria in Kingston, Mulvahill had circulated around the village one more time, trying to get a lead on the men who'd been going door to door asking about the USB drive mentioned by Dante Tassone. It was an exercise in frustration. She confirmed what they already knew, that two pairs of men had been asking around, Leonardo Arcuri and Dante's driver and the white guy in a cowboy hat and the Black guy with dreadlocks.

Cowboy Hat and Dreadlocks seemed to have gone to ground. No one had seen them for a while, and—.

Her cellphone began to vibrate. She dug it out, looked at the call display, and answered. "Ellie March."

"Ellie, it's Jay Lippincott. How are you doing?"

"Well enough, thanks. What can I do for you?"

She heard him take a breath. "Listen, I understand that you're in the middle of a case, and I don't want to bother you, but I have to go back to Toronto very soon and I was wondering if you'd have some time for me, maybe lunch tomorrow, to talk about something important."

"If it's about Ridge Ballantyne's place, I really don't have anything to say about it. Whether you buy it or not is completely up to you."

"It's not about that. Well, um, yeah, I wanted to get your take on it, my buying it, but there's something more important we need to talk about."

"I can't imagine what that would be."

He gave a short, nervous laugh. "Yeah, I know. I understand. But it'll all be clear once we sit down and go through it. Lunch?"

Ellie thought about it. The last thing she needed right now was additional pressure from a wild card like Jay Lippincott. Still, he seemed to be preparing to make his move, to bring out into the open whatever it was that he was going to do.

"I'm in Westport right now and there's no way I'm leaving, not in this snow."

"Of course. I'll come to you. Is there somewhere good for lunch?"

"Not lunch." She thought again. If they could find Cowboy Hat and Dreadlocks in the morning, the day would be hectic. She wanted Lippincott to show his hand, to reveal his intentions, but arresting the probable killers of Alonzo DiMaria was a more immediate priority.

"Dinner. Seven or seven thirty."

"Where will I find you?" The relief in his voice was unmistakeable.

"The Crosby Hotel in Westport. I'll reserve a table, but I may end up calling to postpone, depending on how the day goes."

"I understand completely. Ellie, you have no idea how much this means to me."

"Sure. I'll talk to you later." She ended the call and frowned at her phone.

What the hell was going on with this guy?

Chapter

35

Ellie put away her cellphone and was reaching for her cup of coffee when a sound caught her attention in the doorway of the sun room. Dante Tassone hovered there with a glass of something in his hand.

"I'm sorry to disturb you. I was looking for a place to land. I think they're getting ready for more music in the lounge."

"God, I hope not." She raised her coffee. "I was just going to finish this and go upstairs. The room's all yours."

Dante came in and stood in front of the stove, feeling the warmth of it. This evening he wore grey denim pants, brown slip-on shoes, and a brown corduroy jacket over a light blue shirt. To Ellie it was an odd combination, but she supposed others might find it fashionable.

"My wife is staying with Stella tonight," he said. "Lonnie's wife. She'll do what she can to help her get through it."

"My condolences," Ellie said.

"Thank you." He looked at his glass. "My third. A decent brandy. I don't normally drink this much, but I seem to have a capacity for it when I do."

Ellie finished her coffee.

He sat down in an armchair next to the stove. "Stay for a few minutes, why don't you? I want to talk to someone."

"Where's your sidekick?"

"Leo's up in his room, on the phone with his wife." He shot a cuff and looked at his watch. "It could go on for quite a while yet. They've only been married three years. Everything's still shiny and new."

Ellie said nothing, not interested in the conversation.

"Second time around for both of them." His tone was affectionate. "While Renita and I will celebrate our thirty-fifth this year. And you," he looked at Ellie, "have been divorced for almost eleven years."

Now he had her attention. "I beg your pardon."

Dante nipped at his brandy. "You have your intelligence analyst, Ellie, and I have, well, a whole office full of them. In the business world it's referred to as CI, competitive intelligence. Something I was doing long before my beloved son learned about it at school."

He smiled, not looking at her. "I gave my section head a call, and she provided a thumbnail sketch of the rather remarkable Detective Inspector Ellie March. I always like to know whom I'm dealing with."

It was a given that law enforcement continuously trailed behind organized crime when it came to firepower, resources, money, and information. The playing field was so uneven that it was almost impossible at times to bring these people to justice. Ellie was willing to accept the fact that she was forced to operate under a rather significant handicap in this regard, but she definitely did not like it taking a personal turn.

"You might want to back off," she said.

"Relax. No harm intended." He drained his glass and stood up. "One more of these should do me." He walked to the doorway and snapped his fingers at someone. "Another brandy, please. Ellie, would you like more coffee?"

She didn't remember inviting him to call her by her first name, but she let it pass for now. "Yes."

"And bring a pot of coffee and two cups."

He wandered back to his chair but remained on his feet. "I'll be glad to get home."

Silence fell, punctuated by a loud popping sound from inside the wood stove. After a few moments a server arrived with a large tray. Coffee was poured. Dante was equipped with a fresh drink, and they were left alone again. He sat down.

"My son's very bright," he said, looking at his glass, "but he's young and lacks the wisdom that experience brings."

"How many kids do you have?"

Dante smiled, obviously believing it was a question to which Charlotte McKinley had already supplied the answer.

"Four. Three daughters and a son. Ricardo is the third. The only boy, so his mother spoiled him."

Ellie watched him over the rim of her coffee cup.

"The oldest is Donna. She married a fellow with his own plumbing business in Markham. He's polite, well-mannered, and wants very little to do with our family." Dante shrugged. "Irish."

Ellie lowered her cup.

"Then there's Rosa. Her husband's a real estate broker who buys and sells for one of our companies. Not my favourite person in the world, this guy, but he's very good at what he does."

"I'm sure he is."

Ignoring her tone, he pressed on. "Elisa's the youngest. She's back in Calabria, living with relatives and learning the language and culture. Our family intellectual."

Ellie's special talent as a detective had always been interrogation, driven in large part by her curiosity about other people and their motivations for doing the things they did. She'd found over the years that many of the individuals she'd questioned ended up *wanting* to talk about themselves, wanting to explain, wanting to boast or apologize or rationalize. Something about human nature and the need to confess that she was still trying, after all these years, to understand.

She didn't like what she'd seen of Dante Tassone and had been about to leave the room; but now, here he was, in a talkative mood. She leaned back in the rocking chair and crossed her legs.

"Ricardo's very bright, as I say, but a handful." Dante flipped a strand of hair away from his cheek and hooked it back behind his ear. "Unlike Elisa, he has no interest in our traditions or our language. It puts me in a very difficult position."

"Oh?"

He leaned forward. "Look, there has to be a medium of communication through which people may understand one another. It's difficult for one generation to have empathy for another when young people haven't shared their parents' experiences in life but have only heard about them.

"As a father I can spend hours talking to him about our family history, about our roots in Calabria, about his grandfather and great-grandfather and so on, but as a son it's like he's listening to old music for the very first time that he doesn't particularly like and doesn't find interesting at all. It's just a bunch of sounds. And so for Ricardo, there's no real communication, just a paying of lip service to the whole idea of family obligations and family honour. Without a true appreciation of its value."

Ellie nodded. She didn't quite understand what he was driving at, but she wasn't about to interrupt him.

"He's impatient for success. He holds the mistaken belief that it will come to him without much effort. He went outside the family with numerous business interests and made some bad friends."

He poured cream into a cup and added coffee. "I love him so very much. When he was small, a toddler, he had a grin that was so infectious it lit up the room. Gabriel had just put me in charge of the company at that time, and I was working very long hours trying to pull it all together into something that would be ready to face the twenty-first century. My uncle had grown bored and restless with asphalt and gravel and trucks, and things had fallen into disarray. I had very clear ideas of what I wanted to do, and I didn't hesitate."

He stirred his coffee and set the spoon aside. "As a consequence I saw very little of Ricardo in those early years of his life. It's something I now regret, every moment of every day."

He tried his coffee and nodded. "I should hire this kitchen staff and bring them back to Woodbridge with me. They're really very good."

"Up to big city standards, are they?"

"Just a little homesickness, I suppose. I don't like to travel, when it comes right down to it."

Ellie waited.

"A child is the most precious gift that God will ever give us," he said. "I've been blessed four times, but for a man, to have a son is slightly different than a daughter because you want to pour your entire being into this new version of yourself. Everything you've learned in life, all your most valued possessions, all your fondest memories, you want to pass everything on to this young man who will carry forward your family name and your family pride and family traditions into the future. Perhaps it's the same for a woman and her daughters. Although I understand you're estranged from your two girls."

"We won't talk about me or my family. I thought I made that clear."

"Of course you did. As I said before, no harm intended." He shrugged. "Your life experiences have been so different, though. You grew up with adoptive parents and have no idea who your natural mother and father were. You look Anglo-Saxon, but you could be Irish or even Basque. Who knows?"

He held up a hand as Ellie put down her coffee and started to rise. "No, please. You misunderstand my intentions. It's a pity you've never experienced a true sense of generational continuity, a true understanding of where you come from, and from whom. That's all I'm trying to say."

"Don't patronise me."

"I'm not. Damn it, can't we just have a civil conversation? Please, sit down."

Ellie walked over to the wood stove. "You want to talk?

Tell me who beat Alonzo DiMaria to death."

Dante rose. They stood on either side of the stove, Ellie with her arms folded, Dante with his hands shoved into his pants pockets.

"The two men, the jackals, the thugs I mentioned before. What I've been told is that they followed Lonnie from Woodbridge on Tuesday, intent on taking the flash drive from him. They're Wolfpack. You know what I mean by that, don't you?"

"Wolfpack Alliance?"

"Yes."

Ellie frowned. The Wolfpack was a coalition of young bikers, street gang bangers, and Mafiosi tired of the restrictive traditions of the organized crime groups in which they'd begun their lives of crime. Members were drawn from the Hell's Angels, the Red Scorpions Asian gang, Italian Mafia, and the Independent Soldiers street gang, all of which were normally rival organizations.

The Alliance became a recurrent problem in communities in British Columbia such as Kelowna, Vancouver, and Kamloops before spreading east. Impatient and entitled, they paid little attention to racial or ethnic backgrounds, tended toward extreme violence, and seemed to have absolutely no fear.

"Names?"

Dante clasped his hands behind his back. "They're from Montreal. Henry Samuel was Cheval Noir, and Patrick McQuillan was West End gang. Both now transplanted to Toronto, unfortunately."

"And why do they want the flash drive?"

"Apparently it *does* have financial data on it that Lonnie wanted me to see. Data related to the company."

"And they killed DiMaria. You know this, how?"

"It's what I'm told by someone with knowledge of the subject."

She rolled her eyes at the cliché. "Wonderful. So what would two outsiders want with financial data from your company?"

"Not having seen it, I'm not sure how to answer that question."

"How's your son connected to all this?"

"I didn't say he was."

Ellie moved away from the stove, heading for the door. It didn't take a genius with Charlotte McKinley's advanced IQ to draw the connections Tassone had been more or less inviting her to make. Rick Tassone was young and impatient. He'd gone outside the family and had made bad friends. He was no doubt connected to this Samuel and McQuillan through the Wolfpack Alliance, and perhaps he was also complicit in the DiMaria homicide. But why would his father tell her all of this, potentially placing his son in legal jeopardy?

"When you find the drive," Dante said, watching her walk away, "I'd appreciate it if you'd turn it over directly to me."

Ellie stopped. "No. It's evidence in a homicide investigation."

"I see. Then I should say that I've discussed this at length with Leonardo. He believes that while the existence of the drive as a physical device is relevant to your case, yes, the specific information on it is *not* relevant. You'd have no legal cause to examine the data. Since I'm now telling you that it is confidential information related to my business, Wooden Bridge Investments, and I'm also telling you the company pays taxes on all revenue, and I pay taxes on all earnings I draw from it, you'd have no probable cause to access and examine the specific data on that drive."

Ellie shook her head. "Lawyers, eh? Don't you just love them?"

Dante shrugged. "I want it back."

"Of course you do."

Ellie walked out.

Chapter

36

Rick looked at the call display on his cellphone, sighed, and answered. "This is Rick Tassone."

"Mr. Tassone," a female voice said, "please hold for Mr. Chen."

"Sure." Rick found himself craving a cigarette, although he hadn't smoked for several years.

"Mr. Tassone," Chen's melodic voice buzzed in his ear, "when we spoke earlier, you said you'd call back with an update."

"Yeah, sorry about that. Things are a little hectic around here right now."

"What's going on with the DiMaria situation? Have you found the data yet?"

"Not exactly. We know where it is, but we won't be able

to get it until tomorrow morning."

"I don't understand. I thought this had your highest priority."

"Yeah, yeah, it does. You gotta be here to appreciate the situation, though. It's snowing like we're in the middle of a damned Jack London novel or something. I'm about to ask Dom to break up the furniture and light a fire so we won't all fucking freeze to death."

"What does that have to do with anything?"

Patience, Rick told himself. *The guy's being deliberately obtuse. It's like a test. Keep your composure.*

"The goofball who has the USB drive right now left the village and is holed up in a cottage on a lake out in the bush. The only road in is, like, completely snowed in and we can't get to him right now. The boys are going to rent a Ski-Doo in the morning and drive in there after him."

"I see. In the meantime, you're not afraid this person will disappear on you?"

"He can't. It's like a lockdown around here. Nobody's going anywhere for the foreseeable future, know what I mean?" *Doesn't this guy have an appreciation of the apocalyptic nature of the weather right now?* "What's the snow like in TO?"

"Well, it's coming down, but nothing too drastic. The city's keeping the streets in good condition."

I'll bet they are, Rick thought. *In your neighbourhood, anyway. Or else.*

"Look," Rick said, "once we've got the drive we'll know exactly what to clean up at our end, and we'll get the funds out of escrow and into your accounts right away." Lonnie had locked up the money in question as soon as he'd discovered what was going on, but Tedesco had assured him he'd be able to get it all back out again without a problem. He'd fucking well better be able to, or Rick would feed him to that animal Samuel and find someone else who could.

"And your father doesn't know?"

"No, like I said, no need to worry about that. He knows I'm making investments but he thinks I'm using my own cash. And once we get the clean books in place, he'll be none the wiser. I'll call you tomorrow when it's done."

"Tomorrow, then."

Rick heard the connection go dead.

His hand trembled a little as he put down the phone, and he felt something on his cheek. He wiped at it with his sleeve, realizing that he was perspiring heavily.

In this particular wolf pack, he knew all too well, Thomas Chen was the alpha dog.

Chapter

37

Dante's cellphone began to ring just as he was dozing off to sleep. In his mind he'd been wandering through an office building similar to his own, but not exactly the same. He was about to step onto an elevator when a low-toned bell began to ring. He knew the elevator would malfunction as soon as he got onto it because he often dreamed about being trapped in an elevator in freefall, and he concentrated on the bell, trying to force himself to acknowledge it as a warning not to get on.

Coming awake, he took off his sleeping mask and groped for his cellphone on the side table. "Yes?"

"Mr. Tassone, I hope it's not too late in the evening."

It was Dom. Dante threw back the covers and sat up on the edge of the bed. "No. What's going on?"

"Rick just went upstairs to his room. The two others, McQuillan and Samuel, have gone off somewhere. They said something about breaking into a house they saw outside of town. Rick didn't want them staying here at the B and B."

Dante cleared his throat and reached for the glass of water on the bedside table.

"McQuillan saw some guy with the jump drive. Apparently he runs a clothing store down the street. It looks like Mr. DiMaria stopped and hid it there when he got into town, and this guy just found it."

"Do you have a name?"

"Uh, Scanlan, Mr. Tassone. Matthew Scanlan. Rick thinks the guy has taken off to a cottage he owns. On Wolfe Lake, just west of here. The name of the road is, just a sec, uh, Cottonwood Drive. Last cottage on the road."

"I see."

"This woman here, Couvillon, says the road's probably not cleared yet. No one lives down there, and the cottages are just for summer. The two meatheads, McQuillan and Samuel, are renting a snowmobile in the morning to go in there after him. What do you want me to do?"

Dante set down his glass of water. "Nothing. Leave this with me."

"Yes, sir, Mr. Tassone."

Dante ended the call and put down the cellphone. He hesitated for a moment, brooding. Ricardo would no doubt call this a "high risk, high reward" decision. There appeared to be very little breathing room between his son's involvement in this fiasco and the actions of the two Wolfpack morons who'd killed Lonnie, and Dante wasn't at all sure he could navigate it successfully, feeding the morons to the police while keeping Ricardo safe.

However, Leonardo had explained to him earlier that even if the pair implicated his son after they were arrested, a lack of evidence might prevent the authorities from successfully bringing a case against him. If Dante understood it correctly, out-of-court statements made by an accused against another person regarding the same crime were considered hearsay by the courts and were not admissible. If Dante put McQuillan and Samuel into the hands of the police for Lonnie's murder and they threw blame on Ricardo as a co-conspirator, the Crown would have to produce corroborative evidence separate from these hearsay claims in order to be able to prosecute him. Leonardo insisted that the bar for such corroborative evidence was set very high, and if Rick had been able to keep his hands clean, he might be able to escape unharmed.

It was a risk, Dante knew, and one that would take them very, very close to the edge. But in the final analysis, it was really the best play available to Dante right now.

He picked up the hotel phone on the bedside stand and asked to be connected to the room of Detective Inspector Ellie March.

Chapter

38

The house was quiet. Josh was asleep; Brendan was asleep; Janie was asleep. The strip of yellow underneath Caitlyn's door suggested she was either still reading or had fallen asleep with the light on.

Feet up, tipped back in his recliner, Kevin was also reading. While Caitlyn was halfway through a biography of George Washington Carver, the Black botanist and college professor who developed dozens of uses for the peanut more than a hundred years ago, Kevin was reading a novel: *The Martian*, by Andy Weir. He thought it was remarkable that a story this well written had originally been self-published. Coincidentally, the main character, Mark Watney, played by Matt Damon in the film version, was also a botanist. In his case he was learning how to grow potatoes in a hostile world while using his own body waste as fertilizer.

Car lights shone briefly through the gap in the curtains, drawing his eyes up from the page. They lived on a one-block street on the edge of Sparrow Lake, and traffic was rare, particularly at this hour. A moment later he heard the sound of a car door closing.

As he set aside the book and got up, someone knocked on the side door. He hustled down to see who it was.

Prez Raintree stepped in, tapping his boots to get rid of the snow. "Saw your light and thought I'd stop."

"Come on in."

Raintree removed his jacket and hung it up on a hook that Janie liked to keep clear for visitors. He wore a denim shirt and jeans, and when he pulled off his boots, Kevin saw that his socks were bright purple.

"Come on up. Coffee?"

"Sure, thanks. I hope I didn't wake the kids."

Kevin led the way into the kitchen. There were no sounds coming from the bedrooms, so he relaxed a little. He put a fresh pod in the coffee maker and, while it was brewing, asked Raintree how he took it.

"Black, no sugar. Nice place, Kevin."

"Thanks. We're pretty comfortable here." It was a three-bedroom ranch-style house on an acre lot. Brendan shared a room with Joshua, who would be three in less than a month, and Caitlyn had her own bedroom. Downstairs, the basement had been converted into a rec room, with a small office for Kevin in the corner where he had a desk, a filing cabinet, and bookshelves.

Home sweet home.

Raintree settled down on the couch, his coffee mug on the side table. "I'm not sure if you heard the latest on Tom."

Kevin shook his head.

"The surgery went well, but he's going to be laid up for quite a while. Healing, physio, the whole thing."

"Too bad."

"Yeah. I've been shuffled into the job, so it looks like I'm your new boss from here on out."

Kevin had suspected something of the sort was in the works. "Sounds good to me."

"When he comes back, he'll be reassigned somewhere else. Probably bump him up to staff somewhere."

Relief was the first emotion that passed through Kevin's mind. Tom Carty was a fish, a difficult person to deal with, and an unsympathetic supervisor. An administrative job would suit him much better than one in which he was required to manage people. Kevin tried to remember if he'd heard of any staff sergeant vacancies recently, but couldn't think of one.

Caution was the second emotion that passed through Kevin's mind. He'd known Raintree for a couple of years, since he'd moved into the traffic sergeant slot working out of the Thousand Islands satellite office, replacing Dave Melkin. They'd met at serious traffic accidents or roadside stops on the 401 requiring Kevin's presence and had yakked back and forth. Raintree always came across as friendly and approachable. The back chatter on him, though, was that he was very ambitious and had friends in high places.

Kevin didn't really care about the former. Ambition was fine as long as the person didn't step on other people's hands while climbing to the top. As for the latter, Ellie March was an example of someone with friends in high places who didn't let it go to her head. He would have to wait and see how it went with Prez Raintree.

"We haven't designated a primary for the DiMaria

homicide yet," Raintree was saying. "I talked to Ellie about it, and it looks like you get the nod, Kevin."

"All right." In every major case investigation, a primary investigator was designated to lead the regional team while reporting directly to the major case manager, who was Ellie March. Kevin wasn't particularly crazy about the administrative duties that went along with the responsibility, including resource management, scheduling, and reporting, but it gave him an opportunity to contribute to the direction of the case and influence Ellie in the decisions she made at the top of the chart.

"Whenever you need my help," Raintree said, "just holler. Not my first rodeo, you know."

"Oh?"

Raintree shrugged. "Plenty of homicides where I come from."

"Thunder Bay?" Kevin thought he remembered someone saying that Raintree had been deployed to that detachment before transferring down here.

"No. I'm talking about the APS."

Kevin looked confused.

"APS is the Anishinabek Police Service. I'm from the Pic River reserve, born and raised. Didn't I mention that before? I joined the APS after high school and put in eight years, mostly on the Ginoogaming reserve. About forty kilometres from Geraldton. A lot of gangs up there, a lot of drug trafficking and sex crimes, a lot of very sad kids and suicide and all the rest of it. A lot of murders."

Kevin didn't know very much about northern Ontario, and even less about aboriginal policing. He was aware that Raintree had joined the OPP through a co-operative program about twelve years ago, but he knew very little about him other than that.

"Wait. You didn't go to university?"

"Not then. I was a proud graduate of the Pic River Private High School with a 97.4 per cent grade average, but I couldn't land a scholarship and my family couldn't afford the tuition. Not by a long shot."

"I don't understand. Why couldn't you get a scholarship?"

"I guess the universities I wanted to go to didn't think 97.4 per cent meant much coming from an Indian school way the hell up in Northern Bumcrack, population 964."

"That's ridiculous."

"Doesn't matter. I got a B.A. later through distance learning. Doesn't really mean much except that it's on my résumé at competition time. I learned a hell of a lot more on my own, anyway. Self-educated. Borges was an autodidact, did you know that? Malcolm X wrote down every word in the dictionary while he was in prison to expand his vocabulary. Steinbeck, William Blake, H.P. Lovecraft, all famously self-taught. You're a community college guy, if I remember correctly."

Kevin nodded. "Two-year police foundations at St. Lawrence in Kingston."

"And yet everybody tells me you read everything you can get your hands on about everything under the sun."

"Guilty as charged, I guess."

"So you know where I'm coming from, then." Raintree gulped his coffee. "I gotta go. I have to say I'm not very comfortable with the Italian Mafia presence in this case."

"That makes two of us. Not a lot of exposure to them in rural policing. More the bikers or the Triad cells along the St. Lawrence corridor, that sort of stuff."

"Have you ever met this analyst before? McKinley?"

Kevin shook his head.

"Me neither. Hopefully she'll keep her head down when the time comes to take these guys out."

"You think that's how it'll play?"

"Hard to know for sure." Raintree stood up. "From what I've seen in the papers, these guys shoot first and ask questions later. Thanks for the coffee."

Down at the side entry, after Raintree had pulled on his boots, Kevin held out his hand.

"Congratulations on the new job, Prez. I'm looking forward to working with you."

Raintree pumped his hand, grinning. "Me too, Kev. Me too."

Chapter

39

Rick could hear Dom's voice in the bar as he came downstairs. It was a quiet monotone, too low to catch what he was saying. Angélique Couvillon was locked in her bedroom and no one else was in the place, so Rick figured he must be on the phone.

The carpet on the stairs was thick enough to allow him to creep all the way down without Dom hearing him. He stood in the doorway and listened.

"McQuillan saw some guy with the jump drive," Dom was saying. "Apparently he runs a clothing store down the street. It looks like Mr. DiMaria hid it there, and this guy just found it."

Shit, Rick thought. Anger flared at the back of his head.

"Uh, Scanlan, Mr. Tassone. Matthew Scanlan. Rick thinks the guy has taken off to a cottage he owns. On Wolfe Lake, just west of here. The name of the road is, just a sec, uh, Cottonwood Drive. Last cottage on the road."

Rick tasted an acidic bitterness in his mouth. Betrayal. He clenched his fists as the anger began to spike.

"This woman here, Couvillon, says the road's probably not cleared yet. No one lives down there, and the cottages are just for summer. The two meatheads, McQuillan and Samuel, are renting a snowmobile in the morning to go in there after him. What do you want me to do?"

There was a silence as Dom listened to his instructions.

"Yes, sir, Mr. Tassone."

Rick heard the light clatter of Dom's cellphone as he put it down on the bar. Edging around the doorframe, he saw Dom pick up his glass and turn around on his stool to look at the television. He grabbed the remote and turned on the volume. Yet another hockey game.

Rick crept back upstairs to his room. Anger drove him to the closet, where he'd stowed his travel bag. It was a large, soft-sided duffel-style bag, made of supple black leather. He unzipped an inside pocket and took out his gun.

It was a SIG Sauer, the P229 model. Compact enough for concealed carry. Utterly reliable. He took out a magazine and checked the load. Thirteen 9mm rounds. He snapped it into place, chambered a round, and went back downstairs.

Dom still sat at the bar, watching the TV. Rick stood behind him for a moment. Dom glanced over his shoulder.

"It's a good game. Grab a beer and watch it with me."

Rick slammed him behind the right ear with the barrel

of the gun.

Dom grunted and toppled forward, turning his head so that he struck the bar ear-first.

"Motherfucking ratfuck." Rick hit him again, this time with the heel of the gun, opening a laceration on his left temple.

Dom was dazed. His eyes fluttered and his mouth sagged open, leaking saliva onto the bar.

Rick sat down to give Dom time to come to his senses. He watched hockey for a few minutes. When Dom began to push on the bar, trying to straighten up, Rick got up and grabbed a fistful of the man's shirt. He hauled him off the barstool.

Dom sagged, but Rick pulled him back up, anger fuelling his strength. "Walk, you ratfuck."

"What . . ."

"Shut the fuck up. Walk."

Rick herded him out and across the front entry to the cellar door. He opened the door and reached around Dom to turn on the light.

Dom tried to grab his arm, but his coordination was off. Rick clipped him on the top of the head with the gun and then shoved the muzzle, hard, into the small of his back.

"Smarten the fuck up. Downstairs."

"Rick, what the hell . . ."

"Downstairs."

Weaving a little, Dom went down the stairs. Rick held tightly to his fistful of shirt.

It was a typical nineteenth-century cellar, with a dirt floor and stone foundation. Rick looked around at an oil furnace, a washer and dryer, plastic storage tubs; the usual basement stuff.

"Over there," he said, shoving Dom forward.

"Rick. Relax. Don't do anything hasty. It isn't you."

It was the same old story. Was he tough enough? Did he have the guts to handle business when it got dirty, or was he just another pretty boy with an over-indulgent father?

He'd endured the smart remarks and harassment from the good old boys all his life. He'd turned a deaf ear to all their garbage, but a few times in his life the anger had taken over and driven him to the ultimate act. The first time, when he was fourteen. A high school bully who mysteriously disappeared. His body was never found. That one had been personal, but the other two were business. Executions that were necessary to solidify his position within the organization. Essential acts, but fuelled by the anger that took over when his authority was questioned.

He moved the gun from the small of Dom's back and pointed it at the base of his neck, just below the skull, more or less aimed at the cervical vertebrae at the top of the spinal cord. It was his preferred kill shot; his signature, so to speak.

"Rick, please. You don't understand what's—"

Rick pulled the trigger and Dom's throat exploded outward. He fell, and Rick leaned over and put two more rounds into his head.

The trifecta, as he liked to think of it.

Nobody fucks with Rick Tassone.

Chapter

40

The following morning, Kevin drove into the village at a few minutes before nine thirty. It was a Friday. Janie had a full schedule of bookings at her hair salon in Sparrow Lake, and before he could leave, Kevin had had to wait for her mother to arrive from Brockville to look after Josh, who was still under the weather. Brendan, luckily, had recovered enough from his cold to go back to school.

The snow had stopped overnight and the roads had been cleared and sanded, but conditions were still not conducive to fast driving, so Kevin took his time. As a result, he was running a little late.

As he drove along Concession Street at the edge of the village, he passed a car and trailer rental place next to a gas station. A white Audi S5 Coupe sat in the parking lot beside the little sales office building. A man in a parka and a Brockville Braves toque was waving the driver of the Audi back to a trailer loaded with a tarp-covered snowmobile.

Kevin glanced at the price of gas as he passed the gas station and looked down at his fuel indicator. He should probably fill the tank before going home.

He slowed at the corner of Rideau Street and turned right. He drove halfway up the block and abruptly pulled over, shifting into park.

He closed his eyes and summoned up the after-image of the Audi. The driver, visible through the windshield, had been wearing a cowboy hat, hadn't he?

There had also been someone in the passenger seat.

He concentrated, but could only visualize the first three letters of the licence plate: ASP.

When he tried to pull away from the snowbank, intending to use a driveway on the other side of the street to turn around, he found that he was stuck. His wheels on the passenger side of the car were caught in the heavy edge of the snowbank. He shifted into reverse and backed up about a foot before the wheels began to spin again. Muttering, he shifted back and forth between drive and reverse, rocking the car, until he was finally able to get free.

Turning around, he went back to the rental place.

The Audi was gone.

He pulled into the parking lot and went inside the office. Stamping his boots on the industrial-sized mat to get rid of the snow, he walked up to the counter.

"The white Audi that was just here," he said, showing the guy behind the counter his warrant card and badge, "they were renting a snowmobile, weren't they?"

"Wait a sec." The guy put his hands on his hips. "You're Kevin Walker, aren't you?"

"That's what it says." Kevin flapped the badge wallet between his fingers before stuffing it into his inside jacket pocket.

"I thought so. You don't remember me, do you?"

He was about Kevin's age, mid- to late-thirties, short, pudgy, and as homely as a fish with a buzz cut. When he grinned, he exposed crooked teeth, several of which had stainless steel caps.

"Carp, remember? Andy Carpley?"

Kevin took in the thick lips and the small eyes. The light dawned. "Hey, yeah. Andy. How's it going?"

"Not bad. My dad just died, so that was kind of rough. My mom's in a home now. I see her a couple times a week."

"Oh, jeez Andy, I'm sorry to hear that. Which one's your mom in?"

"Rose Garden Manor. It's okay." Carpley folded his arms. "You did pretty good for yourself. I see you in the news every now and again."

"Yeah, I—"

"I still got that *MAD Magazine* collection, can you believe it? You should come over some time and check it out again, for old time's sake."

Kevin and Carpley had attended public school together in Brockville from Grade Five to Grade Eight. Carpley had been relentlessly picked on until Kevin got tired of seeing the boy's bloody, scabbed face in class every day and had interceded. Because he was the biggest kid in his grade, Kevin had quickly put an end to the bullying of Andy Carpley.

Although Kevin had his own circle of friends, mostly consisting of boys with whom he played hockey in winter and softball in summer, he occasionally accepted Carpley's invitation to come over after school. The boy lived in a home much like his own, a rough-looking two-storey stucco house with a small yard and a cracked driveway along the side.

Carpley's father was a trainman for Canadian Pacific and wasn't home much. Kevin had met him once during an afternoon visit when Mr. Carpley was on sick leave to mend three broken toes injured when a forklift accidentally ran over his foot on a train station platform.

The first thing Kevin noticed was that the man was sober. Unlike his own father. The second thing he noticed was that he was friendly and intelligent. Again, unlike his own father. The third thing was that he wasn't nearly as homely as his son, except for the unflattering brush cut and thick eyebrows. The fourth thing was that he spoke with a slight accent, which Carpley later explained was Welsh. The fifth thing was that he was genuinely pleased that his son had a friend.

Mr. Carpley was a rabid Montreal Expos fan, and outfielder Rusty Staub, Le Grand Orange, was his favourite player. Staub happened to be Kevin's favourite as well, along with a few million other Canadians. They compared notes until Mrs. Carpley came into the living room with her husband's pain medication, and the two boys went into Carpley's bedroom to look at his *MAD* collection.

He kept it on a bookshelf next to his bed. There were several shelves of paperbacks, going back to the fifties with the likes of *The MAD Reader* and *MAD Strikes Back*, and books more familiar to Kevin such as *The Bedside MAD*, *Boiling MAD*, and *Greasy MAD Stuff*. There were also paperback collections featuring the work of Dave Berg, Sergio Aragone, and Al Jaffee.

Other shelves were filled with piles of magazines. They

were mostly *MAD*, but Carpley also had issues of *Cracked*, *Sick,* and *Help!* mixed in.

It was the most extensive collection of its kind that Kevin had ever seen, before or since, and his visits were normally spent stretched out on the floor of Carpley's bedroom, reading.

"Anyway," Kevin said, "those guys that just rented the snowmobile. There were two of them, right?"

"Yep. Toronto hardasses. Rented a Ski-Doo and trailer. Weird couple of guys. One guy had a cowboy hat on and the other guy had a crazy look in his eye. Like he was psycho."

Kevin pulled out his notebook. "I'm surprised an Audi has a trailer hitch."

"It didn't. I installed one for them. They were here almost an hour. Spent the whole time on their phones."

"Can I see the paperwork?"

"Got a warrant, mister?" Carpley grinned and picked up a file folder from the desk behind the counter. "Here's the rental agreement." He opened the folder and took out a document. He spun it around so that it faced Kevin. "There were two of them, so they both had to fill it out and sign it. Here's the security deposit, two grand. Insurance fee, ten bucks a day. They took the five-day rental period. Eight ninety-five. Plus the trailer and helmet rentals, down here. All paid for on this guy's Visa. McQuillan. He did all the talking."

He brought out two other documents. "Here's our copies of the receipt and the liability waiver they signed."

Kevin lined them up on the counter and took photos of them with his cellphone. Then he wrote down in his notebook the names, addresses, and phone numbers that McQuillan and Samuel had provided, their driver's licence numbers, the licence plate number of the Audi (ASP had been correct), the particulars of the snowmobile they'd rented, and payment information.

"Did they say where they were going with it?"

"I asked." Carpley made a face. "I mean, you know me. I like to talk. They weren't saying, though. Hardass types for sure."

"Thanks," Kevin said, closing his notebook.

"You should come over for a visit some time. Really."

Kevin put his notebook away. "How long have you been here?"

"In this job? Six years, I guess."

When he and Kevin finished Grade Eight, they'd gone their separate ways. Carpley and his parents moved away somewhere, and Kevin lost track of him. This was the first time he'd laid eyes on him since.

"No, I mean where'd you go? After Prince of Wales?"

"Kingston. Went to high school there. Then Dad retired and wanted to live near his sister, so we came back this way, to Delta. I'm still living in the same house there. Me and my girlfriend. You should meet her."

"I'd like that," Kevin said, zipping up his duty jacket.

"What about you, Kev? You got married, didn't you?"

"Yeah. Adopted my wife's two kids, a girl and a boy. We've got one of our own now, too. A boy. He'll be three next month."

"Wow. Shit. That's great. Good for you."

Kevin held out his hand. "Nice to see you again, Andy."

"That's one thing I always remembered about you," Carpley said, shaking hands. "The others always called me Carp, I guess because I kind of look like one. But you always only called me Andy. I appreciated that."

"Take care." Kevin pulled on his gloves and hurried out

the door.

As it closed behind him, Kevin heard Carpley call out: "You know where to find me, copper!"

Chapter

41

When he finally rolled out of bed, Matthew Scanlan discovered that the power was out. The fire had burned down in the wood stove overnight, and the baseboard electric heater that he'd optimistically turned up when he'd gone to bed had failed to come on. As a result, the cottage was cold enough for him to see his breath as he hopped across the freezing linoleum floor to the washroom.

He used the facilities and flushed the toilet before remembering that there was only so much water in the tank and that the pump wouldn't come on to refill it from the lake until the hydro was restored. He would have to be careful with what he used, since there was no telling how long the electricity would be out.

After throwing on his clothes, he took a bottle of water

and two energy bars from the fridge. Everything that might interest mice was kept in the refrigerator out of harm's way while he was not here, and although there wasn't much in the way of food right now in the cottage, he always kept a carton of the high-energy fruit-and-nut bars on hand in case of emergencies.

He unwrapped one of the bars while his laptop booted up on the kitchen table. *Breakfast of champions*, he thought, washing a mouthful down with water.

The battery on his laptop was fully charged, and as he fished out the USB drive from his pants pocket he remembered that he'd plugged in his cellphone last night in the kitchen counter outlet. He got up from the table and grabbed it. When he disconnected it from the charging cable and turned it on, he found that the power level was only at 76 per cent.

There was no signal.

Disappointed, he turned it off again and buttoned it into his shirt pocket.

The USB drive contained a number of files that were apparently Excel spreadsheets. He had tried last night to access them, but they were password-protected. He tried again now, with no better luck. He opened the file manager program and fiddled with the settings, looking for hidden files or any other clue to the secrets held by the jump drive.

No dice.

He sat back and closed his eyes, trying to think it through.

Alonzo DiMaria had apparently been murdered by someone looking for this drive. The fact that it contained spreadsheets suggested that someone's financial information was stored here. Or some company's financial information. And since there'd been two different pairs of men—very different, indeed—searching for it, it stood to reason that the data belonged to one pair and was coveted by the other pair as leverage or a weapon of some sort.

In the distance he heard the low growling of a snowmobile. He opened his eyes and sat up. None of the cottages on this road was winterized, and he was certain that no one else was down here at the lake right now. He'd seen no vehicles in driveways on his way in. No lights on. No tracks in the snow. Nothing.

Perhaps someone had come down this morning for a little outing. He listened as the sound rose in pitch. Whoever it was, they were approaching his cottage, which was the last one on the road.

He heard the engine clearly now, steadily approaching. He bolted out of the chair. He snatched the USB drive from the laptop and shoved it into his pocket. He rushed to the front window and peeked around the curtain. Down at the end of the driveway, the snowmobile slowed to a stop.

Shit, he thought, recognizing the cowboy hat.

He threw on his parka and pushed his feet into his boots. He looked at his laptop, but the snowmobile was starting up the driveway toward the cottage. What to do? What to do?

There was an old snowmobile in the shed down near the lake. He'd bought the machine second hand in a burst of enthusiasm not long after purchasing the property. He seldom used it but had it serviced every fall and kept it well maintained, just in case.

It was his only chance to get away. He snatched a helmet from a peg in the kitchen and grabbed the keys. Sparing a last look at his laptop, which would have to stay behind, he hurried out the back door.

Zipping up his parka and donning the helmet, he slogged through the knee-deep snow down to the shed. He scuffed at the accumulated drifts with his boots to clear the area in front of the shed doors. He unlocked the heavy padlock and removed the chain.

The snowmobile was idling at the front of the cottage. They were probably checking out his car.

His snowmobile was a 2004 Arctic Cat Bearcat. Praying that the battery still had some juice in it, he inserted the key and tried the starter. It cranked, coughed, and started. He revved it for a moment and then shifted into reverse, walking it backwards out of the shed.

Over the noise of the engine he heard someone shouting. Unbelievably, the shouts were followed by the crack of a gun.

Sitting down, he shifted into drive and gunned the snowmobile down the sloping yard and out across the frozen surface of the lake, hunching down in fear that a bullet would find his back, ending this absurd flight from danger before it had barely begun.

Chapter

42

Ellie nodded to Kevin as he walked into the conference room. She gave him a minute to pour himself a coffee from the urn in the corner and find a seat next to Mulvahill before clearing her throat.

"We have some new information this morning, and some folks who are going to help out." She pointed her pen at two men on her right. "Kevin, this is Constable Kurt Benson and Constable Rick Goyette. They're on loan to us from the SAVE team out of Loyalist."

Benson had a business-like look to him, his head shaved bald and his mouth turned down at the corners. Goyette was several years younger and several inches taller. Goyette nodded at the faces around the table. Benson stared with intensity at Ellie.

"Chief Superintendent Malcolmsen was kind enough to answer a call for help from me last night," she said, "and these two gentlemen have brought their snowmobiles to lend a hand this morning."

There were three OPP Snowmobile ATV and Vessel Enforcement (SAVE) teams in the province. The closest one to Westport operated out of the Loyalist satellite office in Odessa, twenty minutes east of Kingston, as part of the Lennox and Addington County detachment. The team was staffed with five constables and a sergeant. They were equipped with all-terrain vehicles, snowmobiles, and boats, and they were trained to respond to incidents on lakes and rivers, on snowmobile and hiking trails, and in other areas where their specialized expertise was required.

"By the way," Ellie said, "for anyone who hasn't met her yet, this is Charlotte McKinley. She's here as an analyst specializing in organized crime, specifically the 'Ndrangheta."

Charlotte stared at the open notebook in front of her.

"Detective Sergeant Raintree is now commanding the Leeds County Crime Unit," Ellie said, looking at Benson and Goyette, "and Detective Constable Walker is primary investigator for this case."

"Good to know," Goyette said.

"Kevin," Ellie went on, "you need to be brought up to speed on the current situation and how Constables Benson and Goyette will be helping us."

"Okay." He opened his notebook and clicked his ballpoint pen.

"First, let me apologize for the fact that this investigation seems to be working a little ass-backwards. Information's coming to me before it comes to you, which means I have to brief you and not vice versa."

"Okay." He glanced at Raintree, who winked.

Ellie said, "Let's start with the source of a lot of this information, Dante Tassone. Charlotte stayed up late last night putting together a couple of reports for us that are now online in the case management system. Charlotte?"

The analyst ran through a brief biographical sketch of Dante, where he fit in the overall structure of the 'Ndrangheta in the Greater Toronto Area, and a description of his son Ricardo's role in the family business. When she was done, she shot Kevin a quick look before busying herself with her cellphone.

"This Ricardo," Ellie said, "a.k.a. Rick Tassone, is possibly involved in the murder of Alonzo DiMaria. What Tassone tells me is that his son has gone outside the family to do business with Wolfpack Alliance members, two in particular who may have followed DiMaria from Woodbridge and killed him here Tuesday night. A Henry Samuel and a Patrick McQuillan."

"Oh ho," Kevin said. "I saw them this morning. Cowboy hat and dreadlocks. Renting a snowmobile."

"These are the guys people told us were going around asking about the vic?" Mulvahill asked.

"Right."

Ellie nodded. "Everyone's trying to find a USB drive DiMaria brought with him. Tassone's being coy about it, but we figure it contains sensitive financial information related to Tassone's businesses. It might implicate the son Rick in irregularities that the kid wants to keep hidden from his father, or that the father wants to hide from us."

"It's probable," Charlotte said, "that the two Wolfpack men, McQuillan and Samuel, would like to have the disk for themselves. The alliance part of their group name must be understood as a rather loose concept at best. For the most part, here in Ontario, out in BC, and in Quebec as well, we're talking about a bunch of mid-level drug dealers and millennial high-tech fraudsters acting more against perceived weaknesses in the traditional organized crime groups than as a traditional organization themselves."

"Criminal anarchists," Kevin said.

"No, not exactly." Her eyes flicked up and dropped again. "But it's an interesting thing to say. 'Ndrangheta clan leaders like Dante Tassone probably view them as barbarians at the gate. In general, the 'Ndrangheta clans in Ontario have seen better days. Their reluctance to get involved in the famous Montreal power struggle surrounding the Rizzuto crime family was perceived as weakness, and Wolfpack elements have moved into the GTA to establish their own drug pipelines and online gambling infrastructure. What we see with young Calabrese like Rick Tassone is a generational split, moving their own money out of the family and into these other alliances."

"That's what you think is happening here?" Raintree said.

"Yes."

"And why do they want this jump drive? To extort money from the elder Tassone?"

Charlotte grimaced. "I don't know; it's possible. I think in Rick's case he would want it either to protect himself, you know, to hide the fact he's skimming from the family businesses, or in order to make a move of some kind against his father, to use whatever's on it essentially to rob the family. Certainly there was something in the numbers that upset Lonnie DiMaria so much that he couldn't wait to show it to Dante Tassone."

"These other two guys," Raintree asked, "McQuillan and Samuel. What do we know about them?"

"No outstanding warrants; a few arrests and dismissals; nothing you could use to pick them up right now."

"You said you thought they might want the data for themselves. Again, extortion?"

"As I said, Detective Sergeant Raintree, it's possible. If it's detailed enough, though, they might want to use it to gain access to Mr. Tassone's considerable wealth. Remember, these Wolfpack guys are often very tech-savvy. Knowledge of his financial details, the structure of his companies, and how revenue and assets are distributed might give them multiple opportunities to rip him off before he has a chance to protect himself."

"Particularly with his main money man now out of the picture," Raintree said.

"Yes."

"McQuillan and Samuel don't seem particularly tech-savvy to me," Kevin said. "They look like a couple of brainless hit men."

"They probably are." Charlotte steepled her fingers. "The Cheval Noir gang is notorious for its brutality. I wrote a report on Henry Samuel for you that you can look at in the case file, if you like. He was born in Port-au-Prince and was rumoured to have trained as a boy sniper before emigrating from Haiti. Intelligence suggests he was the shooter when a Filipino peacekeeper was killed by sniper fire six months before Samuel and his brother left the country. In their refugee application they claimed their parents had been killed during the coup d'état in 2004. Anyway, he's been implicated in dozens of murders in Quebec, mostly in Montreal, but has never been charged."

"You said you saw them renting a snowmobile this morning," Raintree said to Kevin. "What's up with that?"

"I can answer that one," Ellie said. "As I mentioned,

Dante Tassone called me late last evening with an update. It seems that DiMaria hid the USB drive in the washroom at Paddy's Threads when he stopped in there just before he was killed. Matthew Scanlan, the store owner, apparently found it and has taken off somewhere. We've been trying to reach him by telephone, with no luck. Tassone said McQuillan and Samuel would be renting a snowmobile to go after him. Where did you say you saw them?"

"At a rental place on Concession Street," Kevin replied. "At the edge of the village."

"I know the one you mean. Apparently Scanlan has a summer cottage around here somewhere that he may have taken off to. On Wolfe Lake. Patrol has already done a drive-by this morning, and the road's snowed in. Conditions will be questionable, so these two fine fellows will get you in there." She nodded at Benson and Goyette.

"Sounds good." Kevin looked at Mulvahill, who gave him a thumbs-up.

"Our objective," Ellie said, "is to secure Matthew Scanlan, first and foremost, and ensure his safety. Secondly, we've got to find this USB drive. Thirdly, we need to arrest McQuillan and Samuel and transport them to the hub office for questioning." She stared at Benson. "Detective Constable Walker will direct this operation and you'll follow his orders. Detective Sergeant Raintree will set up a perimeter around the area and co-ordinate all movement in and out. Any questions?"

No one spoke.

"All right. Get at it."

Once they were alone in the room, Raintree stood up and looked at Ellie as he gathered up his things. "Can you trust what this Tassone tells you?"

"No. Right now his motives for wanting to help are

pretty opaque."

"It looks like he's getting ready to throw his son under the bus. Or am I misreading it?"

"That's a good question. I was going to ask Charlotte about it, but she left in kind of a hurry."

"I'm not a fan of organized crime groups. Not at all."

"Join the club." A thought crossed her mind and she leaned back, watching him make his way around the table toward the door. "How well do you know Jordan Malcolmsen?"

"Mal? We've had a few soda pops together." Raintree stopped in the doorway. "Why?"

"Just wondering. What's your take on him?"

Raintree shrugged. "Lousy chess player, but his heart's in the right place. He'll make a good regional commander."

And thereby hangs a tale, no doubt, Ellie thought, watching him disappear.

Chapter

43

Rick finished the last of his breakfast and pushed away the plate. Angélique slid off her stool and started around the end of the bar to clear off the table, but he held up his hand.

"Leave it."

She shrugged and sat down again.

Rick hadn't bothered explaining to her the absence of Dom. When he had released her from her bedroom this morning, he'd only said that she'd be cooking for one guest today. Hopefully McQuillan and Samuel would wrap up their business quickly and help him get rid of the body before it began to stink. Meanwhile, he wasn't going to let her out of his sight, and she certainly wouldn't be allowed to go down into the cellar.

He wouldn't hear from the pair for a while, he figured. They had to rent the machine, find the cottage road, get the snowmobile going, and cut a trail in to the dump where Scanlan was hiding out. They had to take care of Scanlan, secure the jump drive, and then get back out of there again and down here to the village. It would take some time. He just had to stay patient with the whole thing.

He ordered a fresh cup of coffee from Angélique and mulled over the implications of Dom having been an active spy for his father. Was Dom aware of the theft of funds from the various companies under Rick's control? If so, had he already told Dante about it?

Rick didn't think so. First of all, if Dom had learned what was going on, there was no way he would have kept it to himself for even a second. He would have been on that damned cellphone of his (which was now sitting in Rick's jacket pocket) telling the old man the whole story in all its gory details.

Second of all, if Dante learned from Dom the sad news of Rick's financial misdeeds, he would have put his ass in a sling instantaneously. At the speed of light. Since that hadn't happened, Rick assumed his father still thought he was using his own cash to cut deals with the Wolfpack.

Apparently, the death of Lonnie DiMaria had stopped this information in its tracks. Loco Samuel had at least done him that much of a favour, as stupid and thoughtless as the murder had been.

He realized he hadn't heard from Tedesco this morning. He needed to know where they stood with the cooked books, in case Chen surprised him with another call.

He took out his cellphone and grunted when he saw it was Dom's. He put it back and found his own phone in his other pocket.

"Tommy," he said when the accountant answered, "where's everything at?"

"Mr. Tassone, good morning. I've got your man, Mr. Esposito, here in the office with me. Shall I put you on speaker?"

"No. Just tell him to go sit in your waiting room and bring me up to speed."

It took some time for Tedesco to run through it all, but Rick listened attentively, wanting to make sure he had everything straight in his head. If it all went sideways and his father came looking for an explanation, he needed to be ready.

Three Wooden Bridge subsidiaries were involved: Woodbridge Paving, which handled all the big highway construction projects in the province; Woodbridge Aggregate, which supplied gravel, sand, and other materials to the paving company and many other customers through its own subsidiaries; and Woodbridge Transport, which ran gravel trucks, cement mixers, scrap metal carriers, and other province-wide forms of commercial transportation.

Tedesco's skimming operation involved taking legitimate funds from these three businesses, funds that would normally move up to Wooden Bridge Investments, and diverting them through various channels into an account controlled by Rick. It was clean money, separate from the cash that moved back and forth through extortion, bribery, and other criminal activities on cousin Pietro's dark side of the family business. It was simply now being given a fraudulent twist.

There were several ways that Tedesco was manipulating the books to supply Rick with his ill-gotten gains. For example, Woodbridge Transport contracted out most of their truck maintenance and repair business to a company called McAtee Trucking Service, run by a couple of brothers in Brampton. Since Woodbridge owned a lot of trucks, it generated a lot of business for McAtee and accounted for a substantial percentage of Woodbridge's overhead.

Jordan Walters, the Woodbridge Transport accountant, routinely made payments to a bogus company called McAtee Truck Services for fake work on their dump trucks. The name was close enough to the real company that it should have, by rights, escaped notice. Meanwhile, Woodbridge Paving accountant Donald Atkins was paying another phoney company to run non-existent water trucks out to their construction sites during the busy summer paving season.

Tedesco also co-ordinated a fake roster of employees who continued to draw salaries from each company long after they'd retired or had been fired. Some had simply been fabricated out of thin air. Each payroll contained at least a dozen such phantom workers whose weekly wages were paid into bank accounts that eventually drained into Rick's bucket of ill-gotten cash.

Rick listened as Tedesco patiently ran through the amount of work involved in cleaning up the books in each case. The payroll fraud had been completely covered up, but time was still needed to make the phoney companies disappear. There were other, less significant, schemes Rick had authorized over the last few years that also needed attention before Tedesco would feel comfortable pronouncing everyone safe from further detection.

"How much am I going to have to repay?" Rick asked when Tedesco finally ran out of steam.

"They may bring in an independent auditor, so some funds will have to be returned right now to cover the truck maintenance stuff, for example. Other areas we'll need to wallpaper over as well. I'd say about 40 per cent. The rest you can get away with."

"Christ." Rick rubbed his forehead. Thomas Chen's expectations would exceed 60 per cent of what he'd socked away for their upcoming joint venture, he was certain. Lonnie DiMaria's eagle eye had really put him behind the eight-ball.

"Do you want a list, Mr. Tassone, so you can see where the money's going?"

"Are you fucking nuts? Of course not. Just take care of it, all right? Send invoices and I'll pay them off."

"Yes, Mr. Tassone."

Rick ended the call and slid the phone across the table. It clacked against the rim of his empty toast plate. He clenched and unclenched his fists, willing himself to calm down.

What to do? What to do? How do I get out of this fucking mess?

It was time for Rick to start thinking laterally in a big way.

Chapter

44

Matthew was far from an expert driver when it came to snowmobiles. He headed out onto the frozen surface of the lake, cutting a fresh trail through fifty centimetres of snow, and rounded the peninsula to head past Duck Island and Bateman Island. After passing Whitefish Island he reached the northern shore of the lake. He cruised east along the shoreline until he found a trail that climbed up the beach and headed inland.

He eased his Arctic Cat up through the boulders along the shore and into the opening, struggling to co-ordinate his use of the throttle lever to accelerate and the brake lever to curb the tendency of the machine to jump and buck when he fed it gas.

On second thought, he decided, calling this a trail might

be giving it more credit than it was due. It was little more than a narrow gap between the trees, half-filled with snow and criss-crossed by low-hanging branches that threatened to take off his head as he accelerated underneath them.

He drove for about a hundred metres and stopped, letting the engine idle as he unzipped a pocket and removed his cellphone. He powered it up. The battery charge level was still at 76 per cent, but there was still no signal.

He tapped on the app that gave him GPS information without a satellite connection, silently thanking Angélique one more time for having downloaded it while he was still familiarizing himself with the area. He'd used it a few times and found it handy.

He watched the app open and took a few seconds to orient himself. The trail, it seemed, was cutting through the bush in a northerly direction, more or less. If it remained clear to travel on, it would eventually take him all the way to County Road 36, also known as Mountain Road. Once he reached it, he could turn left and head up to Bolingbroke, or turn right and head down to Westport. Since he knew absolutely no one in Bolingbroke or anywhere along the road in that direction, he figured he'd turn right instead of left.

Over the sound of the snowmobile's idling engine he heard the high-pitched whine of another machine echoing from somewhere behind him.

They were following his tracks around the lake.

He powered down the cellphone to preserve the battery charge and zipped it back into his pocket. Gripping the handlebars reluctantly, he resumed his run up the trail.

He gradually increased his speed, rocketing along each straight stretch, fearful of the men behind him. The lower portion of his face, beneath the visor of his helmet, was numb from the cold. His half-frozen hands felt like they would likely have to be pried from the handlebars once he reached his destination. Thankfully, though, the trail had widened, and he no longer had to crouch in the seat to avoid decapitation from looming tree branches.

Several kilometres flashed by in a numbing haze.

He never saw the snow-covered branch that had fallen across the trail since the last time someone had been along here. The front skis of his Arctic Cat ran over it, and the machine lurched upward and crashed down again. He fought the steering, but his wrists weren't strong enough. He lost control.

He swerved off the trail and clipped a tree. The impact spun him sideways into another tree, throwing him off.

He landed in the snow, gasping for breath, the wind knocked out of him.

The safety lanyard clipped to his parka jerked the key out of the ignition, shutting off the Arctic Cat's engine.

He rolled over, struggling to make his lungs work again. He hadn't felt this specific form of agony since he was a kid playing parking-lot football, and he remembered how much he hated it. He groaned, coughed, and managed to get his breathing back under control.

In the distance, above the sound of the wind in the boughs of the pine trees around him, he heard the howling of the other snowmobile as it came closer and closer.

Chapter

45

Kevin saw the lights of the cruiser ahead of them on the snowy road, blue and red pulsations jumping off the trunks of the trees crowding close on either side.

Raintree had called the municipality, and a grader had cleared the way into Wolfe Lake, followed by a truck spreading sand for traction.

Too late, however, for the white Audi in the ditch and the trailer that had apparently jackknifed on a curve, dragging the car down with it.

Kevin pulled up behind Benson and Goyette, who had stopped just short of the scene. He and Mulvahill walked past the big trailer containing their snowmobiles and gear and came up along the side of their truck. Benson lowered his window.

"City folk," Mulvahill said.

"And their Audis," Goyette agreed, leaning forward to grin at her.

Kevin left Mulvahill to chat while he scoped out the situation. Roberta Raymond was once again the responding officer. She stood on the shoulder of the road, staring down at the mess in the ditch.

"Morning, Bobby. How long ago do you think it happened?"

"Hey, Kev. Not quite sure. The municipal dispatcher called it in to us twenty-five minutes ago. Said their plow driver had just radioed in to tell him about it."

They walked up and down the narrow shoulder, looking it over.

How's Josh doing today?"

"Better, thanks, but still sick. It may be another day or two before he throws it off."

"Ah, too bad. Poor little tyke."

There were a lot of boot prints around the car and trailer in the ditch. Many of them had been filled in and covered with chunks thrown off when the plow had passed, but some were undisturbed. They led from the driver's door to the trailer and back again. Since the right side of the two-door car lay against the snow in the bottom of the ditch, the passenger had been forced to climb up onto the driver's side before scrambling out of the vehicle. There was a large impression still visible in the snow where he'd fallen out of the car and scrambled around before getting to his feet. At the back end of the trailer were similar signs that both men had fallen and thrashed around while wrestling the snowmobile out onto the ground.

"The one guy," Bobby Raymond pointed, "looks like he had cowboy boots on, if you can believe that."

"And a cowboy hat."

"Shit, Kevin, I hate it when you do that. You can't tell from tracks what he was wearing on his damned head."

"I've seen these two whackadoodles before," he grinned.

"Shit."

Off to the right he could see where the snowmobile had climbed out of the ditch and turned right. He looked down that way and said, "One more curve and then it becomes Cottonwood?"

"Yeah. You need me to come with you?"

Kevin looked behind him. Mulvahill had gone around to the passenger side to yak to Goyette. Benson was staring at him through the windshield, and when Kevin made eye contact Benson slowly extended his fingers up from the steering wheel in an exaggerated gesture of impatience.

"No. Stick here in case these clowns try to come back for their car. Raintree's setting up a perimeter, so stand by for instructions from him."

"No problem."

As soon as Kevin got back into his car, Benson threw his truck into gear and edged past Raymond's cruiser. As Kevin followed, he repeated to Mulvahill what Raymond had told him and described what he'd seen in the ditch.

"They might have as much as an hour's head start on us," he finished.

When they reached the end of Cottonwood Drive, Benson turned into the last driveway and slowly rolled in toward the lake, his big tires cutting a swath through the drifts that Kevin tried his best to follow. Between Benson's wheel tracks they could see a fresh snowmobile trail and the faint markings of what was left of car tire tracks.

"Could have been worse," Kevin said, pointing to orange

snow fencing along the weather side of the driveway that seemed to have prevented extensive drifting across their path.

Mulvahill said nothing, worried they were going to get stuck.

Benson slowed and brought his truck around in a half-turn behind a brown Toyota RAV 4. Kevin edged over to one side, careful to allow the SAVE guys plenty of room to unload their machines. He killed the engine and they got out.

Goyette was lowering the tailgate on the trailer. Mulvahill went over to see if she could help. Benson tucked a helmet under his arm and stared at the snowmobile track in the snow. Kevin joined him.

"I don't suppose you know what kind of a machine our targets rented," Benson said without looking at him.

"A 2017 Ski-Doo Renegade Backcountry."

"That's what I'm looking at right now."

"You can tell that just from looking at the track?"

Benson threw him a look. "Yes."

Okay, Kevin thought.

Benson began to follow the track around the side of the cottage. Kevin went with him. When they came to the open doors of the shed down near the edge of the lake, Benson stopped to study the second track.

"This is a 2004 Arctic Cat Bearcat," he said. "I'm guessing it belongs to the owner of this place."

"Matthew Scanlan."

Benson grunted and held up a hand.

Kevin said nothing.

After a moment, Benson turned away. "I can only hear one machine. Still moving away from us. We'd better get our asses in gear and find out what's going on out there."

Chapter

46

Leonardo Arcuri stood in the open door of the conference room. "You wanted to see me?"

Ellie March glanced up. "Yes, come in and sit down. I've got some questions for you."

"Did you want Dante as well?"

"No, just you. Sit down. Shut the door behind you."

Leonardo nodded to Charlotte McKinley as he took a seat across the table from her. When Ellie had called upstairs, he and Dante had decided it was time for the police to assess whether or not the trusted attorney should be ruled in or out as a suspect. Had Leonardo betrayed his boss, gone outside the business to consort with Wolfpack upstarts, and skimmed money from the accounts only to have been caught by the keen eye of Lonnie DiMaria?

He listened to Ellie's boilerplate assurances that he was speaking to them on a voluntary basis and was free to leave whenever he wished. He nodded at the little audio device on the table in front of Charlotte, acknowledging that the interview was being recorded, and he smiled when Ellie reminded him that he could consult an attorney at any time.

"I'm aware of the old saying that a man who represents himself has a fool for a client," he said, "but I'll make that kind of phone call only if I see you stubbornly pursuing a wrong path that could place me in legal jeopardy. Otherwise, I think we're fine to proceed as is."

"How long have you worked for Dante Tassone? When did you two first meet?"

Leonardo turned his chair sideways from the table to give himself room to cross his legs. How much or how little to say? He and Dante had discussed it. Leonardo would tell the truth when answering questions, because it was a personal rule by which he lived his life. He never told a lie. On the other hand, he often avoided answering questions he didn't like, and he refused to believe that to do so was a sin of omission and therefore a violation of the eighth commandment. He considered this assertion to be an exercise in casuistry, but not in a negative way. We must debate within ourselves the meanings of right and wrong, must we not?

Besides which, the Catholic Church no longer controlled his thoughts and actions as it had when he was a child. Post-secondary education had introduced other, equally compelling, ways of attempting to understand the universe, and he now considered himself someone who stuck to his own personal rules and guidelines, rather than those of a hidebound organization skulking behind the walls of the Vatican while the world morphed into strange new manifestations of human will all around them.

After Linda had left him, taking their two young children with her to join a balding cardiologist in a new, 'Ndrangheta-free life in Halifax, the priests to whom he'd spoken had turned out to be spectacularly useless in helping him deal with the situation. As a result, he'd felt vindicated for having trusted his own counsel before that of anyone else.

He smiled at Charlotte McKinley's open notebook. "Does that particular Post-it Note mark the pages that are about me?"

She blushed. "Yes."

"Representative of a somewhat larger file in your intelligence database, no doubt."

"No doubt. I collect information on you folks the way other people collect hockey cards. For example—"

"Us folks. Quaint. May I ask a totally unrelated question before we get this under way?"

Charlotte stared at him.

Ellie held her patience.

"On the drive here, on the 401, I noticed a sign. I saw it because traffic was heavy and we were going slowly enough that I had time to look out the window and see things."

Charlotte tapped her chin with her pen. "And?"

"It was one of your signs. A bridge dedication, right before an overpass while we were going through Oshawa. Is this something 'you folks' do a lot?"

"I believe there are seventy of them so far."

"Detective Inspector Lorne Foran," Ellie said, who kept up on these things. "Killed almost forty years ago in a car accident while investigating the disappearance and murder of a woman near London."

"Yes, that was the name. Foran. Interesting."

"It is, isn't it? Now how about you answer our questions, Mr. Arcuri? How long have you worked for Dante Tassone?"

"Yes, of course. My apologies. I started working for Mr. Tassone in 1989."

"As his personal attorney?"

"Initially, but very shortly afterward he hired me to work for his company."

"Wooden Bridge Investments?"

"No, not at that time."

Charlotte stirred. "It was a company called Calla Holdings, wasn't it?"

"Yes, that's correct."

She flicked a page in her notebook and said to Ellie, "They owned a bunch of pizzerias. It was a front to launder money for Gabriel Tassone. Dante sold it to his cousin Pietro in 1991."

Leonardo sighed but said nothing. He understood he was in a position to learn a little about what kind of information the police held on them, depending on how mature and discreet the young woman proved to be. Intelligence was a two-way street, as Helena Mercuri, Dante's section head, always liked to say.

Just stay in your lane, he told himself, *and see what happens.*

"What did you do for this pizza company?" Ellie asked.

"A little of everything."

Charlotte frowned. "When you first started practising, you were in corporate law, right? An associate with Tettleton, Forrest and Ambry?"

"That must be some notebook."

"Your files primarily consisted of due diligence in mergers and acquisitions. Specifically IP assets. Is that right?"

"That's correct." Leonardo looked at Ellie. "Companies sometimes borrow and lend using their intellectual property assets as security, so when companies merge, the IP situation needs to be thoroughly vetted. I was that guy."

"For three years," Charlotte said.

"Yes."

"At which point you met Dante Tassone and accepted a job from him."

"That's not quite accurate, Ms. McKinley."

"Oh?"

"We first met several years before. In 1983, as a matter of fact."

"Go on."

It was the sort of information he and Dante had discussed, the kind of thing Dante felt could be given away as a display of good faith.

"I was a student at the time. We met on a bus."

"A bus?"

"Yes, a TTC bus. We struck up an acquaintance, later became friends, and it went from there."

"I see." Charlotte scribbled in her notebook. It was the kind of tidbit, their having first met on a Toronto Transit Commission bus, that sometimes made her day. "This was while you were completing your law degree at U of T."

"Correct."

Leonardo and Dante had grown up in different neighbourhoods and had attended different high schools. Leonardo's father was a very successful importer of Italian-made footwear, and it seems he'd known Vincenzo

Tassone, Dante's father, only slightly, through various social encounters within the Calabrian community. At the time, Leonardo had known nothing at all about the Tassone family of Woodbridge and had never heard of Dante.

One afternoon in 1983, Leonardo was riding home on a downtown bus after a long day of classes. At that time the seats behind the back door of the TTC buses faced out into the aisle, and Leonardo preferred them because, being tall, he wanted the extra leg room. Across the aisle from him, a young couple joked between themselves in Italian. They spoke a Calabrian dialect essentially identical to the one on which Leonardo had been raised by his parents, and when the young man came out with a rather ribald play on words, Leonardo laughed without thinking.

He glanced up from the textbook he was reading and saw the young man watching him, a smile playing across his lips. The man ran a hand through his tousled, light brown hair and turned his attention back to his companion. When she got off the bus, he swung out of his seat and sat next to Leonardo.

"*Calabrese?*"

When Leonardo nodded, closing his book, they struck up a conversation. The young man introduced himself as Dante Tassone, raising an eyebrow when the name resulted in no visible reaction. Dante said he was a student at Ryerson, majoring in business administration. When he rose to get off the bus, he invited Dante to a party happening the next night at his rooming house.

The following evening Leonardo cabbed over to the address Dante had given him, but found that the party was too loud and boisterous for his liking. He was about to leave when Dante appeared in front of him, shrugging into a jacket.

"This sucks. Let's get out of here."

Over beer at a nearby bar they became acquainted. Being solitary by nature, Leonardo didn't have a lot of friends, and he didn't socialize much, but thereafter he always looked forward to outings with Dante, who was unfailingly good-natured and respectful to him. When Dante graduated in 1983 Leonardo was in the audience to watch him accept his diploma, and in 1986 when Leonardo received his law degree, Dante returned the favour.

"So you met him in 1983," Charlotte said, "and didn't go to work for him until 1989."

"Correct."

"What happened in between?"

"I graduated; he graduated; I went to work for Tettleton. He learned the ins and outs of the pizza business, I suppose."

"You told Detective Inspector March that the first work you did for Tassone as an attorney was criminal defence. Is that correct?"

Carefully, now. "No, I said that initially I was retained by Mr. Tassone as his personal attorney. No one said anything about criminal law."

"Well, what else would it be?" Ellie said.

"Was Dante arrested?" Charlotte asked. "Did he call you to get him out of jail?"

Leonardo feigned disappointment. "Really. You know as well as I do that Mr. Tassone has never been arrested. *Never.*"

After graduation they'd seen less and less of each other as Dante became absorbed in working for his Uncle Gabriel, and Leonardo spent what seemed like most of his life at his desk in his little cubicle at Tettleton, Forrest and Ambry. Late one night in the spring of 1989, however, Leonardo's bedside telephone rang. He was surprised to hear Dante's voice at the other end.

He was at a club downtown, he explained in a calm voice. Leonardo knew the place; it was not far from where he lived, a watering hole favoured by rich yuppies. Someone had been knifed to death in the men's washroom and Dante's drinking friends were all lawyering up. The police were holding everyone and questioning them. What should he do?

"Don't you have your own lawyer?"

"No, man. You're it. I'd appreciate the help."

Leonardo had already figured out what kind of things Dante did for his uncle, and while it was completely outside his own personal experience, he was surprised to realize it didn't bother him much.

"You're at a pay phone?"

"Yeah. Outside the men's room."

"Stay there. I'm only a few blocks away. I'll call you back in a minute."

"Don't dawdle, my friend."

Leonardo hurriedly dressed and left his building. He found a phone booth down the block from the bar and called the number Dante had given him. Remarkably, his friend was still calm and self-possessed. Leonardo walked him through what to say when questioned. When Dante understood what to do, Leonardo agreed to stay where he was until Dante was able to leave the bar.

He waited more than two hours, but eventually Dante rapped on the door of the phone booth. They went to an all-night diner for coffee while Dante decompressed. It turned out that he'd found the situation somewhat stressful after all.

They talked for a while, and then Dante pitched Leo-

nardo an offer to come work for him. He would double
Leo's current salary for the first year, then double it again.

"I don't know anything about pizza."

"I have guys for that."

"I'm not a money man either, Dante."

"I have a guy for that, too. An old friend of mine who's
a numbers genius. You'll like him. Everybody does. What I
need is a lawyer I can trust. Sitting in the office next to me.
We'll figure it out as we go along."

"Double what I'm making now?"

"Ouch, oww, stop twisting my arm. Triple, then."

"I'm in."

Leonardo wasn't sure if Charlotte McKinley knew this
story. It was possible, since she seemed to be good at what
she did, but he doubted it. It wasn't something either he or
Dante had ever cared to talk about.

"How long have you known Alonzo DiMaria?" Ellie
asked, breaking into his thoughts.

"For almost twenty years. Mr. Tassone talked about
him when we were at Calla, but I never actually met him
until Mr. Tassone assumed control of Wooden Bridge and
I went to work for him there."

"How did you two get along?"

"Fine. No problems."

"He and Tassone were close friends, right?"

"Yes."

"Did that make you feel jealous?"

Leonardo failed to suppress a smile. "No. Why would
it?"

"You two weren't rivals for his attention?"

"Detective Inspector March, I consider Mr. Tassone to
be my friend. A very dear friend. More importantly, though,
he's my employer. I speak for him when he needs me to;

I act for him when he needs me to; I perform whatever job-related tasks he needs me to perform; and I'm a very happy employee. And you're barking up the wrong tree if you think I had some kind of personality clash with Mr. DiMaria. If you'd known him in life, you'd know he was an absolute jewel. Impossible to dislike."

"And yet someone disliked him enough to kick him to death."

There was nothing Leonardo could say in response to that bald statement of fact.

"Were you siphoning money from the business, Mr. Arcuri? Did DiMaria catch you at it?"

Leonardo wanted to laugh in derision, but he refrained. "The answer is no. Mr. Tassone pays me extremely well. He's very generous. I have everything I need. It's simply inconceivable that I would ever betray his trust."

There it was, the key phrase, the one they'd agreed must be placed on the record at this point in time so the police would not go haring off after a false lead instead of focusing on the Wolfpack morons. Dante trusted him, and Leonardo would never betray him.

Ellie stared, and Leonardo returned her gaze with a bland expression.

"You're saying that you're loyal to Dante Tassone?"

"Yes. Absolutely."

"And you haven't ripped him off?"

"No. Of course not."

"If we offered you immunity from prosecution in exchange for your testimony against him, would you take us up on it?"

"Really now. Please. Spare me. First of all, this is Canada. There are no statutory provisions granting total immunity from prosecution, so you're just trying to kid me along. Secondly, there's nothing I could testify about in such a process because Mr. Tassone is a perfectly legitimate businessman who pays his taxes and minds his Ps and Qs to a fault. And thirdly, I am, as I said for the record, loyal to Mr. Tassone. His best interests are my best interests. And his friends, including the late Mr. DiMaria, are my friends."

"And his enemies?"

"Are something I can't comment on. Sorry."

"Did you kill Alonzo DiMaria, Mr. Arcuri?"

"God help me, no. He was such a very nice man. I really, genuinely, liked him."

"Do you know who did kill him?"

One of those difficult questions they'd debated back and forth before he came downstairs. "I have no first-hand knowledge that could assist you in your investigation."

"I'll take second hand."

Leonardo looked at Charlotte. "Are there pages in that notebook of yours containing information about the Wolfpack Alliance, young lady?"

She nodded.

"I really don't think I have anything more to say at this time."

Chapter

47

Kevin was not a snowmobile kind of person. Only once before in his life had he ridden on one, on an ice fishing trip with his minor league hockey team when he was a kid. Several of the parents had gotten together for a Saturday outing hosted by the coach, who owned a cottage on Charleston Lake. They set up a number of huts out on the ice, drilled holes, drank beer and fished, served the kids hot chocolate and hot dogs steamed in aluminum foil, and drove around the lake on their Ski Doos.

Kevin's memories included the delicious taste of the food, constantly being told to move his fishing line back and forth to keep the water in the hole from crusting over, and a nightmarish ride on the back of someone's snowmobile, careening recklessly across the surface of the lake at what seemed like a hundred miles an hour, crashing through snow dunes and fishtailing back and forth like an insane dirt bike rider.

Blinded by driving snow and numb from the cold, he'd decided that it would never be necessary to repeat that experience in order to appreciate what it was like to ride on one of those things. Never, ever, ever.

And now, look. Here he was, not surprised to find out that his dislike of snowmobiling had not changed in the slightest after nearly three decades.

Benson drove out onto the lake, following the tracks of the two other machines. Kevin held on for dear life to the passenger grips on either side of his seat next to his thighs, bouncing and swaying. If either hand slipped, he thought he'd probably go flying off the machine and break his neck. The only other option was to put his arms around Benson and hold on that way, but Benson was clearly not the sort of guy who'd welcome that kind of contact, so Kevin stuck with the grips, which were not much bigger than his gloved fists.

They passed two small islands on the left, tree-covered outcroppings surrounded by ice and snow. Benson pulled up at the spot where the tracks mounted the shore and headed into the woods. He flipped up his visor and listened. Kevin did the same.

"No sounds from either one now," Benson said, raising his voice so Kevin could hear him over the idling of their engine.

"They must be stopped somewhere."

Benson flipped his visor back down without comment and gunned up the bank. Kevin's bottom rose several inches off the seat and his left hand slipped as they crested the slope and banged back down. He grabbed at the post behind his left shoulder, the one topped by a red police light, and managed to avoid falling off.

As Benson zipped into the tree cover, following the narrow trail, Kevin debated whether to try straightening up to reacquire a hold on the left passenger grip, but after a series of bumps he vetoed the idea and stayed where he was. Benson was barely slowing down as the trail wove left and right between the trees, and Kevin didn't want to risk letting go of the light post at the wrong moment.

Thankfully, they slowed down after a while and Benson stopped. He killed the engine and got off. Kevin half-fell, half-slid off the seat onto his knees. Benson ignored him, tromping ahead. Kevin got up and followed. He could see where someone had hauled a fallen tree branch off the trail and thrown it aside. He flipped up his visor and followed Benson, who was tracking boot prints forward on the trail.

Twenty metres ahead, an Arctic Cat snowmobile lay sideways in the snow against a tree trunk. The front ski on the right-hand side was broken. Boot prints were everywhere. One set led north away from the crash site and the other two led back to the trail.

"Scanlan's," Benson said, pointing at the Arctic Cat. "The one from the shed."

"Yeah, okay."

Benson took out his satellite phone and called Goyette, who had remained behind at the cottage with Mulvahill and the other SAVE snowmobile.

"Yeah, it's Benson. The Cat crashed and Scanlan's on foot, looks like. The two targets took off after him up the trail, but I don't hear anything now. They may have already run him to ground."

He listened as Goyette replied.

Kevin removed his helmet, glad to be free of it for a moment. Silence rang in his ears, the total silence of the bush in the dead of winter.

He took a few steps and was startled by an abrupt drumming sound off to his right. A partridge, he realized, taking flight. It arrowed off through the naked trees.

"Yeah, I think that's the best way to do it," Benson said. "All right. I'll keep you posted." He ended the call and put away the phone. "Goyette and your partner are going to stick around at the cottage in case our two guys circle around and go back there. The cruiser's still sitting on their car and trailer in the ditch, and your sergeant just got there, so that's covered."

"All right," Kevin said.

"Let's go further up this trail and see if we can find them."

Back on the snowmobile, Kevin settled down on the passenger seat behind Benson and took hold of the grips in a double-death lock, but Benson chose to take it easy this time, rolling up the trail at a slow pace, following a single track now instead of two. He kept glancing off to his left. After a moment he pointed.

The sun was on that side of the trail, flickering and flashing between the trees, hindering Kevin's attempts to see what had attracted Benson's attention. He lifted his visor. Finally he saw boot prints in the snow where someone, likely Scanlan, had walked parallel to the trail.

After a while, the footsteps angled off deeper into the woods away from the trail and were no longer visible.

Eventually the trail debouched into a clearing that sloped upward. The snowmobile track they were followed weaved between half-covered boulders and disappeared over the crest about sixty metres ahead.

Benson slowed, his helmet turning as he scanned the scene.

Suddenly he jerked. Blood spattered on Kevin's jacket.

A cracking sound echoed in the silence.

Benson sagged.

Kevin grabbed him around the waist and pulled him sideways off the snowmobile.

The key jerked out of the ignition, shutting off the engine.

Kevin bobbed up and heaved the snowmobile over onto its side. He kneed Benson in the back. Prone, Benson scuffed sideways to take cover behind it. Kevin followed.

Thwak-thunk.

Another round struck the underside of the machine, penetrating the track and emerging through the seat a few centimetres above Kevin's hip.

The shot echoed in the silence around them.

They lay still, listening.

Waiting.

On the other side of the slope, a snowmobile engine roared to life. It revved several times, dropped in pitch as the transmission was shifted into gear, and dopplered off into the distance.

Kevin gave it a moment before fumbling in his coat pocket for his pen. He took off his toque and stuck it on the end of the pen. With the OPP crest facing out, he lifted the toque up over the side of the snowmobile.

Nothing happened.

Chapter

48

"Push it back down," Benson said, cradling his right arm. "Can you get it down?"

Kevin got to his knees and, after checking the horizon above them and seeing nothing, leaned his weight against the snowmobile. He shoved hard, and the machine toppled back down onto its track.

Earlier, before leaving the cottage, Benson had attached a disassembled Browning rifle to fittings on the hood, explaining that he and Goyette each carried one with them in case of problems with wild animals while they were out in the bush.

Kevin released the snaps now and freed the scabbard holding the rifle. He leaned it against the snowmobile. "First, let's look at that wound."

"Rifle first."

"Gunshot wound first." Kevin reached for the front zipper of Benson's one-piece snowmobile suit.

"Fuck off. I'll do it myself." Benson removed his left glove and pulled down the zipper. Then he took off his right glove and, with Kevin's help, worked the monosuit down off his right shoulder far enough to expose the site of the wound. There was a blood-stained hole in the thermal long-sleeved top he was wearing as a base layer underneath the monosuit, and a corresponding hole on the back side of his arm.

"Through and through," Kevin said.

Benson grimaced. "Were you hit?"

"No. It was on a bit of an angle, so it must have just missed me."

"First aid kit," Benson said. "Under the seat."

Sparing another quick glance around, Kevin lifted the seat and found a small canvas bag with a red cross on the side. Benson handed him a folded hunting knife from a patch pocket on his thigh. Kevin used it to cut away the sleeve of the thermal top so that he could get at the wound.

He pressed a wad of gauze on the entry hole and held it there for several moments while Benson groaned, clenching his teeth. When he finally lifted the wad, blood was still oozing out.

"Tourniquet," Benson said.

Kevin found it in the kit, a so-called combat application tourniquet with a windlass to tighten it once it was in place. He looped it around Benson's arm, right at the base of the deltoid muscle at the bottom of his shoulder, a few centimetres above the bullet hole. He fed the tip of the strap through the friction buckle.

Benson's hand was already on the windlass, and he tightened the tourniquet as far as he could stand it.

Kevin dressed the wound as best as he could using gauze and an elastic bandage, then helped Benson pull the suit back up as far as possible to limit his exposure to the cold. Benson leaned back against the snowmobile, legs splayed out, and closed his eyes, exhaling raggedly.

After a few moments he opened them again and fumbled in his pocket for his satellite phone. When Goyette answered, he took a long breath before speaking.

"We've taken fire somewhere on the trail south of Mountain Road and I've been hit. Right arm; through and through. Yeah. Walker helped dress it and a tourniquet has been applied, but we're going to require backup and a med evac."

He listened, watching as Kevin removed the rifle from its scabbard and began to assemble it.

"No, they won't come back unless they catch Scanlan up ahead of us and use the same trail to get back to the cottage. They might not know they could just go down Mountain Road and take Porter Road back to their car.

"Yeah, you're right. Well, maybe they're dumb enough to think they can just call CAA and wait around for a tow truck to pull them out. Anyway."

He listened again, watching Kevin as he shouldered the rifle and used the scope to check out the top of the slope above them.

"Just follow the GPS. Sat phones must be good for something, right?" Benson smiled grimly. "Roger that."

He put the phone away and held out his hand. Kevin dropped down beside him and gave him the rifle. Benson put it across his legs and closed his eyes.

"Cavalry's on its way," he said.

Chapter

49

Matthew struggled through knee-deep snow, grimly battling uphill through narrow gaps in the scrub brush. His boots skidded off hidden rocks, sending him careening into tree trunks he was trying to maneuver around. Branches forced him to crouch and crawl on his hands and knees.

It was exhausting work, and when he finally reached an outcropping of rock that was mostly bare, it was like a gift from above. He clambered up onto it, as though he were climbing onto the hood of a half-buried car, and he found he could stand upright and walk ten or twelve metres up to its summit.

He took out his cellphone and powered it up. No signal. He checked out the GPS. North was . . . that way. He turned slightly to his right and looked at more upward-trending rock, saplings, scrub, and snow. Staring at the trees on the horizon, he thought he saw a faint flicker of movement. Not an animal; something travelling in a straight line. A bird?

He suddenly saw the same sort of movement, but from the other direction.

Cars! Mountain Road! It had to be! He looked at the GPS again, more closely this time, and saw that the little icon signifying his current position was indeed sitting almost on top of the yellow strip representing the highway that was his target. Thank God; he couldn't take much more of this.

Below him was a bit of a gully between rock faces, five or six metres below his boots. He had a choice between going down into it and up the other side, maintaining a more or less linear path, or finding a way around it. To the left were solid trees, evergreens that looked impenetrable. To his right, the outcropping on which he stood sloped downward toward a less dense area where he thought he could find an easier way around.

He debated whether or not to turn off the phone or leave it on. He was close to the road where he could wave down a passing car and get safely back to town, so he didn't need to worry about conserving the battery at this point. He'd keep it on because he wanted the GPS display in front of him to make sure he'd continue moving in the right direction. There was no more time to be wasted stumbling around.

Earlier, he wasn't sure how long ago it had been, he'd heard a couple of gunshots in the distance behind him. They were far enough away that he knew they hadn't been directed at him. Were Cowboy Hat and Dreadlocks confused, firing at animals or birds in the bush, thinking they were him? They certainly weren't outdoorsmen, that was patently obvious, so it was possible they were flailing around almost as much as he was.

Of course, they had the advantage of their snowmobile, the sound of which had resumed shortly after the shots had been fired. They must have been closing the gap on him while he beat his way through the bush, trying to avoid the trail.

He realized that he could no longer hear the droning of the machine's engine. He'd stopped listening for it a while ago when the upward climb had become particularly arduous and all he could hear was the sound of his own ragged breath, in and out in gasps, and the noise of his uneven progress through the snow and the bushes.

He frowned and looked behind him, down the slope the way he had come. Were they closer than he thought?

Something hissed, and he felt a tug on his sleeve. His arm flew out, all on its own, and his cellphone went sailing off, down into the gulley.

He felt pain and shock.

His knees buckled and he pitched head-first downward after his phone, landing on his shoulder and rolling, rolling, rolling until he finally came to a stop, face buried in the snow.

Pain, shock, and icy cold.

Faintly, he heard the echo of the shot as it rattled through the trees and faded into nothing.

Chapter

50

Kevin knew it was important for him to help Benson ward off shock while they waited for the med-evac team to arrive. He'd found a small emergency blanket under the seat to keep Benson warm enough; he'd given him a bottle of water to maintain hydration; and he was watching him closely to make sure he remained conscious and reasonably calm.

It was this last step that was proving to be a challenge. Kevin knew there was value in talking to someone in order to keep them from going into shock, but Benson was pretty far down on the list of people Kevin would have chosen to engage in conversation. He was a surly, opinionated, condescending son of a bitch, and Kevin really didn't have much to say to him as it was, let alone while the guy was wounded and in need of assistance.

As it turned out, Benson had been thinking along the same lines. "How long you been with the force, Walker?"

"Eight years. Nine years before that with a municipal department that was disbanded."

Benson nodded. "I've got eighteen in so far. Placed on a sergeant's list a few years ago but turned it down because this came up. Best decision I ever made."

"Climbing the ladder's not for everyone."

"Fucking A. I was made for this job, man. You should see my place. Eight acres just outside Camden East. Little ranch bungalow with just enough room for my wife and me and our two kids. Built all the outbuildings myself from scratch. Winter storage for three boats, summer storage for five snowmobiles, plus three pickup trucks, two cars, two off-road vehicles, two hogs, and a little dirt bike. I even got four bicycles, for whatever. I'm fully equipped, man."

"Sounds like it."

"Goyette and I work the trails, policing the ATVs in summer and the snowmobiles in winter. Then we rotate over to the water to ride herd on the boaters."

"Sounds like you were made for this kind of work."

"Absolutely. I gotta say, though, sometimes I get pissed off, know what I mean? Most of the problems, including the fatalities, are booze-related. Almost half the boating deaths, and 40 per cent of snowmobile ones. Fucking crazy. What the hell's the matter with people?"

"For some, it's an addiction. For others, I guess they're just a little brainless."

"You drink?"

Kevin shook his head. "Alcoholic father."

Benson shot him a look. "Me too. Both parents. Fixed me for life on the stuff, believe me. Anyway, a lot of the people who need some help on the trails are okay. They just got lost or their machine broke down or some other shit. You don't mind giving them a hand. It's just the other fucking jokers who want to spoil it for everyone else."

Kevin checked his watch. It had been fourteen minutes since Benson had called it in.

Benson shifted position and grimaced from the pain. "Where the hell are they?"

"Want me to call for a sit-rep?"

Benson glanced at the satellite phone in his lap. "Nah. I gotta give them time. It just seems like forever. Do you hear them coming?"

"Not yet."

"Fucking snow. Slows everything down to a fucking crawl."

Kevin watched him as he fell silent. His breathing seemed a little laboured, but not seriously. There were no signs of confusion or disorientation. All in all, he seemed to be holding it together well enough.

"They better not try to put me on the shelf," Benson said. "Fucking pencil necks."

"I don't hear the shooters any more," Kevin said, referring to the snowmobile they'd been chasing. "Haven't for a while."

"Yeah, I know. On foot. Maybe stalking Scanlan."

"I hope not," Kevin said. "I—"

They heard the distant sound of a gunshot. Far enough away not to have been directed at them.

"Shit," Benson said. "Shit, shit, shit."

Chapter

51

Matthew struggled to his knees and brushed snow from his face with his left hand. His right arm, just above the wrist, burned as though he'd been stung by a bee. A very large, very angry bee.

There was a tear on his coat sleeve and a small amount of blood on the lining that stuck out from the rip. He'd been shot, he realized, but not seriously. He felt all right. Well enough to stagger to his feet and stumble along the gulley toward the spot where the outcropping edged downward. If he could get to the less dense area where the gulley ended and the upward slope was much less severe, he thought he could continue on in a northerly direction to the highway.

Wait. Where was his cellphone?

He cast around in the snow for it, without luck. It wasn't

anywhere that he could see. The snow was soft, having just fallen in such a great amount, and it must have knifed down out of sight, below the surface, when it flew out of his hand. He couldn't see where it would have landed. He thrashed around, flinging snow everywhere in desperation, but all he uncovered was more snow.

It was gone.

"I think I got him!"

A man's voice. Behind him on the other side of the rock ridge, not all that far away. Heavily accented. Dreadlocks?

"Dammit!" Another voice. Cowboy Hat? "My boot's stuck. Give me a hand!"

Matthew abandoned the search for his phone and waded through the snow down the gulley to the spot where it emptied out into the partial clearing. To his relief, he spotted a deer trail almost immediately, a narrow space that wound through the bush heading upward. He began to follow it, listening to the cursing and swearing of the two men behind him, grateful that they were having more difficulty navigating the terrain at the moment than he was.

Faintly, behind him, he heard the muffled sound of his cellphone ringtone.

Unbelievable, he thought. A signal, after all this time and effort, and he had to leave it behind. Typical of his perverse luck for sure.

"That's him!" Cowboy Hat shouted. "He's right there! Come on, pull me out!"

Matthew emerged into a small clearing. He bent over, breathless. After gasping for a moment he looked up and found himself making eye contact with a white-tailed deer. The deer stood stock still, staring at him. Its tail twitched, and it suddenly bolted away, through the clearing and into the trees.

"Listen!" Dreadlocks shouted. "There he goes! That way! Come on, McQuillan, get your ass in gear!"

Matthew didn't move. He heard the beating and thrashing of the men behind him, and he realized they were being drawn off by the deer, thinking it was him.

He stayed where he was, listening intently. The sounds receded off to his left until eventually, thankfully, he could no longer hear them.

He took off his gloves and pulled at the bloody edges of the tear on his coat sleeve, just above his wrist. His shirt cuff was also torn. Blood had soaked into the material, but not enough to frighten him. He tugged at the edges and used a finger of his glove to wipe away the mess. All he saw was a long scratch on the back of his wrist, little more than a welt, really, where the bullet had grazed him on its way past.

Only a flesh wound! Relief surged through him. He was the Lone Ranger, Brett Maverick, the Rawhide Kid; every Western hero who was ever winged in a gunfight and lived to save the day! The impact had been enough to knock his phone out of his hand, but it hadn't penetrated his wrist at all. He was incredibly lucky.

He pulled his gloves back on and got moving. It was more of the same, the trail narrowing through rocky brush and widening a bit when it reached a cedar copse that served as a deer yard for the white-tails whose hoof prints he'd been following. The snow was stomped down in multiple directions where they'd moved around, feeding on the low-hanging cedar boughs and taking advantage of the thermal cover provided by the trees.

He passed through a gap and followed a single set of hoof prints into a clearing.

But it wasn't a clearing at all.

He stood in a ditch on the side of the road, looking up at a black pickup truck as it flashed by him on its way downhill toward the village.

It was Mountain Road. He'd made it through.

Chapter

52

Kevin's ride back to Matthew Scanlan's cottage was somewhat calmer than the ride out had been.

Goyette arrived at the scene towing a rescue toboggan behind his snowmobile, with a paramedic perched on the back seat. While the paramedic, whose name was Kassem, examined Benson and got him ready for an intravenous bag, Kevin watched Goyette fuss with straps and belts inside the toboggan.

"I've never seen one of these being used before," Kevin said.

"No?" Goyette grinned. "I take it you don't go skiing much. Standard equipment at the big resorts."

"Me? Ski? Never. Too dangerous."

Goyette laughed. "You'd be surprised how often we've

deployed this thing. Fiberglas and Kevlar hull, polyethylene runners, aluminum handles. Lightweight and easy to haul around in our trailer. How you guys coming?"

"Almost ready," Kassem replied. "Good job with the tourniquet, by the way."

"Thanks," Kevin and Benson both said at the same time.

"All right," Kassem finally announced, "let's get you into your ride."

With Goyette's help, the paramedic lifted Benson into the toboggan and got him situated so that he was sitting on the bottom, legs straight out under the hood and his back against the seat. Kassem secured him with straps and a belt before sitting down above him, holding up the intravenous bag so that gravity could do its work.

Goyette swung onto the snowmobile and looked at Kevin. "Coming?"

"What about the other Ski-Doo?"

"We'll come back for it. Right now we've got a guy with a gunshot wound who's our first priority." He started the engine and revved it aggressively.

Kevin hastily clambered onto the back seat. His hands found the grips an instant before Goyette shifted into gear and started back down the way they'd come.

Raintree was waiting for them at the cottage. He helped them get Benson out of the toboggan and took one side as they walked him over to the ambulance. The other paramedic, who'd stayed behind while Kassem rode with Goyette, was ready with the back doors open.

Raintree stood by as they turned Benson around and sat him down on the edge of the open doorway. "Doing okay?"

"Sure. Ain't nothing. Couple of stitches and I'll be right

back out here."

"No rush. We've still got Goyette."

"The guy's useless. Why do you think I left him back here?"

Goyette laughed.

"Give us your sat phone, will you?"

Benson handed it over.

As he and Goyette watched the ambulance ease down the driveway, Kevin and Mulvahill joined them.

"What happened?" Raintree asked.

"We got to a clearing and Benson slowed down for a look," Kevin said. "There was a rifle shot and he took a round in the shoulder. We hid behind the Ski-Doo and there was another shot or two, then they took off and left us there."

"If Samuel's a sniper, he mustn't be keeping up with his practice schedule. Sounds like he had ample opportunity to take you both out."

"Thanks, that makes me feel real good inside. Anyway, we found Scanlan's snowmobile, so he's on foot. Cutting through the brush on his way up to Mountain Road. Samuel and McQuillan headed after him, then we heard the snowmobile stop, and afterward there was a shot."

"Stalking him. Wonder if they got him?"

"At this point," Kevin said, "there's no way to know for sure."

"Yeah. I'm trying to set up a perimeter, but it's the devil's own work this morning to get bodies into vehicles and down here. Everybody's short-handed, and the roads are a bitch. Lanark's sending me a cruiser, and they're coming down from Bolingbroke with an ETA of ten minutes, so I'm going to have them close off the upper end of Mountain Road. I've got one of ours moving up to the Porter Road intersection, so that's our lower perimeter. It also prevents them from going in after their car and trailer with a tow truck or whatever. I'd rather have Raymond stay where she is, but I need coverage here at the cottage in case Scanlan tries to come back or the two suspects do, so—"

His radio squawked, interrupting him. It was Bobby Raymond.

"Bad news, Sarge. Casper went off the road and can't join the party."

"Damn." Raintree took out his cellphone: no signal. They'd probably tried to reach him but couldn't get through, so they were relaying through Raymond.

Kevin and Mulvahill checked their phones with the same result.

"All right," Raintree said, "looks like we're going to have to economize. Goyette, how about you take your truck down and leapfrog Raymond? You'll take up Casper's position at the intersection of Porter and Mountain Road as the lower perimeter. I'll follow you to set up a command post there."

"Sounds good," Goyette said.

"Kevin," Raintree said, "you go with Goyette. If they try to break through, I want adequate firepower at that spot. Mulvahill, I want you to stick here. I don't want to leave this place uncovered in case they come back this way. Kevin, give her your keys. Goyette, put my number into your sat phone and give it to her."

"Great," Mulvahill said. "I love getting to sit on the bench."

"That's not it at all." Raintree recited his cellphone number to Goyette and fished out his car keys. "Surely there's cellphone connectivity out there on the main road. It's not like we're on Mars or something, is it? Mulvahill, listen up."

She caught the key fob Kevin tossed her and accepted the satellite phone from Goyette. "I'm listening."

"If they show, do not, repeat, do not attempt to intercept. Call me on the sat phone and try to reach Raymond on Kevin's car radio. Report what you see and that's it. Do not engage. Got it?"

"I've got it, Sarge."

"Good." He looked at Kevin. "I feel like I'm playing chess with three-quarters of my pieces missing."

"Yeah, but it's what you're good at, right?"

Raintree shook his head. "I'd better be."

Chapter

53

Normally Rick didn't do much driving. With much more important matters to occupy his mind, he usually slid into the back seat and left the driving to employees. However, with Dom lying dead on the cellar floor at Couvillon House and inconveniently unable to take the wheel, Rick had no choice but to troop downstairs, poke through Dom's pockets for the key fob, and head outside to do the dirty work himself.

Thank god the damned thing had an automatic transmission. He didn't have the first clue about how to drive a stick-shift vehicle.

He checked Google Maps for his directions and started out. McQuillan and Samuel had reached Mountain Road on foot, discovered they miraculously had a signal on their cellphone, and called him for a pick-up.

Did they have the USB drive?

No, of course not.

Did they at least have Scanlan, so they could find out what he'd done with it?

No, of course not.

Were they both absolute and total worthless fucking wastes of space?

What do you think?

As he drove, squeezing the steering wheel in a death grip, he felt frustrated with himself. Maybe it was the weather, this incessant snow, maybe it was being cooped up in Santa's Village while events unravelled around him, but he felt as though his IQ had suddenly been cut in half.

When he'd called McQuillan Tuesday morning, he'd thought it would be a simple enough favour to ask. Drive over to DiMaria's place, take the jump drive from him, and hang onto it until Rick got back to Toronto.

A. Simple. Fucking. Request.

How was he to know that McQuillan would grab Samuel to ride shotgun with him, that the damned psycho would take a shot at DiMaria and spook him, and that events would fall apart to the point that they'd kill Lonnie without getting the drive and bring this ridiculous clown show down on his head?

He found Mountain Road and started to follow it north, keeping his speed down. He hated to drive, and the last thing he wanted to do was go off the road or slide and hit another car or some damned thing. The snow plow had been along here and the pavement was partially clear, but he worried about patches of dark ice or whatever else might cause him to lose control and have an accident. He cursed McQuillan and Samuel again for being a couple of damned screw-ups.

Thankfully, the road was quiet. The only vehicle he saw was a battered old pickup truck driven by an old man with another man on the passenger side. Otherwise, he had the highway to himself.

He started checking out the snowbanks on either side. McQuillan had said they would leave a snowmobile helmet where he could see it as a marker for their pick-up point. So far, no helmet.

He wasn't really sure what to do next. Samuel thought he'd shot Scanlan, according to McQuillan, but they hadn't been able to find his body or the drive. If the guy made it back to the village, he'd go straight to the police and hand over the data along with a story that would put Rick in a very difficult position.

Should he cut his losses right now and run? On the advice of another Wolfpack partner, a biker who was considerably less psychotic than the pair he was currently dealing with, he'd set up a contingency plan in case he needed to disappear. Fake identification and passport, a couple of domestic bank accounts in various names for needs that might arise here in Canada, and an offshore account with a reasonably decent retirement fund he could live off of in his Caribbean hideout, should it come to that.

Was it coming to that?

Was it time to jump out of the airplane and pull the damned ripcord?

He passed something round and red sitting on top of the snowbank on the opposite side.

Helmet. McQuillan's marker.

He slowed, checking his rear-view mirror. There was no one behind him, thankfully. He stopped and began a complicated trial-and-error K-turn or whatever it was called, praying that a car wouldn't come along at top speed and broadside him while he was vulnerable, sawing away at the steering wheel and trying not to put himself in the ditch as he maneuvered back and forth.

Christ, he hated driving.

Finally, he was straightened around and pointing back downhill, the way he'd come. He eased forward until he was even with the helmet and shifted into park. He honked the horn.

After a couple of beats, McQuillan's cowboy hat showed over the snowbank, followed by a handgun and a grim-looking face. The gun was lowered when McQuillan saw who it was, and Rick watched impatiently as he and Samuel scrambled out onto the road and jumped in the back seat.

"What fucking took you so long?" Samuel demanded, pulling off his gloves and settling his rifle stock-first between his knees. "I thought I would damned nearly freeze waiting for you to get here."

Rick glanced at McQuillan in the rear-view mirror. The man removed his cowboy hat and, balancing it on his knee, ran his fingers through his wet hair.

"Hank thinks he winged him," he said, "as I mentioned, but there was no body and we lost him. He's bound to head back to the village and go looking for the cops, so we might want to stake out the hotel where they're set up and head him off."

"Got me a cop, too." Samuel grinned. "Wind gusted so I only hit him in the shoulder. Gave them something to think about, though."

Oh, great, Rick thought. *Now he's shooting cops, too.* It was definitely getting too hot to stick around. But he needed to make one more attempt to get his hands on the spreadsheets before bugging out.

"I've never even seen Scanlan," Rick said, glancing at McQuillan again in the mirror. "What does he look like?"

"Short guy, dark hair going grey, beard that looks the same." McQuillan coughed and spat on the floor between his cowboy boots. "Blue thermal coat, blue jeans, snowmobile boots. Pretty nondescript little prick."

"I can't believe you guys didn't catch him."

"Oh, here's the big man." Samuel leaned forward and pounded the back of Rick's seat with his fist. "You think you're better than street people but you never come out and do the dirty work. *White* collar criminal, this guy. Safe inside with his cappuccino and his newsfeed."

Rick bit his lip, controlling his temper. What he wanted to do was tear this guy a new asshole, but he knew he needed to bide his time. "Look, you said your car is in the ditch, right? So they've already found it and traced it back. Maybe you should jack a car and bug out for TO while you still can."

"Maybe," McQuillan shrugged.

"Where the fuck we supposed to find a car to steal in this little asscrack dump, man?" Samuel glared at him. "Are you delusional?"

"Well, I don't know, *Hank,*" Rick retorted. "Why don't you put your mind to it and find one, since you're the fucking master criminal around here?"

"Don't take that tone with me, man."

"Boys," McQuillan said. "Down."

As Rick passed an intersection on the right, he saw a big black pick-up truck approaching on the side road. The truck had white doors with the OPP logo unmistakeably plastered on it. Behind the truck was an OPP SUV.

Christ!

"Get your heads down," he ordered. "Cops."

"Where?" Samuel said, craning around to look out the rear window. "I don't see nothing."

"Get down, Hank." McQuillan pulled sharply on his arm as he scrunched down, his cowboy hat toppling to the floor.

"Don't do that, Pat." Samuel glared at him before slouching down.

Rick kept looking in his mirror, expecting to see the vehicles swing out onto the highway, rack lights flashing. For a moment there was nothing, and then he saw the truck roll out onto the highway and stop, blocking the way. The SUV edged out and took up a position behind it, lights flashing.

They were barricading the road, and he'd slipped through with only seconds to spare.

"I got an idea," Samuel said. "Remember, a few places down from where we were last night? Also gone away, but someone plowed the driveway this morning."

"Yeah," McQuillan said, "I remember. Saw it when we drove by. There's a Jeep Cherokee sitting there."

"You shovel it out, and I'll hotwire it."

"Deal, compadre."

"Let's take one more shot at finding Scanlan," Rick said, "and then I'll drive you out there. We'll just go through town and see if we can see him.'

"If not, we clear the fuck out," McQuillan said.

"Absolutely," Rick agreed.

Contingency plans were good to have, though, and he was already wondering if he could trade the Couvillon woman for the drive, if Scanlan wouldn't give it up any other way.

Chapter

54

The old fellow who picked up Matthew along the side of the road was named Bill Yeats ("William Butler Yeats, mind you"). A widower, he had a farm on Big Crosby Lake Road, and he was driving into town to buy a few groceries.

"This is my good truck," he told Matthew as he ground the transmission back into gear and pulled away from the snowbank on which Matthew had been perched, thumb stuck out. "I got a couple others I use in summer, but they don't run too well in this kind of weather."

Matthew buckled himself in, looking at the cracked vinyl on the dashboard and the twisted piece of wire that was holding the glove compartment closed. The engine sounded to his untrained ear like a 747 jet on the wrong kind of fuel, and the smell of exhaust hung in the cabin like a reminder of past responsibilities left unaddressed. If this was his good truck, Matthew would hate to see the other two.

He kept his right arm down, out of Yeats's sight, so the old man couldn't see the tear in his sleeve and the streaks of drying blood. The wound still stung, but otherwise he seemed to be all right.

Yeats glanced at the helmet on Matthew's lap. "Ski-Doo break down?"

"Had a little accident. Then I lost my phone, so I couldn't call for help. If you could drop me off at my store on Church Street, I'd appreciate it."

"I've seen you before," Yeats said. "At shows and what not. And I go by your place. A little too pricey for me, though."

A black Lexus sedan drove by on the other side of the road. Matthew had a quick impression of a driver and no one else in the car. He turned around and looked behind them. The car drove slowly up the hill. There was no other traffic in sight, car or snowmobile.

"Scanlan's a North Crosby name," Yeats said. "You spell it with an 'a' and not an 'o' if I'm not mistaken."

"That's right."

"Where are you from, if you don't mind me asking?"

"No, I don't mind. I'm from Montreal, but my father's family was from around here."

Yeats was a sight to behold. His long, white hair stuck up all over the place. His white moustache and thick side whiskers were trimmed in what used to be called burnsides, after the American Civil War general of the same name. His clean-shaven chin was deeply cleft, and his eyes were a pale blue.

"What do you farm?" Matthew asked.

"Oh, I'm an apiarist."

"A beekeeper!"

Yeats smiled at him. "Maybe you've seen my product in the stores or at the summer fairs. 'The Murmuring Bee.' I do light and dark, both."

"Yes, I've seen it. That's Shelley, I think. Isn't it? 'To Night,' if I remember correctly. 'Thy sweet child Sleep, the filmy-eyed, / Murmured like a noontide bee.' An allusion to death, I think. It's been a while. Brave choice of a name for honey, although no one would get it unless you told them. Are you a poet?"

The old man laughed. "No. You're thinking of my name, I guess. My father was well read, a self-taught man, and he particularly liked the Irish writers. I'm not much of a reader, myself, although my sisters are. Both went to university. I stayed at home, with him. He kept a few cows until he passed. I looked after them as pets until it was time for them to go too. Anyway, looks like they've been busy trying to clear the streets."

Yeats had followed Mountain Road right into the village, and at the T-intersection that marked its termination he'd turned left onto Bedford Street and then right onto Concession. The streets had been recently plowed and were in reasonable condition for careful driving.

As they passed St. Edward the Confessor Catholic Church, Yeats grunted.

"Big funeral there on Monday," he said. "Made the mistake of coming into town with some stock for Whalen's and got caught up with the procession. Bunch of Mafia types, from what I heard. If you can imagine that."

"I heard the same," Matthew said.

"I'm not Catholic, but I can't figure why their church caters to crooks and that sort. Doesn't seem as though a real heaven would have a place for drug dealers and their leg breakers, but that's probably just me."

Matthew shrugged. "They're human beings too, I guess. Well, most of them are. Some are closer to Neanderthal than *Homo sapiens*."

Yeats turned onto Spring Street and drove down to the corner of Church Street.

"Just let me out here," Matthew said. "I'm two doors down."

As he watched the old man drive away, Matthew thought of the reference in Yeats's autobiographical novel *The Speckled Bird* to an altar in a nobleman's house that had been built in honour of Shelley but later converted to a tribute to the Virgin Mary after the nobleman's health began to fail. Since reading the novel as an undergraduate, Matthew had always fastened on that small anecdote as a reminder that for most people, Romanticism as a world view was a matter of convenience or fashion, and that when crunch time came it was often jettisoned for more pragmatic and self-serving religious rituals. To Yeats, who had studied Shelley and written about him extensively, it had also likely been a lesson in humility and a reminder that fame, however radiant in the moment, was fleeting.

No one that Matthew knew read Shelley these days, unless they were paid to do so, either for pleasure or for insight. Including himself. And very few read Yeats, either, come to that. Then it struck him that he'd just met a man who'd obviously read both.

As he walked up the steps onto his verandah he saw that his front door was ajar, the frame splintered and the glass shattered. Matthew remembered with a thud that Cowboy Hat had kicked it in while he was getting away. Trying to think of whom he could call to get it fixed, he went inside and pushed it closed. It rocked open again. He looked around for something he could use to keep it closed and lighted on a cast-iron figure of a tailor sewing a pair of trousers that he'd found at a flea market and kept in the store as a novelty. He dragged it over and shoved it against the door. Hopefully that would keep it closed. There wasn't much he could do about the broken window at the moment, though.

It was cold inside the shop. He looked at the thermostat and saw it had dropped to 11 degrees Celsius. The furnace was running in a vain attempt to warm it up.

The telephone rang.

He jumped. He remembered his cellphone was somewhere in the bush, lost in a snowbank, likely for good. This was his landline, his business number.

He had a bad feeling it was a call he didn't want to take.

He walked over, picked up the portable, and thumbed the button.

Chapter

55

The barricades and yellow tape having been removed from the vicinity of the hardware store last evening when it was decided that the crime scene would yield no further physical evidence of any use, Rick was able to drive right up Bedford Street to Church and turn right. He noticed that the hardware store was not open. One or two of the other small businesses on the street were, but most weren't. The killing of Lonnie DiMaria had evidently shaken people up quite a bit.

Whatever. Rick slowed in front of Couvillon House and shifted into park.

"What if you call the guy?" McQuillan suggested. "Might save a lot of fucking around."

"Maybe." Rick thought it over for a moment and then

remembered that he'd kept Angélique's cellphone on him as well as Dom's. He was wearing the same jacket and, when he reached into the inside breast pocket, his fingers found it.

He shut off the engine and handed the keys to McQuillan. "Go in and bring her out. She's upstairs in her bedroom."

"I'll get her," Samuel said.

"No, you won't." Rick wasn't worried; the back passenger door on Samuel's side was centimetres from the snowbank, and he couldn't get out.

McQuillan slid out of the car and found his way through a narrow gap onto the sidewalk. Rick watched him go into the house.

Samuel slid over on the back seat and opened the door.

"Easy," Rick warned.

"You do your thing. I'll do mine." Samuel got out and shut the door. Rifle in hand, he climbed up onto the trunk of the car and eased down across the roof until he was prone, rifle extended, in a sniper's position.

It was probably a good idea, Rick decided. God only knew how this thing was going to play out. He could always drive off and try to shake Samuel loose, if it became necessary. At least he wasn't still sitting behind him with that goddamned rifle in his hands.

He turned his attention back to the phone. Opening the Contacts list, he dialled the first number with Scanlan's name. It went immediately to voicemail.

"This is Matthew Scanlan. Please leave a message and I'll get back to you."

His cellphone, probably out of service by now.

He pressed the second one, which he remembered was

the number for the landline in his store. It rang three times and then, surprisingly, was answered.

"Paddy's Threads. May I help you?"

"Mr. Scanlan, how very nice to hear your voice."

A pause. "Who's speaking, please?"

"Oh, I'm a customer, make no mistake, Mr. Scanlan, but not for clothes. You have something of mine, and I'd like to buy it back from you."

"Who is this?"

Rick sighed. "The person who's now best friends with your friend, the lovely Ms. Couvillon. And as a group of friends, I'm sure we can work this all out in a, uh, friendly way. What do you think?"

"Where is she? What have you done to her?"

"Good lord, Mr. Scanlan, what are you thinking? I haven't done anything to her. She's fine, just fine."

Rick saw McQuillan emerge onto the front verandah with a firm grip on Angélique Couvillon's arm. The woman looked really pissed, and McQuillan's cowboy hat was slightly awry, as though there'd been a little physicality involved in getting her downstairs and out the door. He held his gun in his free hand, pointing down.

"In fact, I'm looking at her as we speak. Tell you what. Bring me the jump drive, right now, and you two can have a good, old-fashioned reunion. I'll pack my bags and go, and that'll be the end of this whole sad little affair. How does that sound to you?"

"What are you suggesting? If I give you this data disk, you'll let her go and leave? Is that it?"

"That's it. Sounds pretty simple and straightforward, doesn't it?"

"What—"

"Oh, please," Rick interrupted, "let's not do the 'What

guarantee do I have that you'll keep your word?' thing. It's so clichéd. There are no guarantees in life, Mr. Scanlan. There are only percentages. Look, all I want is the damned disk and to get the hell out of this godforsaken dump. The percentages look pretty good in your favour that I'll keep it nice and simple to get that done, don't you think?"

"You'll let her go if I give it to you?"

Rick watched Angélique struggle to pull away from McQuillan, who calmly cuffed her on the side of the head with the butt of his gun until she subsided. "Yes, Mr. Scanlan. I'll let her go. Can we please do this and move along with our lives?"

"All right, all right. I'm coming down."

The call ended.

The roof above Rick's head creaked and popped as Samuel adjusted his position for a slightly more favourable trajectory.

Rick reached under the dashboard and felt around until his fingers encountered a leather holster velcroed into place. He pulled it out and slid out the gun, a Beretta PX4 Storm compact model. He checked the magazine and chambered a round.

Time to rock and roll.

Chapter

56

Ellie was halfway up Bedford Street from the hotel, smoking a cigarette and talking on the phone to Prez Raintree. The sky overhead was white, and stray flakes were finding their way down on air currents that had finally dropped below the level of a stiff wind.

"We've got the highway covered at both ends," Raintree was saying, "but we're kind of stuck in place right now. I can't move closer in case they come out on their snowmobile behind us, so I've got to wait for Lanark's ERT to bring their Ski-Doos down so we can get in there to see what's what."

"I understand."

"Presumably they've all been following a trail, Scanlan and the two suspects, and it likely comes out onto the road somewhere inside our perimeter. Mulvahill can cover her end back at the cottage, but we need to know if they've already egressed from the bush onto the road. Finding tracks would tell us that. Of course, finding *them* would be even better."

Ellie took a last drag on her cigarette. She stooped, stubbed it out in a snowy patch on the sidewalk, flicked the stubbed tip with her thumb, and put the butt into her coat pocket. "What about Goyette?"

"Yeah, I considered it, but I want him down here at the moment in case they try for their car. Same with me. I'm sticking here for the moment as well."

She heard sounds behind her. Turning, she saw that Dante Tassone had come out of the hotel and was standing on the sidewalk, looking up the street at her. She turned back and resumed walking toward the corner.

"You need more back-up," she said. "These guys are armed and dangerous. They've already shot and wounded an officer. I don't like this situation at all, Prez."

"I know. I talked to Mal about it."

"You did?"

"Callaghan's in a meeting and can't be disturbed. I've got a situation on my hands, and he's giving me that? I took it as a signal to go around him, so that's what I did. We'll get the back-up, but it's going to take time for them to get here. Everyone's knee-deep in the shit right now. My best move at the moment is containment."

"Okay." It was his show, and Ellie understood his reasoning.

She was almost at the corner. A car was approaching from the opposite direction, daytime running lights bobbing up and down as its tires ran over scattered brown chunks of ice left in the street from other vehicles. She watched it slow down and turn the corner in front of her.

It was a black Lexus, one that she hadn't seen before. The driver, whose hands gripped the steering wheel nervously, was unknown to her, but he matched the description she'd received of Ricardo Tassone, a.k.a. Rick Tassone, son of Dante Tassone.

There were two men in the back seat. She couldn't see the one on the passenger side, but the guy on her side wore a cowboy hat. McQuillan. He glanced at her. He didn't react, not knowing who she was.

She kept her face straight, not wanting to give herself away, but said into her cellphone, "Prez, I've got a visual on them. In the back seat of a Lexus driven by an individual matching the description of Ricardo Tassone. Think you could get your folks to scramble on down here? You wouldn't want to miss the party."

"On our way, Ellie. See you in five."

Chapter

57

Kevin called Mulvahill on the satellite phone while Goyette concentrated on driving at a breakneck speed without putting them into the ditch.

"Pull out," he told her, his shoulder banging against the doorframe as the truck swung onto Concession Street, the trailer fishtailing behind them. "Suspects are down here in the village. We're going to try to take them right here."

"Always stuck in the bleachers, Walker. This sucks."

"Don't wreck my car."

"A little stunt driving won't hurt it."

"I'm getting enough of that right now." He ended the call and dropped the phone into its charging station on the console. Raintree had called to order them back down into town, and he'd told Kevin to use the satellite phone to pass the word along to Mulvahill, her cellphone signal still being nonexistent.

Their position on Mountain Road had only been four kilometres from downtown Westport, so Kevin had barely finished the call when Goyette pulled up in front of Scanlan's store and killed the engine. They got out and Kevin ran up the stairs. He was about to pound on the door when he saw that the glass was broken in and the doorjamb was splintered.

"Walker!"

He turned around. Goyette was beckoning to him.

"I think that's him!"

Kevin hurried back down and stood beside him in the middle of the street. Someone was crossing the intersection, walking away from them, hands in the air.

"Shit." Kevin drew his service weapon and moved forward. Goyette threw the back of the trailer open and went inside for his rifle.

As Kevin drew even with the back yard behind the church on the corner, Matthew Scanlan had made it across the intersection and now paused in the middle of the street, hands still up.

"I've got it here!" Scanlan called out. "Don't hurt her! I'll bring it right down to you."

Kevin crept up alongside the church to the corner. Goyette joined him, rifle ready. Down the block, Kevin could see a black Lexus parked in front of Couvillon House. Someone was lying on the roof of the car in obvious sniper-fashion, propped up on his elbows, rifle aimed at Scanlan. The driver's door was open, and another man stood behind it.

"Nice and easy!" this one called out. "Play it smart, Scanlan."

"No, Matty!" a woman's voice called out. "Get away from here! I'm all right!."

Kevin could see two people standing on her front verandah, a woman and a guy wearing a cowboy hat. Angélique Couvillon and McQuillan, presumably. The guy on the roof of the car, then, would be Samuel.

"Shit, Goyette." Kevin dropped to a knee. "This could get bad in a hurry."

Goyette had left his side. He'd taken up a position behind the Spring Street snowbank where he had a clear view of Scanlan, the car, and the two people on the verandah. His rifle rested on the top of the snowbank in front of him, ready for an order to shoot.

At that moment, down at the far end of the block at the hardware store, Kevin saw two black-and-white OPP vehicles turn the corner, barricading the street at that end.

It looked like the proverbial shit was about to hit the fan.

Chapter

58

As Prez Raintree arrived at the corner and positioned his SUV to block off the foot of Church Street, Ellie walked over and motioned for him to lower his window.

"We've got a stand-off shaping up," she said. "The Lexus has two shooters, one on the roof with a rifle and the other guy behind the driver's side door with a handgun."

Raintree shoved the gearshift into park and got out, nodding.

"A third shooter's on the verandah of the B and B," Ellie added, pointing, "with a hostage."

"I've got a backup unit two minutes behind me," he said, studying the scene, "and Kevin and Goyette should be in position at the other end of the block. Mulvahill's ETA is five. She'll back up Walker and Goyette."

"Okay. TRU, Sergeant."

"Agreed." Raintree pulled out his radio to make the call. According to OPP policy, an officer at the scene of a hostage rescue situation or a barricaded persons situation should request assistance, through the provincial communications centre, from the nearest Tactics and Rescue Unit. The request would be directed to the regional headquarters duty officer in Smiths Falls. This duty officer would assess the situation based on the information Raintree would supply and, if a TRU intervention was deemed necessary, which it clearly would be in this case, they would inform the TRU commander and the General Headquarters duty officer in Orillia, at which time a unit would be dispatched to their location. Ideally the team would be mustered within thirty minutes, but it was impossible to say how long it would take them to arrive from Odessa.

Ellie suspected this situation would not last nearly that long.

"Ricardo!" Dante Tassone suddenly shouted from right behind her. "Put down that gun and call this off immediately!"

Crouched behind his open car door, Rick Tassone swung around at the sound of his father's voice, his gun pointing in their direction. On the roof, Henry Samuel looked over his shoulder.

"Christ!" Ellie grabbed Dante and pulled him behind Raintree's SUV. "Get down. Be quiet. Let us handle this."

Dante struggled in her grip. "It's Ricardo! I can't let anything happen to him."

Ellie took his coat lapels in her fists and gave him a shake. "It's gone way beyond anything you can do to help. This is in our hands now. Stay here, and stay down."

"Damn you! I don't want him shot."

Raintree grabbed a bullhorn from his SUV, his call for a TRU intervention having been completed. He crouched behind the open door.

"ATTENTION! HENRY SAMUEL, PATRICK McQUILLAN, AND RICARDO TASSONE. LAY DOWN YOUR WEAPONS AND PLACE YOUR HANDS ON TOP OF YOUR HEADS!"

Through the windows of the SUV, Ellie saw Samuel slide off the roof into the narrow space between the car and the snowbank. He swung the rifle in Raintree's direction.

At the same time, Rick ducked into the open car door to sit sideways on the seat, trying to find cover from his rear while also keeping an eye on Matthew Scanlan, who was standing stock still in the middle of the street about twenty metres away.

"ATTENTION, PEOPLE OF WESTPORT. PLEASE REMAIN INDOORS. REPEAT, REMAIN INDOORS."

Ellie saw several doors open along the street as people looked out to see what was going on.

"MR. TASSONE. WE CAN END THIS PEACEFULLY. NO ONE NEEDS TO GET HURT. TELL YOUR MEN TO PUT DOWN THEIR WEAPONS RIGHT NOW."

"All I want is the disk!" Rick shouted. "If he gives it to me, I'll leave and that'll be the end of it. No shooting."

Ellie gave Dante another little shake. "Stay put."

He sat down, legs crossed. His eyes were closed. Tears rolled down his cheeks.

Drawing her service weapon, Ellie crawled around the end of the SUV and moved up to Raintree's position behind the door.

"TRU's rolling out," he told her, "but who knows how long it'll take them to get here."

The realities of rural policing in a jurisdiction exceeding

one million square kilometres province-wide.

"EMS's also en route," Raintree added.

"Until TRU arrives, this is your show."

"Affirmative."

Ellie turned at the sound of a vehicle behind them. A black-and-white cruiser disgorged two uniformed constables she recognized from the Lanark County detachment. She knew them because Lanark was part of her jurisdiction as eastern Ontario's primary major crimes manager. They trotted forward in a low crouch. One of them, Winslow, had his hand on the stock of his holstered Glock while the other, whose name was Hart, carried a standard-issue Colt Canada C8 rifle. They both wore body armour and looked ready for anything.

Ellie pointed at each of them in turn and identified them to Raintree.

"We're in a defensive posture," Raintree said. "Winslow, get this civilian back behind your vehicle and maintain a position there. Hart, stay with us."

Winslow pulled Dante to his feet and, pushing him down into a crouch, hurried him back behind the cruiser.

Raintree keyed his radio. "Goyette, what's your twenty?"

The speaker on Raintree's radio coughed. "In position at the intersection of Church and Spring. With Walker and Mulvahill. I have a visual on Scanlan and also on the target in the Lexus on the driver's side."

"Copy. Tell Walker to contact Detective Inspector March using his cellphone."

"Copy that. I have a clear shot at the suspect behind the wheel, through the windshield."

"Understood. Hold your fire until I give the command."

"Affirmative. Sarge, lower your head about six inches, will you?"

Raintree ducked down, looking at Ellie. She rolled her eyes at him and was going to say something, but her cellphone vibrated. It was Kevin. Raintree had ordered him to call because he was without a radio at the moment and the sergeant wanted everyone in the communication loop while directing this confrontation.

"Kevin," Ellie said, "I'll put you on speaker."

"Hey, Ellie. Sarge, I still have a visual on Matthew Scanlan. Permission to approach to get him out of harm's way."

"Denied." Raintree snapped. "I don't want to do anything right now to destabilize the situation."

"Come on!" Rick shouted. "Bring me the jump drive and let's get this over with!"

"Sarge," Kevin said, "this is going to go south in a hurry. Use the bullhorn to tell them I'll take the disk from Scanlan and bring it over to them. That way he can back off and get to cover."

"No. It's a given in crisis negotiation that you never exchange personnel for hostages, Kevin. It's off the table. Period. Acknowledge."

"Acknowledged," Kevin said.

Raintree looked at Ellie. "I need to be talking to them. Time is our greatest ally. I need to string it out, distract them. Damn, there are three different focal points here. Tassone in the car—the leader. Samuel the sniper—the wild card. The hostage on the verandah. Man."

He raised the bullhorn. "RICK, AS A GESTURE OF GOOD FAITH, CAN YOU TELL YOUR TWO MEN TO PUT DOWN THEIR WEAPONS? I THINK IT WOULD BE A REALLY GOOD IDEA TO DE-ESCALATE THIS WHOLE

THING SO NO ONE GETS HURT."

"Fuck you, asshole!" shouted Samuel from between the Lexus and the snowbank.

Raintree looked over his shoulder at Hart. "Do you have a visual on that guy?"

"Not at the moment, but that can change in a hurry."

"Do it." He looked at Ellie. "In the absence of Tactical, I need options in place." Meaning that if a shot needed to be taken, he wanted to have the ability to take it.

Ellie watched Hart ease down into a prone position and, after a quick peek, prop himself up on his elbows and sight his rifle along the bottom of the snowbank toward the Lexus. After a moment he rolled back.

"Too much crap in the way." He got up onto one knee and, after another quick peek, eased his rifle around the end of the SUV for another attempt.

"Target acquired."

"Hold for my order."

"Copy that."

"Which way's that damned rifle of his pointed?"

"Uh, currently out into the street, Sarge."

"Probably at Scanlan." Raintree raised the bullhorn and was about to speak when Ellie put a hand on his arm.

"Hold on. Something's happening."

Raising her head as high as she dared, she saw that the door of a shop on the far side of the street had opened. The shop was situated between the Lexus's position and the spot where Matthew stood.

As Raintree lifted the bullhorn again, a man in his sixties, maybe early seventies, stepped into a gap in the snowbank. He was hatless, his wavy grey hair combed back off his forehead, and he wore a six-button navy topcoat and zippered galoshes.

He raised a gloved hand for balance as he started to ease out onto the street. It was obvious from his behaviour that he had absolutely no idea what was going on. Behind him, from the door of the shop he'd just left, someone shouted. He turned to catch what they were saying.

"What the fuck?" Rick shouted, pointing his gun.

Behind him, Henry Samuel came out of his crouch, thumped his rifle on the roof of the car, aimed, and fired.

Chapter

59

Time slowed down to a crawl for Ellie.

She straightened, took a step to her left to get clear of the open SUV door, and raised her firearm in an isosceles stance.

The man in the navy topcoat threw up his arms and fell back onto the sidewalk, out of sight behind the snowbank.

Rick Tassone came off his car seat and fired at where the man had been an instant before.

"Tassone!" Ellie shouted. "Drop the gun!"

Rick turned and pointed the gun at her. He fired a wild shot that went over her head and struck a telephone pole.

Ellie fired twice into his body mass. He banged against the open car door and fell to the ground.

Matthew Scanlan threw himself down flat in the middle

of the street and covered his head with his arms.

Raintree threw his bullhorn into the SUV and drew his gun.

From the other side of the SUV, Ellie heard Hart firing, once and then once again.

Henry Samuel flew sideways and disappeared down between the Lexus and the snowbank. His rifle slid off the roof and clattered across the hood of the car.

Behind her, at the end of the street, she heard Dante Tassone screaming something in Italian.

"Don't shoot!" McQuillan shouted from the verandah. "Don't shoot, don't shoot!"

Ellie pointed her gun in his direction. His hands were up, the gun pointing upward. Angélique Couvillon jerked away from him and started down the steps.

From the far end of the street, Kevin was running in a tight crouch toward Matthew, gun out.

Raintree moved around Ellie and began advancing on the Lexus, gun first, his eyes on Rick, who lay motionless on the ground.

Hart rolled over the snowbank onto the sidewalk, got to his feet, and scuttled toward the spot where he'd seen Samuel disappear beside the Lexus.

"Verandah!" Raintree shouted at Hart.

"This one's out," Hart said, pointing down at Samuel. He slung his rifle across his back and drew his handgun.

Ellie took another sideways step, still covering Rick.

"You, on the verandah!" Hart shouted. "Throw your gun into the snow! On your knees! Hands on top of your head!"

Ellie saw McQuillan toss his gun over the verandah railing and drop to his knees.

Raintree waved her forward.

She reached the open door of the SUV and saw that Rick's eyes were open and lifeless. She looked up and saw Kevin pulling Matthew Scanlan to his feet as Angélique ran out toward them. Hart was on the verandah, securing McQuillan's hands behind his back with a plastic zip-lock tie. McQuillan's cowboy hat fell off his head and rolled across the verandah.

Holstering her weapon, Ellie ran across the street to the civilian that Samuel had shot at. He was lying face down on the sidewalk, but his arms were moving. He tried to lever himself up, but gasped in pain and flopped down again.

A woman, the one who had shouted from the door of the shop, leaned over. "Is he all right?"

"Ma'am," Ellie said, "please go back inside."

"The ambulance is already here," the woman said, pointing down the street. Ellie looked. Just past the church, she saw lights flashing as the EMS vehicle edged around Goyette's truck.

"Sir," she said, kneeling beside the wounded man, "don't move. The paramedics are here. It'll just be a minute."

She looked at the back of his topcoat, where blood was seeping through from a wound just to the right of the vent at the bottom of the coat.

"He shot me in the wallet," the man said through clenched teeth. "Jesus, it hurts."

"Sir?"

He rolled partly over and looked at her. "It's an expression, Ellie. Argghh. You know. Where I usually keep my wallet? Uhhh. He shot me in the ass."

It was Jay Lippincott.

Chapter

60

Ellie always made a conscious effort not to use foul language when she was working, as she felt it was important to maintain a professional disposition at all times, but in her defence she was rather upset and stressed.

She held her tongue as the paramedics examined Jay and cut away his topcoat and trousers to apply field dressings. They started him on an intravenous fluid and eased him onto a gurney, face down. They assured her that he was stable, that the shot had passed completely through his right buttock on an angle without causing serious damage, that blood loss was not excessive, thankfully, and that their main concern was avoiding shock, hence the intravenous and the blanket they'd covered him with.

She followed as they pushed him through the snow to

the back of their ambulance, which they'd driven right up to the scene as soon as Raintree had given them the all-clear, but as one of the paramedics opened the back doors she held out a hand.

"Just a minute." She glared at Jay. "Right now, you need to explain to me what the flying fuck is going on. What the hell are you doing here?"

"We had a . . . dinner date, Ellie. I was a bit early."

"Early? You were a bit early? You walked right into the middle of an active hostage situation and got shot and all you can say is that you were *early*?"

"It's cold," the paramedic said. "We need to get him inside the bus."

Ellie waved them forward and watched as they levered Jay up into the back of the ambulance. They slid the gurney forward and secured it for transport. She held up her hand again.

"I'm not done talking to him yet."

The paramedic hissed through her teeth. "Can't it wait?"

"Don't leave." Ellie climbed up into the ambulance and crouched down. "Who the hell are you? What do you want here?"

"I told you who I am, Ellie. I just wanted to talk to you. Get to . . . know you better."

"Get to *know* me better? What the hell is that? Are you an associate of these Italian mobsters?"

"Who?" He seemed genuinely confused.

"Tassone and his gang. Or the Wolfpack. This whole fucking mess. What's your part in it?"

"Ellie, I . . . don't know what you're talking about."

"Bullshit you don't."

"I just wanted to get to know you. I . . . have something

important to tell you."

"Detective Inspector March," the paramedic said, "we need to transport this patient *now*."

"What?" Ellie demanded, ignoring the interruption. "What's so important you couldn't wait to tell me tomorrow, or next week, or next month, for chrissakes?"

"I . . . I wanted this to be a little different. Appetisers, a glass of wine."

"What the fuck are you talking about?"

"Detective Inspector," the paramedic said.

"Ellie," Jay tried to smile and didn't quite make it, "I'm your father."

SEVEN WEEKS LATER

MARCH 12, 2020

Chapter

61

Ellie's attorney was Veronica Savage, a partner in a high-powered Toronto law firm. She specialized in police law, labour law, and related litigation, and she was highly sought after by senior members of the law enforcement community who found themselves in need of legal assistance.

Two years older than Ellie, she was married to a prominent oncologist. They lived in a multi-million-dollar home in Markham with their daughter, who was sixteen, and a small herd of miniature Dachshunds. She was short and wiry, she wore clothing Ellie had only seen in magazines, she was pretty if not beautiful, and her hair was styled in one of those women's smooth-bob business looks that cost a small fortune to acquire and another small fortune to maintain. She was put-together, brilliant, and damned near perfect. The kind of woman that always made Ellie feel as though she should just grab her mop and get back to cleaning the courthouse floors.

Veronica had driven up to Orillia last night and was staying at the Marble Works Spa and Inn, a luxury boutique hotel with the highest rates in the region. Ellie, on the other hand, had been in Orillia for two days and was camped out at the Best Western, which was close to the GHQ campus and cost quite a bit less per night.

Because she was client-centric, Veronica insisted that they meet in the coffee shop next to Ellie's hotel for breakfast, since it was on her way to their 9:00 AM meeting. As Ellie worked on her bowl of oatmeal smothered in honey, Veronica pulled apart a toasted bagel and chattered about her daughter.

"She wanted to go to Florida next week, it being March break, but we decided it might not be a good idea this year. Her grades are excellent and she's certainly earned it, but I don't like what's happening down there right now. The entire country's gone off the rails. It's like mass insanity or something.

"And then," she went on, "I just heard on the news driving over that we're extending the school break by two weeks because of this coronavirus thing. They're saying the doors will probably stay closed for the foreseeable future. And apparently early next week the premier will announce a province-wide state of emergency."

Ellie spooned up oatmeal, listening. Veronica was a talker, but she was also wired in at the highest levels. Ellie was interested to hear what she had to say.

"That means no public events over fifty people. Libraries, theatres, and daycare centres will have to close down, and restaurants will have to go to take-out and delivery only. It's completely and totally bizarre."

"The cases are starting to climb," Ellie offered.

"As of yesterday, forty-two in Ontario, and the WHO's just announced it's reached the level of a pandemic worldwide. God only knows where it's going to go from here."

She ate a piece of bagel and shoved the plate aside. "The other thing," she said, reaching for her coffee, "is that on Monday the Attorney General's office will announce the suspension of all trials in the Ontario Superior Court system until the end of May. I mean, we're talking about one of the busiest trial courts in the world, Ellie. Shut down for the next two and a half months? What a nightmare. I expect that's why we've been summoned by His Nibs. He wants to brief us on what's happening in your investigation before the roof falls in."

"But that's good news, right? That we're getting the word now?"

"That's my understanding."

Ellie finished her coffee. Immediately after the shootings in Westport, the Ontario Special Investigations Unit had been called in. For the second time in a week, Church Street was barricaded as the SIU brought in a team of investigators, including their own forensic technicians, to process the crime scene that had resulted from the ill-fated attempt of Rick Tassone to obtain possession of the USB jump drive left by Alonzo DiMaria in Matthew Scanlan's washroom.

Ellie and Provincial Constable Hart were the subjects of the investigation, as the SIU undertook to determine whether their lethal use of force in the situation was warranted by circumstances or was excessive and unwarranted. If the latter, the SIU might level criminal charges against them.

In 1988, in response to the shootings of two Black men by police, the Ontario Solicitor General had formed a task force to address problems experienced by visible minority communities in their interactions with law enforcement. Recommendations of the task force led in 1990 to the creation of the SIU, a civilian oversight agency reporting to the Attorney General. The SIU was mandated to investigate officer-involved shootings and other complaints including sexual assaults, vehicle deaths, and other injuries and deaths resulting from police activities. The objective was to ensure that police conduct would be subject to independent and objective scrutiny, and that the public would have confidence in the rule of law and the administration of justice in this province.

As a result, the SIU now had oversight over some 28,000 municipal and provincial police officers. During 2019, 314 cases were opened, eight of which involved firearm deaths. In total, 3.6 per cent of cases closed in 2019 resulted in charges being laid. The public generally felt that this percentage was too low, while many in law enforcement felt the SIU was intrusive and unnecessary.

When Ellie and Veronica walked into the commissioner's boardroom at two minutes before nine o'clock, SIU Director Bernard Holmstead was sitting alone at the foot of the big table, swiping his cellphone.

He looked up, nodded, and went back to what he was doing.

Ellie chose a seat halfway down, set her briefcase on the table, and removed her overcoat, which she draped over the chair next to her. On her left, Veronica did the same. Before they had a chance to sit down, Commissioner Cecil

Dart swept into the room, closing the door behind him.

"Bernie, sorry I couldn't see you when you got here, I was on the phone." He walked down the length of the table and shook Holmstead's hand.

"No problem, Cecil. I'm already in retirement mode. Light as a goddamned feather."

"I wish I could say the same." Dart walked around to the other side of the table to shake Ellie's hand. "Glad to see you. Holding up all right?"

"Just fine, sir." Ellie sat down.

"Counsellor, good to see you again." He nodded at Veronica, who generally never shook hands with men. "You drove up yesterday?"

"Last night. But the roads were good."

"I was talking to Craig this morning," Dart said to Ellie as he sat down. "He said to say hello."

"Oh. Thank you." Ellie was somewhat surprised. "How's he doing?"

"He's fine. Actually likes Sudbury. Met a girl, and they plan to get married this summer."

In the winter of 2015, Dart's son Craig was a detective constable in the Leeds County Crime Unit. During a homicide investigation managed by Ellie, he'd fallen through the ice on Sparrow Lake while being chased by an armed suspect. Ellie had risked her own life to pull him to safety, and Dart, much to Ellie's dismay, had remained grateful ever since.

"Well, tell him congratulations for me."

"Thanks, I will. Bernie, you didn't come up here to listen to idle gossip. Why don't you tell us what you've got."

"Glad to." Holmstead had turned off his cellphone and dropped it into his jacket pocket. There was nothing in front of him on the table, no file folders, no neatly stapled documents, no laptop or tablet. His briefcase remained unopened on the floor behind him, leaning against the wall.

"Detective Inspector March, we've never met before, but I've had the chance to review your file in some detail and I must say it's impressive."

"My client appreciates the compliment," Veronica said.

"Yeah. Fine. Cecil, this one was completely straight-forward. I'm talking about both cases, March and Hart. Everyone took good notes for once and handed them over promptly, the interviews all went smoothly, civilian witnesses were completely forthcoming, the detachment gave us all the policy updates and what have you, and at the end of the day it was a goddamned walk in the park. The shootings were warranted and justified in both cases. No charges will be laid."

"Well, that's a good thing, isn't it, Bernie?"

"Sure it is. I feel wonderful about it. Piece of cake." He made a face. "We've been averaging one hundred and thirty-five days to close a case and the frigging premier and his A.G. sidekick think one hundred and twenty days is *perfectly reasonable,*" his voice rose to a sarcastic falsetto, "despite the fact they've chopped our budget to the bone and we don't have nearly the resources available any more to conduct most investigations to that standard. But here we are, wrapping up these two after only forty-eight days The Unit will never hear the end of it."

"Again," Dart said, "it's a good thing, though, right?"

Holmstead pushed his glasses up onto the top of his bald head and rubbed his eyes. "They still harp on the fact that some of our investigators are ex-cops, and how in the hell do you preserve impartiality when you've got ex-cops investigating cops? Excuse me if our low-level investigators have a law enforcement background because that's where the skill sets are going to be found right now. But what about me? I'm not an ex-cop. The guy before me? Also a civilian; also a former Crown Attorney. And the guy before him and the guy before him? Civilian prosecutors, all of us. Pro cop? Give me a break. March, how did Bass seem to you?"

Ellie shrugged. "Fine. Competent." Frank Bass was the lead investigator assigned to her case, along with a team of two investigators who assisted with interviews and document reviews.

"As you may or may not know, we're supposed to have fifteen lead investigators but we only have thirteen right now on strength, and Bass is the only one who's former law enforcement. The *only* one. I've never received any complaints at all about his impartiality, but no, the bunch of them are all too pro-cop despite the fact that *all* the rest of them are civilians? Yeah. Right."

"I thought he was rather surly," Veronica said.

Holmstead snorted. "That's when he's trying to be charming. You should see him when he's in a bad mood. Anyway. I'm just tired of feeling like the bologna in the middle of a very old and very stale sandwich. I really am."

He got to his feet and grabbed his winter parka. "Don't mind me. On Monday I'll make the announcement on these two cases, and right after dinner Margot and I will be on a plane to Saint Lucia. We're never damned well coming back if I can help it. I'm digging a goddamned hole down there and pulling it in after me."

He pushed back the hood of his parka, which had flopped over his face when he reached down for his briefcase.

"Hopefully this coronavirus thing won't interfere,"

Veronica said.

"Tell me about it. I've got a feeling the roof's about to cave in."

Dart walked down to the end of the table. "Gene went to Walmart yesterday to pick up a few things and the shelves were empty. No toilet paper, no paper towels, no hand sanitizer. No canned beans or soup either, for crying out loud."

"Same thing in Markham," Veronica added. "Empty shelves everywhere."

"Our brilliant Health minister suggests people might want to stockpile," Holmstead groused, "and the next day people are filling vans with cases of toilet paper and selling them on the Internet at ten times the price. Insane. All I want to do is to sit on a beach, practise my French, and work on my tan. Is that too damned much to ask?"

Dart shook his hand. "Bon voyage, Bernie. It's been a pleasure."

"No it hasn't, but thanks anyway." He bustled for the door, parka rustling. He nodded to Veronica and disappeared.

"Well," Dart said to Ellie, "I guess that means we can take you off administrative leave and put you back to work."

"Can't come soon enough, sir."

"Yeah, I'll bet."

Chapter

62

Lunch was a leisurely affair on the terrace, shared with Renita's father. Tall and thin, Salvatore Fortuno was a quiet man in his late eighties who ate like a sparrow but still walked in his bergamot orange groves every day and was a better card player than Dante. He was pleasant and thoughtful, and when he did speak, it gave Dante a chance to practice his Greko, an Italian-Greek dialect that was Fortuno's preferred language when at home.

The view was spectacular. From where he sat, Dante could admire Fortuno's groves, tidy rows of orange trees that still generated a respectable revenue through the essential oil sold to high-end makers of eau de cologne. On the left, he could see a strip of beach and the crystal-blue beauty of the Tyrrhenian Sea, and on the right, an abandoned village on the mountain slope. The Aspromonte range featured a number of such vacant stone ruins, and as Dante understood it, this particular one dated back to the eleventh century. Like the stumps of ancient broken teeth, it reminded Dante that while the blue sky above might be eternal, the works of man below it were not.

Lunch began with light pastry appetizers filled with sausage and spinach, followed by an antipasti platter of sun-dried tomatoes, marinated olives, and fresh local fish and clams. As a remembrance of Ricardo, Dante followed this with a pizza and a light dessert of strawberries and coffee. Thankfully, Fortuno had seen to it that oranges were not included in the meal, knowing that Dante found the smell of bergamot somewhat nauseating.

The weather was pleasant, a far cry from what Dante had left behind in Toronto. The temperature was a mild 18 degrees Celsius, and the breeze coming off the sea was gentle. It had rained yesterday, but after the fog had burned away this morning, the skies had cleared and the sun was shining brightly overhead. Fortuno found it somewhat cool and was wearing a thick cable knit sweater, but Dante wore a yellow linen blazer and khaki trousers to commemorate his escape from the frozen hell that was Canada.

They would not be going back. Disconsolate in her grief over the loss of her only son, Renita had refused to speak to Dante for more than a week, blaming him for not keeping their boy safe from harm. It was a nightmare Dante hoped never to repeat in his life. His wife was his partner and his best friend. The bitter anger she directed toward him was like acid thrown in his face.

When Renita's mother's health took another downward dip, upsetting her further, Dante broke through her wall of silence with the suggestion that they travel home to

Calabria so that she could attend to her in person. It was a wise decision, and a week after arriving, Renita declared she had absolutely no desire to return to Canada. They talked about it—finally, they were at least talking again—and Dante agreed. They would dispose of the house in Woodbridge and most of their possessions, ship the rest over here, and never look back.

Their daughter Elisa, the family intellectual, soon joined them and lent her support to her mother and grandmother in their time of distress. The three women quickly formed a triumvirate that now ruled Casa Fortuno with an iron fist. Dante and Fortuno were grateful for whatever brief respites, such as lunch on the terrace, might be afforded to them to escape this tyranny.

The beauty of Renita's family home helped ease her pain, and Dante moved ahead with their decision to relocate. His first thought was that his international holdings in Holland, for example, might provide an opportunity to move to Amsterdam, which to all accounts was a fine and exciting city. Neither of them spoke a word of Dutch, however, and Renita had no desire to learn. Neither did he, when it came right down to it.

When Dante mentioned Catanzaro, the capital city of the Calabrian province, with more than 150,000 inhabitants in its various metropolitan components, Renita became more receptive. Dante owned a villa just outside the town of Soverato on the coast, a property passed down from his father, and he'd made a few inquiries. It was still in good repair, according to his second cousin Matteo, who was currently living there as a caretaker and handyman, and there was a cottage on the property Matteo could live in if Dante should decide to move there.

Renita was noncommittal, but Dante saw her nod to

herself as she thought about it. Catanzaro was a city in which she felt comfortable. It had decent shopping and it wasn't too far from here, so she could travel back and forth to be with her mother. As a peace offering on Dante's part it was a judicious choice, and Renita eventually agreed that it would be the next destination on their long road together.

A chance to put the loss of their son into a new and hopefully less painful context.

After coffee and dessert were finished and the lunch dishes were cleared away, Fortuno excused himself. It was time for his postprandial nap, after which he would be driven down to the sea for a stroll along the beach. As always, he invited Dante to join him for the drive, if not for the walk, but Dante politely declined. He knew it was Fortuno's alone time, and he didn't wish to intrude.

Once he was by himself, Dante took out his cellphone. The villa featured a powerful wifi connection and a satellite link to the world outside rural Calabria, and Dante remained in close contact with his key people in Canada and around the world. Despite the losses of Ricardo, Lonnie, and Dom, all three of which had left large holes in his heart, he still had a large multinational corporation to run, and he found that work helped him manage his own considerable grief.

He'd kept it turned off as a courtesy to Fortuno, who maintained an intense dislike of modern technology. When it had powered up and connected, Dante saw that he had several e-mails. A few were from cousin Pietro and others were from Pietro's son, Carlo. Dante had chosen Pietro to become chief operating officer of Wooden Bridge Investments, responsible for its day-to-day operations, and he'd further decided that Carlo, a very competent young businessman, would become Rick's replacement.

Pietro was steady, unimaginative, and glad to move out of the illegal side of the business after so many years and Carlo was a loyal, loving son who would work well with his father. It would be just fine.

An e-mail from Leonardo caught his eye, and he opened it.

Thought this might be of interest.

It contained a link to a story that had run yesterday in one of the Toronto newspapers. It was short and to the point:

Wednesday, March 11 2020 – 8:35 am

Toronto Police Service's homicide division is investigating the death of a man at the Toronto South Detention Centre.

Police say there was a fight between two inmates at the facility Tuesday evening in which one of the men was stabbed repeatedly with an improvised knife.

Paramedics rushed the victim to hospital with life-threatening injuries but he died before arrival.

Patrick Casey McQuillan, 28, was a Montreal native who relocated to Toronto two years ago. He was a former member of the notorious West Side Gang with known connections to organized crime in the city.

Thanks, Dante replied, after reading it. *Stay well, my friend.*

Chapter

63

The weather tended to move in narrow bands across this part of eastern Ontario, and one such band had passed through Sparrow Lake overnight, leaving behind another six centimetres of unwanted snow. Kevin leaned on the handlebar of his snow scoop, the way that Montreal Canadiens goaltender Ken Dryden used to lean on his stick after whistles, and surveyed the scene.

His eyes followed the tracks left by Janie and Joshua from the end of the driveway down to Sarah Street, where they disappeared around the corner. Janie had had a flu cancellation this morning, but she had two appointments in the afternoon that were still a go, so she'd gone to clean off the sidewalk in front of her salon on Main Street. She'd probably stay inside for awhile and fuss around a bit, making sure everything was in its place and ready for business. She was a perfectionist that way.

They probably wouldn't see the snow plow in the village until early this afternoon. Kevin would have to come out again with the scoop to clear away the barricade the plow would leave behind, but he didn't mind. The driveway was small and he enjoyed the exercise. Janie occasionally asked if he wanted to invest in a gas-powered snow blower, but he always told her he'd rather just use the scoop.

Caitlyn was cleaning off the front step with a plastic shovel that Kevin kept in the back of the Grand Cherokee in winter in case it got stuck while away from home. The porch was a small cement affair with three steps and an aluminum covering above it, and although everyone used the side entrance under the carport, Caitlyn liked to make sure the front door was also accessible, in case of emergencies. She also insisted that the back deck be cleared off and likewise available for use. Kevin detected a little insecurity in it all, and he worried that he was contributing to it. His name had been in the news again, in connection with the Westport happenings, and it had not gone down well with the family that he'd not only been shot at while riding on a snowmobile but had also been in the middle of a street gun battle that had resulted in two deaths and an injury.

In the living room window, Caitlyn's cat Boo Boo had jumped up under the curtains and was crouching on the window sill, watching her. The cat was very dependent on her, and she loved it dearly. As Kevin watched, she stopped shovelling and waved. The cat stood up, arched its back, and settled down again. Maybe, he thought, he was reading too much into things.

"Daddy!"

Joshua came running down the street. Behind him, Janie trudged along, parka hood up, her face half-hidden behind faux fur. She lifted a hand and waved.

Kevin jammed the scoop into the snow bank and bent down to lift his son into the air. "Man, look at you! Winter Boy!"

"I helped Mommy clean."

"Did you? What did you do?"

"I put towels in the dryer and I helped fill the bottles of soap."

"Wow, that's great." He put the boy down and thumped him on top of the head.

Josh ran up the driveway. "Hey, Cait! What are you doing?"

"Shovelling snow. Want to help?"

"Sure!" He strode importantly up the little sidewalk to the steps.

"I thought you'd have this all done by now." Janie threw back her hood and grinned at him.

"It's all these distractions." Kevin leaned down and kissed her.

She grabbed him and pulled him in for another one.

Car tires crunched behind them and a horn tooted. Kevin reluctantly unclinched and stepped back. An OPP SUV rolled to a stop next to them and the window went down. It was Raintree.

"Sorry to interrupt all the smooching."

"Sure, no problem. Janie, this is Detective Sergeant Raintree. He's replacing Carty in the crime unit."

"Charmed, I'm sure." Janie pulled her hood up. "I'll let you boys talk business."

Kevin watched her walk into the carport, calling for Josh to follow her into the house.

Raintree shifted into park. "Was it something I said?"

"Just bad timing. What's up?"

"Look, I know it's supposed to be your day off. The word's coming down that the SIU will announce they're finished with the investigations and no charges will be laid in either case. Both shootings are ruled as justified in the circumstances."

"That's great. Really fast, though."

"Yeah. They're also done with me."

"Oh?" Kevin knew that Raintree's actions as incident commander at the time of the shootings had been subjected to an internal investigation. Had he followed established departmental procedures? Had the orders he'd given to his officers, including Constable Hart, been appropriate and correct? Had he managed the scene correctly, or had he carelessly placed the community and its civilians in jeopardy?

"It was noted," Raintree said, "that I warned people over the bullhorn to stay indoors while the thing was going on. But they thought if I'd repeated it a couple more times, Lippincott might have stayed in the store and not gotten his ass shot. So they're putting a reprimand on my file, but apparently it's too much effort to move me, so I'm staying with you guys for the foreseeable future."

"Good," Kevin said. "I'm glad. That you're staying. Not about the reprimand."

"Understood. Anyway, I need you to come in and give Leung a hand this afternoon. We're bringing in a bunch of witnesses related to that arena fire in Delta that the fire marshal's calling arson and I need you to take some of them."

"I don't know. Janie's got a few appointments this afternoon and she needs me here with the kids."

"Appointments?" He looked concerned. "Doctor's appointments? Is anything wrong?"

Kevin laughed. "No, hairdressing appointments. She runs the hair salon on Main Street. Business, Sarge. Business."

Raintree grinned, a little sheepishly. "Okay, sorry. Good to know. Look, let's see if we can get some of the witnesses to come in tomorrow morning instead and you could handle them then. Sound okay?"

"Sounds great. Thanks." Kevin hid his surprise. Supervisors who understood the importance of family were rare birds, indeed.

Raintree started to put the window up, then stopped. "You don't play chess, do you?"

Kevin shook his head. "I know how to play, but I don't like it. I'm more of a euchre kind of guy."

"Oh. Okay."

"I hear Leung's pretty good at it, though. You might want to try him."

Raintree tapped the steering wheel. "I'll do that. See you in the morning."

Kevin watched him drive slowly down to the corner and turn left onto Sarah Street, which would take him south in the direction of the detachment office.

"Kevin!" Caitlyn called out. "I'm all done. Did you do the deck yet?"

Kevin pulled his scoop out of the snow bank. "Not yet. Want to help?"

"It would be my distinct pleasure, sir."

He laughed, banging snow loose from the blade of the scoop.

Kids. Nothing quite like them.

Chapter

64

Ellie followed Cecil Dart from the boardroom to his suite of offices in the back corner of the floor. In the outer reception area, Dart's executive assistant, Hannah Waller, came out of her office to talk to the secretary about something. With her was Gavin Elliott.

Gavin folded his arms and gave Ellie an expectant look. "Good news, I hope."

"Good news," Dart said over his shoulder, on his way into his office. "Get her back to work, will you?"

"Congratulations," Waller said.

"Thanks."

Waller picked up a file from the secretary's desk and followed Dart into his office, closing the door behind them.

"Walk with me," Gavin said.

Ellie followed him out of commissioner country and through a glassed-in atrium bridge to the next office block.

"I have a file that needs a desk review," he said, holding the door open for her. "It'll give you something to do over the weekend. As soon as the SIU does their press announcement, then there'll be something else for you."

"Sounds good," Ellie said.

"I read your note on McKinley." He stopped and leaned against the wall. There was no one else in the corridor at the moment.

"I thought she did well." Ellie had written a memo to Colin Hailey thanking him for the loan of Charlotte McKinley and praising the analyst's contributions to the DiMaria case. She'd copied Gavin and Charlotte on the memo.

"I was impressed. A name to remember." He folded his arms. "Look. You know I don't make a habit of interfering in other people's business. Particularly colleagues. What you do or don't do about this, that, or the other thing is entirely up to you. I don't like to get involved." He sighed. "Having said that, there are times when I feel I should speak up, offer my take on a situation, maybe provide a little advice even though we all know that free advice is worth what you pay for it."

"For godsakes, Gavin. Spit it out."

"Yeah. Okay. There's a visitor in my office waiting to see you."

"A visitor. I'm not expecting anyone. A civilian?"

Gavin nodded. "He's attending the conference downstairs."

"I don't know who that would be. What conference? I

mean, I know there's one going on right now, but I don't know what it's about."

"The future of police transportation, or something like that. He was the keynote speaker this morning. Very Important Person. Anyway, I made him explain why he wanted to see you before I'd let him sit in my office."

"I don't . . ." Ellie rolled her eyes as it hit her. "You've got to be kidding me."

"He's says you've been avoiding him. Says you won't return his calls or reply to his e-mails."

"Damn." Ellie leaned against the wall next to him. "I don't want to deal with this."

"He seems like a pretty good guy, El. Very sincere. I'm a fairly decent judge of character, you know."

"Yeah, Gavin. I know. You used to do it for a living."

"Well, I still do. In a manner of speaking. It's like riding a bicycle; you never really forget how it's done." He turned to face her. "Come on, you can't duck him forever. Just deal with it and get it over with."

"That's your free advice?"

"Yep. Take it or leave it."

She sighed. "All right. I guess I'll take it."

Chapter

65

Jay Lippincott stood up as she walked into Gavin's office, closing the door behind her. "Thank you for seeing me, Ellie. I really appreciate it."

She sat down behind Gavin's desk, swivelled back and forth in Gavin's chair, and folded her arms. It was Gavin's office, but two years ago it had been her office while she acted as the superintendent in command of the Criminal Investigation Branch. It was a familiar place. The walls and cabinets were covered with Gavin's stuff and not hers, and the winter coat on the coat rack and the boots in the tray were Gavin's, but the room reminded her of the authority she'd wielded in the job for twelve months, and she tried to pull it around her now, like body armour. Emotional kevlar. Protection against an unwanted threat to her personal space.

"I called and left messages," he said. "Superintendent Elliott said that you were under investigation for the shooting and couldn't talk to me because I was a witness."

"That's correct." Gavin had done her a favour, planting an excuse for her, but the fact of the matter was that she wouldn't have returned his calls even if she hadn't been under investigation.

"Maybe you didn't believe me," Jay said. "What I said to you. When I told you who I was."

She realized he was still standing, leaning a little unsteadily on a cane, tipped slightly to the port side. He was still favouring the wound, which apparently had not yet fully healed.

"Sit down, for crying out loud."

He picked up a bottle of water Gavin's secretary had given him and limped over to a seating arrangement at the side of the office. The chairs were a little more comfortable over there. As he eased down into one he groaned faintly, tipping himself so that his weight was resting on his left cheek rather than on the right.

In fact, she did believe him. While sitting around doing nothing on administrative leave for forty-eight days, she'd reached out to Tom Faust, a former CIB colleague who'd gone private after retirement. He worked for a Toronto-based investigation and intelligence security firm that had connections at mysterious, high levels. Faust had run a backgrounder on Jay Lippincott that verified everything Charlotte McKinley had told her before. He'd also looked up her adoption records, using whatever roundabout means people used in the private sector to find out things that sworn officers like herself couldn't legally access. When he'd started to go over his findings on that score, though, she'd stopped him.

"Give it to me in one word, Tom."

"In one word?"

"Yes."

"Legit."

Now here was Lippincott, in her boss's office, playing one of the oldest power tricks in the book, switching the seating arrangements to take the big desk out from between them and forcing Ellie either to remain where she was and talk to him from across the room or to get up and join him at the little round table where they could have a reasonable conversation on more equal terms. It was something experienced executives did instinctively. One of many tactics that seemed to be part of their DNA.

Speaking of which.

She got up and crossed the floor. Sitting down, she said, "I don't see much of a resemblance."

He smiled and shook his head, clearly relieved that she'd decided to talk about it. "You got all your looks from your mother, thank god. She was so beautiful."

Ellie's expression darkened. "I take it we're not talking about Jeannette Kennedy."

"No. May I tell you the story? Do you have time?"

"Gavin's gone for coffee. He's a dawdler. We've got time."

He took a drink of water and found a handkerchief in his pocket to wipe his lips. "I expect you've run a background check on me already."

"Yes."

"A wise first step. Look, when I was twenty-four, I was still very immature. I had an MBA from the Wharton School of Business in my back pocket, and I was young and brash, working for my dad's company. We made components for

Pratt and Whitney Canada aircraft engines. I had my own apartment in a very exclusive building downtown; I had a nice car, nice clothes, Italian shoes, you name it." He smiled sadly, wagging his head in self-mockery. "I thought I had a certain something."

Ellie leaned back, trying to take some of the tension out of her posture. These were details she'd already heard from Tom Faust and Charlotte McKinley, although in a tone that leaned much more heavily toward law-enforcement-slash-intelligence chapter and verse. She now found herself wanting to hear the information from Lippincott himself. She wanted to hear his version of the past, his spin on things. Since he was, apparently, legit.

"I was engaged to Jeannette at the time. She was the daughter of Patrick Kennedy, a Pratt and Whitney vice-president, and the marriage would be very important to my father's business and obviously to my future with PWC. She was a bit of a fish, kind of on-again off-again as fiancées go, but she was bright and ambitious and I thought I loved her. Well, I did, I guess."

He took another pull at the water. "There was a girl who was hired to work as one of the secretaries in my dad's office. I'd see her whenever I went upstairs to talk to him about something or other. I was a sales rep for him at the time, and I liked to share little tidbits I picked up in my various meetings, so I'd hang around the outer office until he was free. While I was there I'd chat up the girls, since I thought I was particularly charming. This one girl started to draw my attention more than the others.

"Her name was Juliet Magennis, Ellie. Irish-born, raised in Dundalk, County Louth, not related to the Guinness Anglo-Irish who brew the stout. Her family being working class poor, she had to earn her way through university on grants and part-time jobs. She studied poetry and was a poet herself. Imagine that. She had a falling out with her parents about the Catholic church and their treatment of women, and she ended up dropping out of school. A friend of hers had already made arrangements to come to Canada, and at the last minute Juliet joined her. The friend was able to get admission into the English program at U of T, but Juliet's grades weren't quite good enough, so she had to find a job instead. She ended up working for us."

Ellie sat quietly, watching his face. It was obvious that after forty-odd years the memories still held strong emotions for him. It softened her resolve against him ever so slightly.

"When she told me she was pregnant and that the baby was definitely mine, I didn't know what to do. Then she said she'd decided against an abortion and was going to carry it to term. No, not it. Her. You, Ellie. You. She'd decided after all, despite her feminist leanings and all the rhetoric surrounding the right to choose that swirled around the campuses and in the newspapers and magazines of the day, that her choice, this time, was to become a mother. Your mother."

Ellie nodded, feeling herself inexorably pulled into the current of his emotions.

"Her parents back home completely disowned her. A baby out of wedlock! Not a thing good Catholic girls allowed to happen. There was no option for her to return to Ireland, then. I talked to my father and mother, and that didn't go very well, either. My mother threw me out of the house and stopped talking to me. My father was almost as upset. His unequivocal advice was to cut all ties, walk away, and never look back. And what about Jeannette?

What would she do if she ever found out? Did I realize what I was jeopardizing, the future I was putting at risk, with such juvenile, irresponsible behaviour?"

His fingers moved restlessly on his cane. "I was a coward. There's no other word for it. I pretty much left her to deal with the pregnancy alone. Her roommate, Eleanor, was the only one who really helped her through it. And when she was taken to the hospital to deliver the baby, it was Eleanor who called to tell me what was happening. So now I had a final choice. I could turn my back and walk away, pretend it wasn't happening. Go on with my life and forget her altogether. Did I have it in me to do that? To be that cold?

"I went to the hospital. I saw her briefly before they took her in. She said, 'If it's a girl, I'm going to call her Eleanor. If it's a boy, John.' Then she was wheeled away."

He fell silent. Ellie continued to watch him. His head was down and his eyes were closed. She gave him the time.

"When they came out to tell me," he finally said, "I was devastated. A blood vessel had burst and they weren't able to stop it in time. She'd bled to death. The baby was healthy. A girl. I told them its name, *your* name, was Eleanor. Then I left."

He pinched the bridge of his nose. "It was the worst thing I've ever done in my life. I left. I walked out. I went home and got drunk and that was it. They called the Children's Aid Society. You were put into foster care, and four months later you were adopted by Paul and Mary March."

"Four months." Ellie frowned at him. "So when was I actually born?"

"The third of January 1973. I understand you've always celebrated your birthday in April, but you're actually a

Capricorn and not an Aries."

"I don't pay any attention to that kind of stuff."

"I'm not surprised. Your mother, by the way, is buried in Mount Pleasant Cemetery. At least I had enough brains after the fact to make those arrangements for her. Her plot's actually not very far from Glenn Gould's. Mackenzie King is also buried there. The list goes on and on. Timothy Eaton. Hart Massey. Sir Frederick Banting. Egerton Ryerson. Punch Imlach and Dick Irvin, Senior. Northrop Frye. My parents. And your mother. God rest her soul."

Ellie nodded once again, surprised that the information was important to her.

"I want you to understand, Ellie, that I haven't stalked you all these years. I don't want it to seem creepy, because it wasn't. I stayed away. I paid a lot of money, yes, to track down the adoption records and find out where you'd gone. After that it was just a mild sort of surveillance, if that's what you law enforcement folks would call it. I saw copies of your high school transcripts because I wanted to know what subjects you were good at. I knew you'd enrolled at Ryerson and that you got your bachelor's degree in criminology, and when you were hired by the OPP I was surprised. I admit, I thought you'd follow in your mother's footsteps and lean toward the arts, but here you are. An exceptional career law enforcement officer. I couldn't be more proud."

"I don't know what to say."

"That's the thing, Ellie. You don't have to say anything. You don't have to do anything. I just wanted you to know. That's all. For all these years I've felt immense guilt over having abandoned you, and having seen what amazing things you've done with your life I feel a little less guilty, but it's still there. I was hoping that by coming forward, by finally telling you the truth, I could make amends at least enough to ease up on the self-punishment a little and feel a bit better going forward. I'm on the last lap here, Ellie. I don't know how long I've got left. Getting shot was like hearing the sound of death's wings for the first time, stirring somewhere behind me, like a warning of what was coming. I'd like to be able to breathe a little more easily from this point on, you know, in whatever time is left."

She looked at him. "This is for your sake, then, more than for mine."

He winced. "No. I'm not saying this at all well. Look, what you do with this information is entirely up to you."

"Let me explain something," she said. "I don't have a family. It's not who I am. My adoptive parents both died last year, within a couple months of each other, and I wasn't in contact with them before they went. There's a dose of guilt for you. A former neighbour said something about it in a Christmas card. I hadn't even known."

"I'm very sorry," Jay said.

"Thanks. My ex-husband remarried, my two girls hate me, and I've let go of them completely now because that's what they want and I'm fine with it. I'm a loner. That's how I'm used to living. Alone. That's who I am. I don't know what to do with any of this you're handing me now. I just don't know how I'm supposed to feel about it."

He raised a hand. "I understand completely. Look, Ellie, if we never speak again after today, then that's how it'll be. It's entirely up to you."

Ellie said nothing.

"You should also know I'm not really interested in buying the place next door to you. Although it's really nice. That was just a pretext to see you, to introduce myself. I won't intrude on your space up there."

"I see."

"I do have something to give you, though." He leaned a little further to port and pulled something out of his jacket pocket.

"This is all that I have of your mother's." He held it out to her. "It's a chapbook of her poetry, written when she was pregnant. Eleanor got it printed up for her just before you were born. Before she . . . died. Eleanor had a close friend at the U of T Press, and they published it and ran off a hundred copies for her."

Ellie took the book, a slender paperbound volume. The cover was cream coloured and featured an illustration of a green Celtic harp. The title, printed in an Irish-looking font, was *Songs to a Looming Spirit*, by Juliet Magennis." It was fifty-two pages altogether. She opened it randomly and looked at a poem entitled "Mother and Child":

> Looming in darkness,
> My flesh weaving yours in careful silence,
> You contemplate solitude that begins and
>   never ends.
> You and I together, then apart, then thrown
>   away into
> Another darkness in which you cry, and I cry,
> And forever we reach out for each other;
> We reach out for love that cannot be regained.

She closed the book. "Thanks."

"You're welcome. At first I was going to buy all one hundred copies, but then I realized if I did that then no one else would ever read her poems. Eleanor sent them out to a few bookstores downtown and eventually they all disappeared. That's the only one I have. It's yours now.

Your legacy from her."

She held it in her hands, trying not to look at it again.

He edged forward on his seat. "That's all I wanted to say to you. But I have one favour to ask. Would you put my number in your Contacts list? I'll send it to you now if you'll let me."

"Sure. Why not."

He took out his cellphone and started tapping. Ellie took out hers and saw it appear. "It's there."

"Great. Thanks very much." He put the phone away and struggled to his feet. "I've taken up enough of your time. I have to go back downstairs to make another appearance and then I'll be flying back home after that."

"Flying?" She stood up to get the door for him.

He grinned at her. "Come on, Ellie. A state-of-the-art helicopter that supports day and night operations, has enhanced safety features, and is loaded to the gills with the latest tactical gear? It's sitting on the helipad waiting to take me home, but while it's here, it's demo time, baby. The RCMP have already bought in, so it's time for you guys to get on board while the discount price is still good. It was my excuse to come up here in the first place. Multi-tasking. It gave me a way to save face if you refused to see me."

"I didn't, though."

"No, you didn't. And I'm eternally grateful." He stopped in the doorway and turned. "If we *do* ever speak again, which as I say is entirely up to you, I just wanted you to know that you never have to call me Dad or Father or Pop or whatever. That would be beyond the pale. Just call me Jay. All right?"

"All right. Jay."

"Perfect."

She watched him hobble past the secretary's desk and

out into the corridor beyond.

Gavin Elliott was sitting in a chair next to the desk, pretending to read a report of some kind.

She looked at him. "That was . . . different."

Gavin nodded at the chapbook in her hand. "You took it. I'm glad. He wasn't sure if you would."

"I took it."

"Good. Did he mention the will?"

She frowned. "What will?"

"His will." Gavin dropped the report and stood up. "I grilled him pretty good, El. Friends looking out for friends, you know?" He patted her arm. "The guy's worth billions. He's got an ex-wife and three adult sons who'll get the lion's share, but he told me you're in there, too. When he kicks the bucket, you're going to be very, very rich."

"Bullshit. Excuse the language."

"Well, now, I don't know. I thought he was telling the truth. Remember, I used to—"

"—do this for a living," she finished. "Yeah, I know."

"Be gracious about the whole thing, Ellie. He seems like a very nice old guy who's just pretty damned lonely."

"Mmm."

"Since you're going to be so filthy rich in the not-so-distant future, how about the Jack Daniels being on you tonight?"

"I'm driving home this afternoon."

"Rain check, then."

"Rain check, Gavin."

Chapter

66

Three weeks later, as an early-April rain turned the snow into slush, Ellie found herself bored and depressed as the sun went down and the storm settled in. The COVID-19 virus had been ramping up, and all non-essential businesses were shut down for the duration. The state of emergency in Ontario had been extended, and there was talk that people needed to remain at home as much as possible to begin flattening the curve of the contagion. The elderly were particularly at risk because the vast majority of them had pre-existing conditions that increased their vulnerability.

There was nothing on television to watch, and she'd gone through her current stock of DVDs. Thinking about the elderly led her thoughts to Jay Lippincott, for the millionth time. She hoped he was taking care of himself in that big-assed mansion of his in York Mills. Apparently he had a live-in housekeeper and chef who could manage things for him so that he wouldn't have to go out unnecessarily until the scope of the pandemic was better understood.

Reggie drank noisily from his water dish and drooled all over the floor as he wandered into her office to curl up on the oval mat in front of her desk. One of his favourite spots to catch a few winks.

She picked up her cellphone. There were no new messages, no e-mails, no notifications of any kind that she needed to check out.

She opened her Contacts list and scrolled down.

She looked at his name.

Her mind went blank for a moment, and then she poked the contact and made the call.

Oxford Station, October 8, 2020

Acknowledgements

As aways, it's important to note that this book is a work of fiction. Although the Ontario Provincial Police, the Leeds County Crime Unit, and most of the locales, including the village of Westport, Ontario, actually exist, all people and events in this novel are entirely the invention of the author, and any resemblance to actual people or events is strictly coincidental.

The following publications were helpful during the writing of this novel: Margaret Meikle, *Cowichan Indian Knitting* (Vancouver: University of British Columbia Museum of Anthropology, 1987); William Butler Yeats, *The Speckled Bird*, ed. William H. ODonnell (Toronto: McClelland and Stewart, 1976); and Frederico Varese, "How Mafias Migrate: The Case of the 'Ndrangheta in Northern Italy" (*Law & Society Review*, vol. 40, no.2, 2006, pp. 411-444).

Thanks to Tim McCann for help with cellphone stuff, among many other things, and to Lynn Clark, as always and forever, for everything.

About the Author

Michael J. McCann lives and writes
in Oxford Station, Ontario, Canada. A
graduate of Trent University (Peterborough,
ON) and Queen's University (Kingston,
ON), he served as Production Editor of
Criminal Reports (Third Series) and Law
Reports Co-ordinator for Carswell Legal
Publications (Western) before spending
fifteen years at the Canada Border Services
Agency as a project officer and national
program manager. He's married to author
Lynn L. Clark. They have one son.

**If you enjoyed this crime novel,
you'll also love the debut of
retired detective Tom Faust in**

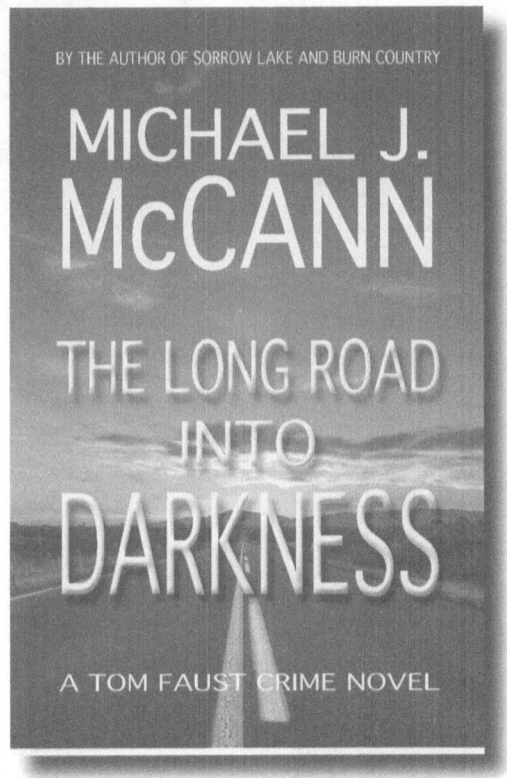

The Long Road Into Darkness
Michael J. McCann
ISBN: 978-1-927884-17-1

Ask your local independent bookstore
to order it today!

The March and Walker Crime Novel Series

Sorrow Lake
Michael J. McCann
ISBN: 978-1-927884-02-7

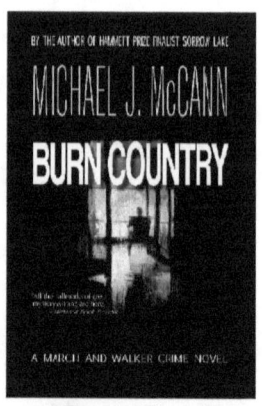

Burn Country
Michael J. McCann
ISBN: 978-1-927884-09-6

Persistent Guilt
Michael J. McCann
ISBN: 978-1-927884-13-3

No Sadness of Farewell
Michael J. McCann
ISBN: 978-1-927884-15-7

Ask your local independent bookstore
to order them today!

www.ingramcontent.com/pod-product-compliance
Lightning Source LLC
Chambersburg PA
CBHW031153020726
47499CB00002B/349